DEVIL'S BARGAIN

Corvin chose his words slowly: "I ask no more than a chance to talk to you, as one friend to another. If you will but grant me this favor, I swear I will not cause you any further pain."

This simple apology moved Guin far more effectively than any endearment. It would be easy to drift with the sweet swells of emotion, to submerge herself and be overwhelmed by his obvious desire. But Guin knew that if she let go of reason she would surely drown.

"You are making oaths that you will not be able to keep," she declared. "We will both be hurt, milord, by indulging in this fairy tale."

"Ah, but they always end happily," Corvin replied. "The ogre vanquished, the princess rescued." His face broke into a smile as he realized that he had won the first round . . .

"Splendid . . . by turns both amusing and touching . . . Rita Boucher demonstrates perfect Regency pitch."

Mary Jo Putney

Other Regency Romances from Avon Books

THE SCANDALOUS SCHOOLMISTRESS

RITA BOUCHER

AVON BOOKS ◆ NEW YORK

THE SCANDALOUS SCHOOLMISTRESS is an original publication of Avon Books. This work has never before appeared in book form. This work is a novel. Any similarity to actual persons or events is purely coincidental.

AVON BOOKS
A division of
The Hearst Corporation
1350 Avenue of the Americas
New York, New York 10019

Copyright © 1992 by Sonia Crowne
Published by arrangement with the author
Library of Congress Catalog Card Number: 91-92411
ISBN: 0-380-76529-2

First Avon Books Printing: May 1992

AVON TRADEMARK REG. U.S. PAT. OFF. AND IN OTHER COUNTRIES, MARCA REGISTRADA, HECHO EN U.S.A.

Printed in the U.S.A.

RA 10 9 8 7 6 5 4 3 2 1

To my three muses of MRW,
Binnie, Linda, and Mary Jo,
who gave of their time,
advice, and encouragement
and lent shoulders as needed.

Prologue

‹‹‹‹‹‹‹‹‹‹‹‹‹

T HE FIRST glow of dawn was beginning to creep into the sky and shafts of light struck through the mist that rose from the Serpentine. As Lord Corvin paused in appreciation, he tried to recall when he had last been awake to savor the simple beauty of a morning. Perhaps Delphine had done him an unwitting favor by ejecting him from her residence at this early hour.

The Viscount was so absorbed in his thoughts that he did not notice the stout gentleman in his path until they collided. The impact sent Corvin sprawling, knocking the wind from him while the man before him remained steadfast and silent. Although he knew the fault was entirely his own, the Viscount's irritation grew as he attempted to scramble unsteadily to his feet. At very least, the fellow could offer him a hand.

"Excuse me," Corvin mumbled as he tried to brush the dust from his knees. His eyes searched for a patent pump that had skittered off into the brush. "It was most clumsy of me."

When there was no reply to his apology, Corvin squinted in the dim light and burst into laughter. He had been asking pardon from a lightning-blasted tree trunk. As he hopped about to replace his shoe the Viscount realized that he was more than a trifle foxed. If the bills he had received from the vintner were an accurate indication, Delphine's cellar was excellent, and last night, he had imbibed far too much of her French brandy, perhaps needing a bit of Dutch courage.

Giving a mistress her congé was always a difficult task, especially for the Viscount, who had always preferred to take his leave personally rather than conclude a long association via some indirect communication. He had gone to St. John's Wood with a handsome parting gift in his pocket expecting the Cyprian to accept the inevitable end with her usual aplomb.

Delphine had ever been the most pragmatic of Frenchwomen, knowing just how much she could demand. The affaire had long been on the wane; their liaison had become more a habit than a passion. Indeed, if the wretched woman had been discreet, Corvin might have been no wiser and continued the connection out of his inclination to custom. However, Delphine had been foolish enough to flaunt her lover. Although she claimed that her infidelity was but a misbegotten effort to arouse Corvin's jealousy, her blatant faithlessness had forced her protector's hand. Under the circumstances, his mistress' outraged reaction had come as something of a shock to the Viscount.

"You have no heart, milor'!" Delphine had shrieked with all the verve of a Gallic fishwife once she had realized that he truly intended to leave her. "You geeve me nothing, nothing of yourself."

Unfortunately, Corvin had not had the foresight to have his carriage wait for him, but had sent it home, as usual. Although he had not expected his mistress to appreciate the news, neither had he thought to be so summarily dismissed at an hour where there was not a hack to be had.

As he continued to weave his way through Hyde Park, it troubled him to realize that Delphine's accusations were, on the whole, true. The wall of reserve built up over the years was a barrier that he allowed few to surmount. He knew that some thought him cold and calculating; but was he, as Delphine had charged, incapable of passion? Certainly, he felt no jealousy. The realization that another shared Delphine had irritated him only because Corvin was paying for the exclusive use of that commodity which she sold. It had rankled him that his bit o' muslin was free with her company.

Did he lack a heart, he wondered? Corvin knew for a fact that many thought so and admired him for it. There was a distinct advantage in the absence of such a vulnerable organ in the world in which he moved. Time and time again, he had watched his friends dash themselves to pieces, destroy their fortunes, families, and sometimes even their sanity for that elusive emotion called ''love.'' He need look no farther than his own family for evidence of such destructiveness.

A sharp stone cut through the thin leather sole of Corvin's pump and he cursed as he limped from the path to lean against the trunk of an ancient oak. He frowned and bent to pluck a blade of grass, twisting it absently in his fingers as he pondered his problems. Emmaline. What was to be done with that sister of his? His father, the Earl of Sinclair, had sent one of his illegible notes, scribbled in a crabbed hand to conserve paper. From the little he could decipher, Corvin had discerned that yet another governess had given her notice, the fourth within as many months. Something had to be done.

He closed his eyes as he thought, savoring the warmth of the new-risen sun upon his cheek. A plan of action was necessary and Corvin spoke aloud to himself in the manner of a man who is often in his own company.

''The first objective is to get Emmaline away from

St. Clair Abbey and our dear stepmama," he ruminated. "The girl should be safely ensconced in some school. But does a school exist in England that would take the Earl of Sinclair's outrageous daughter?" Corvin sighed to himself as he anticipated the difficulty of locating some seminary for young ladies willing to take the minx despite her scandalous reputation.

The Viscount sank wearily to the ground, hugging his knees to his chest in a childish gesture. "And what about you, Daniel?" he asked himself. "A new liaison?" But the thought had little appeal. At the age of one and thirty, the pursuit of a mistress seemed more tedious than exciting to him. His parents, by their licentious example, had caused him to despise adultery. Yet, unless he accepted the favors of those wanton, bored matrons of polite society, who flaunted their availability, there was no alternative to seeking out another Cyprian.

"There is another solution," Corvin mumbled but as he mused upon the possibility, it seemed far more distasteful than pursuit of a mistress. The parson's mousetrap was an obvious answer but again, his father and mother came inexorably to mind. "Unfortunately," he told himself, "one cannot easily dismiss a wife who does not suit."

The sound of hoofbeats interrupted his reverie. The Viscount watched, startled, as a horse came into view. The rider stretched forward against the horse's neck, the animal's whipping mane obscuring the face. Only when the pair were nearly past him did he realize that the rider was a woman.

As she rounded a turn with breathtaking speed, Corvin was about to shout to her to beware of the fallen tree that lay just beyond her sight. But, before a sound could leave his mouth, she was up and over. Obviously, she knew the ground well. At first, he thought that she was racing some unseen competitor, for once she reached a lone beech she raised her hands in a gesture of victory. The echo of her untrammeled laughter broke the morning stillness.

Although Corvin watched, no defeated challenger followed. Minutes passed and not even a groom made an appearance. She was riding alone, it seemed. Who was she, Corvin wondered, this Diana of the Dawn, who raced the wind neck or nothing? As she disappeared around the bend, Corvin realized that although one could not judge too well from the distance, she seemed a pretty looking woman, if a trifle mad. Corvin put the incident on his list of items due for investigation. Another early morning outing in the park might be in order on the morrow. It would be interesting to see if she returned and perhaps, he might get a closer look. The possibilities were intriguing.

One

THE WELL-APPOINTED room was as hot as purga-
tory, the blazing fire in the hearth adding to the
swelter of an August afternoon. Indeed, Guin
thought, her parlor smelled like the gates of hell itself despite the windows being wide open to any
passing breezes. The smell of simmering potpourri
battled to disperse the sulfurous odor that seemed
to pervade every corner. Although Guinivere
Courtney raised her handkerchief to her watering
eyes from time to time, Madame Celeste Vallée did
not seem at all affected by the heat or the stench as
she earnestly stated her case to the schoolmistress.

"*Mais*, Guin," Madame Vallée entreated. "Surely,
for Dorothea some allowance could be made. The
little one is a budding genius."

"No, Celeste, I simply cannot permit it!" Guin
said, shaking her head with an air of finality. "We
strain the proprieties to the limit as is, my friend. If
somehow parents were to get wind that Morton
House has live male models for art classes . . ." The
very thought made the schoolmistress shiver despite
the warmth from the nearby hearth. Guin looked
beyond the art instructress to the parlor's delicate
Grecian furnishings, marquetry table, rich Axminster carpet and ormolu, remembering back just a few
short years to when the room had been bare of any
furnishings at all. No. She and Aunt Hermione had

6

worked too long and too hard to hazard it all. Unfortunately, Guin was finding it deucedly difficult to convince the Frenchwoman that she had no intention of risking the reputation of the Morton House for Young Ladies even for the talented Dorothea Quigley.

Celeste pressed on, rumpling her paint-stained smock in her hand as she spoke. "Not for all the *jeune filles*, Guin, only for Doro. I beg you. How is she to study the male form, the musculature?"

"Hopefully, in due time, she will marry a male form of her own, then study him at her leisure, but not in my school, Celeste," Guin said with a sigh. "Fruit, flowers, profiles, but no nudes."

"Yes, I understand," the woman said sadly, bowing her head in acquiescence. As she reached the door a sparkle came to her eye. "Guin, if it is outsiders you are worried about, what about one of the staff? Goodness knows they are loyal."

"The servants, Celeste, will keep their livery on. Do I make myself clear?" Guin stated in dismissal.

Though Celeste nodded grudging agreement as she went out the door, Guin was left with a distinctly uneasy feeling. Art was sacred to Celeste and the sixteen-year-old Dorothea was a most devoted acolyte. The two would bear watching. Watch! Glancing at the timepiece suspended from the chain at her bosom, Guin saw that it was nearly three o'clock and rang for Perkins.

She met the butler at the door. "We are expecting Lord Sinclair and his daughter at the half-hour. Is there nothing more we can do about the smell?"

"I am afraid not, Mrs. Courtney," Perkins replied apologetically. "For all we have tried, the odor continues to linger. Beyond opening the windows and simmering Mrs. Bacon's concoction upon the hearth, there seem little we can do. The worst of it should be cleared by the time his lordship arrives."

"And Eddy?"

"Miss Edwina is most contrite, madame," the butler said. "T'was she who helped Mrs. Bacon to compound the potpourri."

Guin sighed. "Well, I suppose that we have no choice. 'Tis the only decent room for an interview. Unlock the wine cupboard and bring up a bottle of the best brandy. I shall ring when I wish tea served." She started up the stairs, then stopped midway. "Oh, Perkins?"

"Yes, madame."

"Tell Miss Edwina that I will wish to see her at seven."

"Yes, madame." The butler's lip twitched at the edges and he spoke with the familiarity of an old servant. "If you will forgive me for saying so, Mrs. Courtney. She meant no harm. Miss Edwina was only trying an invention of hers to start fires up easily. It worked wondrous well."

"I'm sure it did, Perkins. Only now my parlor smells like Lucifer's den. I shall see Edwina at seven," she said, squeezing past a gaggle of girls as they came trooping down the stairs.

The schoolmistress was looking forward to a few peaceful moments alone before the interview with the new pupil and her parent, so she was dismayed to enter her bedroom and find Aunt Hermione waiting. As Mrs. Haven rose from a chair, patrician grace was patent in her every move, making her simply styled clothes seem the height of fashion.

The older woman sniffed delicately as she spoke, "I thought that you might need some assistance dressing. You smell like rotten eggs, child."

Guin spilled some water into the basin. "I doubt that anyone will notice since the whole place smells of sulphur."

"Eddy again, no doubt. Whatever were you thinking of to allow that girl a laboratory, Guin?"

"Stillroom, Aunt Hermione, stillroom," Guin replied as she reached for the buttons at the back of her grey morning dress. "It is very important that we have at least the appearance of propriety."

"Are you sure that you do not wish me to conduct this interview, Guin? Your voice is barely above a croak. I should not wonder if your sore throat turns putrid. How foolish of you to go riding in the morning. The miasma that rises from the Serpentine carries all kinds of illness," Aunt Hermione said rebukingly. She opened the wardrobe and took out the black bombazine dress that her niece habitually wore for interviews, frowning at the ugly garment as she shook out the folds.

"Unfortunately, it is the only time that I can ride safely without a groom, Aunt," Guin said as she reached in vain for a button at the small of her back. "Really, a spoonful of lemon and honey and I shall be good as new."

"Here, let me," the older woman said.

"No, Aunt Hermione, I can get it," she said, stepping hastily behind the Chinese screen. "Would you hand me my dress?"

"This excessive modesty of yours, dear child, is beyond belief. You behave as if you were as wrinkled an old crone as I," she said draping the dress over the top of the partition. "You should be dressed in lovely gowns that display that wonderful figure of yours, for I vow, you are the image of your dear mother in her youth. I sponsored her debut, you know. She was exquisite; could have had her pick of any of a dozen of the most eligible men in England."

Guin listened with half an ear as her aunt's familiar speech began to waft from beyond the barrier. Although she could not see the old woman, memory could supply the facial expressions and gestures that accompanied each word.

"It is all very well, Guin, for me to be headmistress of Morton House, for all that I am a baroness. There are few alive who might recognize Hermione Haven Burnett, the widow of Lord Cathcart, and deride me. Dear me, how the mighty have fallen! Bloodlines without lines of credit, child, there is nothing sadder. Still, if you would but shed that crow's raiment of yours, noone would need know that you had worked for your livelihood these years. We could scrape an adequate dowry together."

"I have no wish to return to the ton, nor would they accept me if I did," Guinivere said, trying to suppress a growing annoyance. "Why do you persist?"

"Because I owe you so much, my dear. My capital was disappearing pence by pence, for when Lord Cathcart departed this world, he left me little but fond memories."

Guin heard a familiar note of pain in the older woman's voice and tried to remind herself that her aunt meant no harm. Indeed, the lady was entirely ignorant of the anguish she caused her niece by this foolish notion of reinstatement into polite society. "The pittance that was left would not have sustained a household for much longer." Aunt Hermione's voice wafted from beyond the screen. "Were it not for your clever idea, child, I have no doubt that I would have ended my days in some shabby but genteel boarding house, mending my gloves and drinking watery tea. Still, despite the school's success, I cannot help but think that this is no life for you."

"I love the girls, Aunt, and you know that I am far happier here than as a governess. Have you consulted with Mrs. Bacon regarding the menus?" Guin said, trying to change the theme of conversation.

"You deserve more," the old woman said, hanging doggedly to her thread of thought. "I still cannot understand why your papa left all of his affairs in your husband's hands. It seems that your father was the only man alive who did not know that Alfred Marshall was a fool and a spendthrift."

"You well know Aunt Hermione, that the fault for Papa's disposition of his fortune was more than partly mine. My caprices with Caro Lamb and her wild crowd pushed me well beyond the realms of propriety. Caro was so witty, t'was almost intoxicating to be with her," Guin reminisced. "And she was so kind to a young nobody in her first season."

"Kindness had little part in the lady's attentions, I would wager," Aunt Hermione said cynically. "Your adoration flattered her vanity. No one truly kind would have embroiled an inexperienced maiden in her schemes to regain Lord Byron's waning affections."

Guin opened her mouth to defend her friend, but fell silent as she realized that there might be more than a grain of truth to her aunt's assessment. As Guin reached over her shoulder to adjust her shift, she felt the hardened seam of skin above her shoulder blade. Although she could not see the scars without the aid of a mirror, she could trace every line in her mind, as if she was standing naked before the glass as she had on that morning . . . Guin firmly put those thoughts behind her as she slipped the black dress over her head. There was so much that her aunt did not understand, so much that the dear woman could not know about her niece's life with Alfred Marshall. Guin had long vowed to keep that shame to her bosom. By buttoning some of the bottom fastenings beforehand, she made sure that she had no need of her aunt's assistance.

"Still, your husband . . ."

"Alfred had no idea that he was going to die in that duel and it was for my sake he fought, for my honor," Guin cut her aunt off rudely, hoping that she would drop the subject. Through the screen, she could hear a disbelieving snort.

"That may well be, but at least your husband's family could have helped you," the older woman said with an unlady-like sniff.

Guin stepped out from behind the screen and turned to look at herself in the glass as she arranged the starched white fichu. Wordlessly, she took up her brush pulling back every wisp of her mahogany colored hair into a severe knot at the nape of her neck. The mention of her husband's family caused the bristle to scrape at her scalp. By the time she had jabbed the pins into place, Guin found that she could face her aunt calmly.

"As everyone else, they held me responsible for his death." Despite her efforts to contain herself, Guin's voice was angry. She set the mob cap upon her head to complete her disguise. "When I settled our affairs, almost all our assets had been invested in one of Alfred's bubble schemes, or gambled away on the baize, my dear. I suppose the Marshalls did not wish to throw good money after bad. As for their obligations to me as their daughter-in-law, 'Good riddance to bad rubbish' was the way Alfred's mama put it."

Guin felt a lump rising in her throat as she saw unshed tears gleaming in the older woman's eyes. Although Lady Cathcart spoke of what she owed, Guin's debt was far greater. When the rest of the world had scorned Alfred Marshall's widow, Aunt Hermione had taken the scandal-haunted girl into her Cornwall home. Even though Guin was only a distant relation, not truly Lady Cathcart's niece, she had shared the little that she had. When, between jobs as a governess, Guin had come to Aunt Hermione with the idea of a school for unmanageable young ladies, the old woman had been willing to risk her small hoard of capital on a wild dream and serve as the figure-head principal of Morton House.

"I'm sorry, dear," Aunt Hermione's voice trembled as she put her hand on Guin's shoulder. "It just hurts me to see you looking like some dried-up stick at seven and twenty. There is still a chance for you."

Guin squeezed the wrinkled hand and said with an attempt at lightness, "I have had my chance and lost it. What cannot be changed must be borne, Aunt Hermione. You, yourself have told me that more times than I can remember."

"Don't quote me to myself, young lady. There is nothing more tedious than having your own silly homilies spouted back at you. Yes, we must endure, but perhaps the time has come when we can give you a second chance. The school is doing well," she said as she pinned the watch to Guin's dress.

Guin set the final part of her disguise upon her nose. She had no need for the spectacles but the light refracting off the glass dulled the gleam of the eyes that one of her more poetic suitors had years ago likened to twin gems of lapis lazuli. The stranger that faced Guin in the mirror was the very caricature of the prim schoolmistress, an angular bombazine crow. Guin wrinkled her nose in disgust at the picture she presented; a far cry from the fashionable Miss Elaine Guinivere Morgaine Borne, the pampered daughter of Sir Jacob Borne of Woodbourne.

There was little chance that any parent she had encountered in that long-ago life would now recognize her as the scandalous debutante who had broken nearly every rule of accepted behavior, one of the most whispered about young ladies to cross the sacred threshold of Almack's. The Gorgon's guise had the additional dividend of reassuring the parents that their wayward daughters would be in firm hands.

"No, Aunt, I am afraid that we have crossed the border into the mushroom land of Trade, and even if society were to overlook that important detail, I fear that the scandal of Alfred's death would still put me beyond the pale. Goodness, is that a carriage I hear?" Guin asked. As she had hoped, Aunt Hermione was distracted.

"It is not stopping," the older woman said as she peered through the window to the street below. "I had thought you said that the new pupil was not due until the half-hour."

"With a man like the Earl of Sinclair, one never knows," Guin said shrugging her shoulders.

"Sinclair? Dear Heaven, Guin! Never say that you are thinking of taking his daughter on as a pupil. Why that little minx is nearly sixteen and has been an enduring source of *on-dits* since she was barely out of leading strings." Aunt Hermione's eyes acquired a martial gleam as she spoke. "Why the Countess of Sinclair and her myriad lovers made Lady Harley, with her miscellany, appear the very model of moral rectitude. Not that I am saying that Sinclair is any better; married that Drury Lane doxy of his the moment his wife stuck her spoon in the wall."

"I know all about it, Aunt," Guin said. "When have I ever accepted a pupil without researching her background thoroughly? With a family like that, do you wonder that the girl is incorrigible? It is clear that the poor child desperately needs help. Would you have me deny her because of the sins of her parents?" she asked, bending to brush her aunt's cheek with a kiss.

"The sinning tendencies of the parents are usually the inheritance of the children. Guin, please, I know that you have pity on strays. Every wounded creature has always had the power to catch your heart, but please, don't take the chit. She will be naught but trouble.''

''I have not taken her on yet; that is the reason for this interview. Imagine how it will enhance our reputation if we succeed with her as well as we did with Mary Abernathy. Why, we would have to beat the potential pupils from our door. The Earl of Sinclair represents one of the oldest and wealthiest families in the ton.''

''Rakes and lightskirts, every last one of the Stanton family and I challenge you, gel, to name me one that is not. The stories that I could tell you would curl that straight hair of yours, Niece. But you know that I dislike gossip above all things.''

Guin hid a smile at this blatant untruth. ''I will report the outcome as soon as they depart. You will wait upstairs?''

''Of course, I may be in my twilight, but I am no fool. I doubt that Sinclair would recognize me since Cathcart and I did not spend much time in town, but why take the risk? La, this farce is exasperating, everytime anyone near my age pokes his head in the door, I must disappear to my bed.''

''That is by your own choice, Aunt, although I do not believe anyone would think the less of you if they recognized you as Lady Cathcart. You certainly would not be the first of the ton forced to earn their bread. The consequences would be far worse if anyone were to recall my true identity. Still, I doubt that anyone would suspect that Mrs. Guinivere Courtney is Elaine Borne,'' she said, grinning ruefully as she pirouetted with mocking grace. ''And you have become something of a legend, Aunt, the redoubtable Mrs. Haven, headmistress extraordinaire. The severity of your countenance, your almost martial dignity are the talk of the ton,'' Guin said, laughing as she looked at the woman's disbelieving expression. ''Only yesterday, Countess Von Schoenhaus was telling me how much her husband admired you for the state of discipline that you maintain here.''

''Locked all the brats in their rooms did you?'' her aunt asked with a skeptical sniff.

''Truly, they think that you are a sorceress. Their daughters come in to Morton House, sullen, intractable and gawky, and they come out poised, confident women, ready to take their place in the world. Our record is enviable,'' Guin said.

''Luck is what I'd call it! Lucy Putnam marries an earl. Mary Abernathy weds a duke and suddenly, Morton House is all the rage. And a merry dance those hellions will lead their husbands. Don't insist on pressing your fortune, my girl, lest it desert you and then see how fast this place empties.''

''Not all of it is luck,'' Guin said, tucking a stray wisp of hair beneath the cap. ''We give our girls what they need, care for them with affection and nurture their talents. Any female with the brain of a monkey can simper her way across the social scene. 'Tis the bright ones that have the worst of it.''

''Well, I still say that its lucky that we have got a good sum salted away if Sinclair's minx pulls the school down with her. I should forbid you to do it, but I know better. You have that stubborn look. Just do not come crying to me after you take that little spitfire on!'' the older woman declared as Guin closed the door behind her.

As Guin descended the stair she could hear a bustle below. She hurried down and arrived at the entry just as Perkins was ushering in their guests. As the young lady's light mantle was removed, the sight of her unseemly attire almost caused the schoolmistress to echo her aunt's opinion. The gown beneath the girl's cloak revealed far too fully the premature charms of a blooming beauty. Curly blond hair was cropped according to the prevailing fashion and arranged artfully to frame a heart-shaped face set in porcelain skin. The look of disdain in those intelligent brown eyes was barely disguised.

"I am Mrs. Courtney." Guin's greeting came out as little more than a hoarse croak as she extended her hand to the girl. There had been no time for the lemon and honey.

The girl ignored her and spoke to her companion. "The place smells, Daniel!"

Mrs. Courtney turned her gaze to the man who was handing his hat to the footman. He was just the far side of thirty, she would surmise, and dressed in the height of fashion. From the well-cut jacket of blue superfine that bespoke the hand of a master tailor, to the gold tassels that reflected upon shining Hessians, his attire was impeccable. The obvious expense of such fine raiment was as much as a declaration that this was not the miserly Earl of Sinclair. According to her information, his lordship dressed in the fashions of the previous century, wigs, patches and all. The eccentric Earl was reportedly a gouty, rotund fellow in his sixth decade.

"Mind your manners, brat," the man said, not unkindly, moving the unwilling girl forward for an introduction. "This insolent chit is my sister, Emmaline. I am Lord Corvin; my father has asked me to act in his stead."

"I am afraid that I, too, am a substitute, milord. Mrs. Haven is indisposed and I will conduct this interview in her place," Guin said.

"Interview? Father said nothing of an interview, Daniel. How ridiculous! I agreed to look the school over, Daniel, to see if it is agreeable to me and I already find that it is not! This place stinks worse than Billingsgate."

Guin managed to contain her smile. Experience had taught that any show of softness was usually interpreted as weakness by parents desperate for discipline. "I must admit, you have the right of it,

Lady Emmaline," she said. "We have had a mishap in the stillroom. As for looking the place over, you will be free to do so after I have looked *you* over. First, I must speak with your brother. Perkins will show you to the library so that you may occupy yourself until you are called."

The girl's jaw fell open. Clearly, she had thought her acceptance at Morton House was a fait accompli. Well, Guin thought as she ushered Lord Corvin into her parlor, let her chew on that for awhile.

Luckily, the schoolmistress' researches had also extended to Lady Emmaline's brother. Although Guin knew that Lord Corvin had spent most of his time upon the Continent, there was still some minor chance that their paths had crossed in society and that possibility caused her no little uneasiness. Still, it was unlikely that they had met, for she surely would not have forgotten a man like Lord Corvin.

As he seated himself in the chair before her desk, Guin took the opportunity to surreptitiously study the Viscount. His countenance was not as striking as his sister's but his eyes were the same peculiar shade of brown. In the light of the entry they had seemed like autumn leaves, now they seemed almost black. Unlike his sister, his looks were swarthy, his skin olive in tone, his hair almost jet with streaks of premature grey. Only the slightly skewed imperfection of his nose marred the perfect patrician profile. Still, there was a clear resemblance between the siblings in their proud carriage, that air of unconscious elegance that is like a second skin to people who are sure of their place in the world. In keeping with that inborn arrogance, the look that he gave her as he settled himself in his chair, was coldly appraising, then impersonally dismissive. It was obvious that the Viscount had already consigned her to the rank of minor functionary. It seemed that he had not recognized her and she breathed an inward sigh of relief.

"I too had thought that matters were fixed, Mrs.—" the Viscount fumbled.

"Courtney, milord," she supplied, as she pulled a folder from her drawer and tried to cover a rising sense of annoyance at his rudeness. Didn't even bother to remember her name; Guin was surprised to find that his unconscious arrogance was unsettling.

She kept her voice calm and businesslike, the hoarseness making her sound a bit like a creaky door. "I am sorry that your father did not apprise you that your sister has not yet been accepted as a pupil here. Some matters remain to be discussed, that is why Mrs. Haven wished to speak to the Earl and chat with the girl herself," Guin said.

"My father has empowered me to act on his behalf," he said in wary tones. "Just what do you wish to speak about?"

"How much do you know about our school, milord?"

"Very little, Mrs. Courtney. Only that it was recommended most highly by Lady Derwent, whose daughter Catherine is one of your pupils, and my cousin, Lady Abernathy, was quite pleased with her daughter's education."

"How is Mary?"

"I visited the Duke and Duchess of Berlenton a fortnight ago. The Duchess seems quite well."

Guin's eyes twinkled at the subtle emphasis on the title. So, he thought to put her in her place, did he? Well, Lord High and Mighty needed her desperately, if the information that she had gathered was correct. Corvin's sister stood at the very edge of respectable society. Only her youth had brought her pardon for her more reprehensible escapades, but the girl was nearly a young woman.

"Let me tell you something about our school then, milord. As you know, we have a reputation for dealing with, shall we say, willful girls?"

The Viscount sprawled back in his chair. "Do you?" he drawled.

"Come, milord, let us drop all pretense here. Do you wish to help your sister?"

Lord Corvin looked at her. "Yes, of course," he said. "She is a very unhappy child."

His forthright reply was startling. Guin was surprised to see a glimpse of real concern on his face. Lord Corvin really did care for the girl. That thought gave her the courage to plunge forward into the most unpleasant part of the interview.

"This, milord, is all the information that I could find regarding your sister," she said as she proffered a sheaf of papers to Lord Corvin.

He began to read then looked up at her, a tempest brewing in his eyes. "Does Mrs. Haven hire the Bow Street Runners to investigate all potential pupils, Mrs. Courtney?" His voice had a razor's edge.

"No, milord," Guin answered keeping her calm with effort. "All this is common knowledge."

He leafed through the pages. "I vow, your sources must be listening at our keyholes, for there is precious little that you missed. Father never told me that Em's escapades were being bruited about in public."

"I do not see how you could have failed to hear, milord." Guin wondered how a brother could neglect such blatant misconduct. Some of her disbelief must have crept into her voice.

"Your temerity amazes me, Mrs. Courtney," he said, his anger apparent in his cold, clipped tones. "If you have the knowledge of my family situation that you claim, you must know Em was in my mother's charge until her death last year. Byron, Princess Caroline and their harum-scarum ilk were the Countess's intimates as she gallivanted across the Continent. My stepmama is scarcely a more respectable substitute.''

His eyes narrowed; his lips compressed to a tight, angry line. ''I begin to understand, Mrs. Courtney. Having had a glimpse of my sister, you find that the already piratical sum that was agreed upon is insufficient for the trouble of her tuition. Very well.'' He pulled a piece of foolscap towards him and scribbled, then pushed the paper in front of her. His look of contempt was worse than a verbal insult.

The amount was outrageous; double the usual fee.

''Are you so desperate, milord?'' Despite herself, her voice shook. ''Is your family so anxious to get the child off your hands that you will pay any sum to absolve yourselves of responsibility? Do you think us some genteel form of gaol that will accept any prisoner for the proper price?''

''How dare you? You speak of a situation that you know nothing of,'' he grated, rising and leaning over the desk.

Guin felt a familiar stab of the old fear but kept herself from shrinking back at his intimidating proximity.

''I joined the army in my seventeenth year, Mrs. Courtney, to leave the family Bedlam. Then I spent time in diplomatic service. My friends kept the worst of the whispers from my ears and even if they had not, madame, I could do nothing about Em's situation. She was in my mama's charge.''

Guin marshalled her courage before she spoke again. ''I apologize, milord, if you think that I presume to criticize your family. I am merely trying to determine why you believe that our school can help your sister.'' She tried a more conciliatory tack. ''I must know something more about her than the fact that she is the daughter of the eminent Earl of Sinclair. I had hoped to glean from your father some understanding of her personality, her likes, dislikes, talents and aspirations.''

Lord Corvin stared at the schoolmistress as if she were a lunatic.

Perhaps I am, Guin said to herself as she crumpled the piece of foolscap in her hand. ''The tuition that was mentioned in the letter to the Earl will be sufficient, unless your sister should have some special need that we are not equipped to supply. If you will sit down, milord.''

He obeyed, his expression puzzled. ''You mean that you will accept Emmaline, despite what you know?'' he asked.

''Pending a talk with the young lady herself, I am inclined to think that we can find a place for her here,'' Guin said, raising a hand in caution when she saw a smile of relief dawning on Lord Corvin's face. ''But I cannot agree to take her on until I know more about the girl, understand as much as possible about the forces that have shaped her character. I realize that what I am asking is a violation of your privacy and I give my oath that not a word will go beyond this room.''

''What is it you need to know?'' He was guarded once more.

''Some of the things that are not in those papers, milord. The more of her misdemeanors I am aware of, the more easily I can help her avoid pitfalls. Tell me of the life that Emmaline has led.''

''Can you not guess from the information that you have already gleaned?'' He settled back in his chair.

''We at Morton House have often found, milord, that minor details are often the difference between success and failure,'' Guin said.

''You ask a great deal,'' Lord Corvin said as he rose.

''I am sorry then, milord. I hope that you will find

another place for your sister." She pushed her chair back and handed him the file. "Do with this as you please, for I have no need of it any longer."

"Dammit! You know full well that no other respectable school will have her," he said, throwing the papers to the floor.

"A governess, perhaps?" Guin suggested.

"She's had a string of 'em. Most will not stay beyond a month. I will give you triple your fee, damn you."

"Do not curse at me, milord. I have told you what the school requires. I have no desire for failure, and your sister seems destined to distinguish herself in a spectacularly scandalous manner. To be blunt, sir, it would destroy Morton and the reputation of the girls who are already our pupils."

"The Misfit Maidens of Morton," the Viscount mumbled.

Guin barely caught his words. "Is that what they call us?" she asked. Despite herself the corners of her mouth twitched and she stifled a chuckle.

The Viscount nodded with the ghost of a smile.

Guin's good humor was restored. In fact, she was a bit ashamed at herself for being so harsh with him. He was clearly desperate for his sister's sake. "I know that I ask a great deal, milord, but you must consider my position. The child has lost her mother and the only way of life that she has ever known. From what I gather, her stepmama will not supply the affection that she so desperately needs. I rather believe that her escapades have been an effort to gain attention."

"I had not thought of that." Lord Corvin leaned back, the tension in his posture relaxing as he considered.

"Did you ever do something that you knew was forbidden as a child, milord? And risk the consequences just to see if someone cared?" As his expressive eyes widened, Guin wondered what it had been like for him as a boy, growing up in the bizarre atmosphere of St. Clair Abbey. Certainly, the schoolmistress knew from the recognition upon his face that she had struck the correct chord.

"The governesses all claimed it was a matter of discipline," Lord Corvin said, uncertainty creeping into his voice.

"It is," Guin said, praying that her voice would not fail; it was barely above a whisper. "Discipline and routine can be extremely important to a young girl, but mere rules are worthless unless we make her see that we are seeking her ultimate well-being. Without the cooperation of those who truly care about her we have little hope."

He looked at her intensely, as if trying to assure himself of her motives. She met his eyes with all the confidence she could muster. His gaze was an unsettling question. She could almost see the calculations that were taking place in his thoughts. Doubt, anger, and mostly mistrust.

Apparently he found an answer that satisfied him. Lord Corvin eased himself into the chair once more and sighed. He brushed aside a lock of hair that had fallen before his eyes. "Very well, Mrs. Courtney. You have me at a disadvantage," he conceded. "What can I tell you about Emmaline?"

The bedroom was decorated starkly, with but a few framed samplers and paintings adorning the walls about the tiled fireplace. The girl's hand rested upon the mantlepiece as she bent with her head nearly inside the hearth itself. Upon her frowning face was an attitude of fierce concentration. She did not notice as the door opened silently and a dark-haired young lady slipped into the room and moved up behind her.

"Did you hear anything, Cat?" the girl asked in a whisper.

Catherine Derwent jumped up with a start, giving her head a sharp crack against the mantlepiece.

"Eddy, you half scared the life out of me." She rubbed her hand through her flaxen hair, feeling for a bump beneath the blue velvet ribbon.

Eddy fingered her friend's head gingerly. "Skin isn't broken. I don't think it will swell much. You will live."

"Thank you for your sympathy, Dr. Edwina," Cat said with mild sarcasm. "All that trouble and I did not hear a single word. Miss Matlin kept me after class to talk about a story, and by the time I got here it was all over but for the clink of teacups and the farewell pleasantries."

"Corvin, you say? For pity's sake, I thought that the new girl was a Sinclair."

"I had forgotten that you are from the Colonies." Eddy's glowering look caused Cat to realize her slip. "I mean America, Eddy. My father fought at Saratoga, you know. At home, we still refer to them as the Colonies if we know what's good for us."

"Your father sounds like the most awful bear of a man."

Cat frowned and took a handkerchief from her pocket. She wiped the soot from her fingers as she spoke. "My sister gets on with him fine. I wish that I had Elizabeth's way of wrapping everyone round her little finger."

"I would hope not; for if you were anything like her, I could never be your friend," Eddy declared. "Elizabeth is the slyest cat that has ever walked on two feet. All sweetness and smiles in public, then pinches and nastiness in private."

"The dandies at White's have styled her 'Perfection.' 'Tis no wonder that Lord Corvin is paying such marked attention to her.''

"The man has my sympathies if he doesn't see past her face. You are beautiful too, Cat, both inside and out.''

"Not like her. Elizabeth's kind of beauty draws the eye. She does everything so well—rides, dances. I am clumsy and frightened of so many things. When I am in a drawing room I do not know what to say or do. I am here because I am an embarrassment and a failure.''

"You are not!'' Eddy declared. "Why, you and Doro are my best friends in the world. You may not draw every man's eye immediately, but you're kind and sweet and loyal, Cat,'' she said, putting a comforting hand upon her friend's shoulder. "You are not a failure. Writing is a talent, a gift that very few people have.''

"Hardly a respectable talent for a marquis' daughter.'' Cat's laugh was bitter. "Anyway, let me explain this business of titles to you, Eddy. Lady Emmaline's father is the Earl of Sinclair. His oldest son and heir has a title of his own, a viscountcy. When the Earl passes on, Viscount Corvin will become the Earl of Sinclair, and inherit several minor titles as well. His eldest son will, in turn, become Viscount.''

Eddy frowned. "That's ridiculous.''

"Perhaps, but it becomes more complex yet. The Sinclair family name is Stanton.''

"For pity's sake! It's a wonder that any of you titled people know who you are.''

"Well, whatever you wish to call him, he is extremely good-looking. I vow, I would not give the Duke of Belvent a second glance if a man handsome as Corvin came to court, for all that the Duke is one of the wealthiest men in England,'' Cat said, rubbing at the rising bump once more. "Unfortunately,

Belvent is one of the few men who seems immune to Elizabeth's charms."

"I thought your sister was enamored of Lord Corvin," Eddy said.

Cat colored.

"So Lord Corvin is the spare horse?" Eddy asked sarcastically. "I cannot say I am surprised that Algy won't throw his cap at your sister. She is not an heiress and he adores money for all that he has plenty of his own. The only thing that pleases him more than riches is science."

"Algy?"

"The Duke of Belvent. He is my cousin on my mother's side, you know. He spent some time with us in Philadelphia working with my father on the effects of electrical forces on gaseous matter. What happened was—"

"Eddy! Spare me please!"

"It was highly interesting." Eddy looked at her friend in puzzlement. "But getting back to Algy—he is married to science."

"I did not realize that you were related to a duke."

"Oh, my lineage is quite impeccable, although I come from the *Colonies*. What with a countess for an aunt on Papa's side and a duchess for a grandmama, they all expect me to make some spectacular match, for pity's sake. How I envy Algy! He is a friend of Davys' and Faraday—Hush!"

Eddy stuck her head into the hearth and listened for a few moments to hear if there was anything going on below in Mrs. Courtney's parlor. "Nothing!" she said, in disappointment. "Anyway, Algy is particularly interested in the study of gaseous matter. He is somewhat inclined to resemble a bullfrog when he speaks, but I suppose wealth and a title cause people to overlook such superficialities."

"Well, Elizabeth has not got any money of her

own, as I have.'' Cat said, brushing her dirty hands with her handkerchief as she tried to justify her sister. ''I am sure Papa will give her a generous settlement, but it is not the same. My Great-aunt Catherine left me her entire fortune. Is there any more soot on me?''

''You would defend Satan, himself, for pity's sake, if he were a relation of yours. Turn around,'' Eddy commanded, carefully eyeing her friend's blue sprigged muslin and brushing at a mark at the back. ''There! So, we know nothing new about the 'Scintillating Stanton,' for pity's sake.''

''Scintillating Stanton. You do occasionally turn a good phrase, Eddy,'' Cat said. ''It does seem a shame that I missed it all, especially after all the trouble you went through.''

Eddy flopped down on the bed and put her hands behind her head watching a spider spinning in a dark corner of the ceiling as she spoke. Arachne's web was progressing beautifully providing an excellent nature study in her own bedroom. ''I did not believe that it would stink so. I just wanted an excuse to make sure that the flue was open. The voices carry so much better.''

There was a faint rap at the door and a whisper.

''Eddy? Cat?''

Eddy opened the door to let another girl slip inside.

''No need to make a secret of it, Doro,'' Eddy said. ''This is your room too, you know.''

''But none of us are supposed to be in here. I held madame off as long as I could.'' Dorothea Quigley scratched a spot of paint from her hands. ''I excused myself to get a new smock. Madame Celeste will be looking for you, Cat, if you are not in the studio, *vite! Vite! Vite!* Did you hear aught of the new lass?''

''Not a word,'' Eddy shook her head. ''Too late.''

"Pity." Doro pulled a smock from the drawer and made a moue of annoyance as she discovered a smear of gentian across the bridge of her nose. "But we shall find out about her soon enough."

A voice came drifting up the flue. "Mrs. Courtney? Is Eddy with you?"

Eddy jumped up from her bed. "I had forgotten. Today is my turn for kitchen duty. Mrs. Bacon must be looking for me."

"Where is that much vaunted brain of yours, lass?" Doro asked. "Mrs. C. is angry enough at you as is. If you miss your turn at kitchen, she'll skelp you sure. Now both of you, hurry!" Doro said, her Scot's accent becoming more pronounced in hurry as she grabbed a smock and bustled out the door.

"Don't see why we have to play at scullery maids once a week. It's a waste of precious time, for pity's sake. I have experiments to run," Eddy grumbled as she and Cat walked down the stairs.

"Oh, do shut up, Eddy and stop complaining for once, *for pity's sake*. It does make sense, you know, to understand all the workings of a household," Cat said.

"Granted, but the woman is a fanatic. None of us will ever have to work a day in our lives. It is just about the only thing that all of us have in common. Our parents are rich and well-born," Eddy said.

"And have daughters that drive them to desperation. True enough!" Cat said with a boisterous laugh. "I wonder about the new girl, though. Do you think that she will be anything like her mother. They say that the Countess of Sinclair could not keep the name of her lovers straight there were so many."

"I do hope she is accepted," Eddy said eagerly.

''Morton House has been so awfully dull since Lucy Putnam left to have her Season.'' Eddy sniffed the air. ''Ah! Cat, I think my luck is about to turn. Mrs. Bacon is making currant buns!''

Morton House has been so awfully different Lady Durham felt to have her Season! I bade smiled the an. "Ah! God, I think my luck be about to turn. Mrs Bacon is blasting clearly, hurs.

TWO

◄◄◄◄◄◄◄◄◄◄◄

LORD CORVIN maneuvered his carriage skillfully through the afternoon traffic of Mayfair, narrowly squeaking by a high-perch phaeton.

"A ham-fisted clunch if ever I saw one," he muttered. "Did you see that pair, Em? All flash." But the girl at his side did not respond.

Whatever had Mrs. Courtney said to Emmaline? Lord Corvin wondered. During the trip to Morton House, the girl had chattered nonstop, providing an amusing running commentary on everything from his taste in horses to the type of snuff preferred by Lord Byron. Her continued silence was becoming worrisome.

Corvin was surprised to find that his sister had become far more than a duty thrust upon him by his father's neglect. He was actually enjoying her company. Emmaline's keen intelligence seemed almost at odds with a curious type of naiveté, an innate sense of honesty. She was much like her mama in character, a worldly innocent, with all the contradictions that implied.

Although Corvin had tried to eliminate his mother from his thoughts, in Emmaline's company, he could not help but think of Mama. The girl's conversation gave him new insights into the life that his mother had led in her exile and Corvin was rapidly gaining

31

a new understanding of the woman whom he had alternately hated and adored.

Life with the Earl of Sinclair must have been absolute hell for a woman of Mama's passionate nature. Yet she had done her duty, stayed with Father through three miscarriages, until, at last, she produced an heir. Having fulfilled her obligation, Lady Sinclair had begun her odysseys, trekking across Europe, the Holy Land, the Americas, even Africa, bringing back presents to intrigue and delight a small boy whose greatest wish was to leave with her and see the world beyond the dismal walls of St. Clair Abbey.

"Well, Emmaline, what do you think of the place?"

She shrugged her shoulders. "As good as anyplace else," she said in listless syllables. "Mama always said that it is the people that make the place, not the other way around."

"Then I suppose that I should ask you what you think of the people?"

"The teachers seemed well enough, although I was barely introduced. I cannot quite decide though, about Mrs. Courtney. She is an enigma."

"How do you mean?"

"She is quite pretty you know. Beneath that disguise of hers. Her eyes are almost the color of Lake Geneva on a summer's day."

The prim and proper Mrs. Courtney, a secret beauty? The daylight that had shone through the window at the schoolmistress' back had rendered her little more than a talking black blur to him. Still, what the woman had said made a good deal of sense. There was a sharp mind beneath that abomination of a mob cap. She might be just the ticket to turn his wayward sister around.

Emmaline seemed like a young lady in so many ways. Still, just when he had been lulled into believing that the girl was almost a woman grown, Emmaline would launch into one of her childish leaps of imagination. For all her sophistication, she was a child still and Corvin was glad that he had not wholly missed those years of wonder, when schoolmistresses could be secret princesses. Corvin's lip curled in a smile at the girl's fancy.

"You think that I am foolish, don't you?" Emmaline had misinterpreted his smile and was wounded. "*She* does too, says that I daydream too much."

There was no need to ask who *she* was. The new Lady Sinclair seemed determined to make poor Emmaline's life a misery.

"No, Emmaline," he said too quickly, "not at all." But the fragile thread of companionship had been broken. Emmaline retreated once more to a sullen silence.

Corvin cursed his foolishness. The girl was as skittish as a pup and who could blame her, never knowing whether she was going to be petted or kicked in the backside? Norah had a great deal to answer for and, if the truth be told, so did he. He should have returned home immediately upon hearing of his mother's death and father's hasty re-marriage. Corvin recognized that he had been reluctant to deal with the problems he had run away from in his youth. It was far easier to resolve the difficulties of strangers.

The many wounds and grievances created by the long years of war against Napoleon were only beginning to heal. Corvin had floated across the Continent in the service of maintaining the fragile peace. He had told himself then that his diplomatic skills served the greater good. However, Emmaline had needed him far more than his government ever had.

Corvin watched as the girl fidgeted with the ribbons of her outrageous bonnet. She looked like a

young tart; more of Norah's work he would wager.
He cast about for a way to mend fences.

"Em?"

"*She* says that I am too old for childish nick-
names."

"Does she now?" Corvin's brow went up. "Well,
if I may address Lady Emmaline Henrietta Caroline
Stanton?"

Emmaline giggled and smiled in apology. "I'm
sorry, Daniel, for being so snappish. It is just that . . ."
She shrugged her shoulders expressively, tipping her
head slightly toward the tiger behind them.

Corvin was pleased at his sister's show of discretion
before servants. There was hope for the chit yet. Even
though she had left her thought unfinished, her
brother needed no further explanation. He too, would
be somewhat snappish if compelled to live at St. Clair
Abbey under the new regime.

Morton House was certainly a far better alternative than Norah's care, but the child needed a home.
His bachelor's quarters were most definitely unsuit-
able for a young girl, but if all went as planned, he
would not be a bachelor much longer. For Emmaline's sake, Corvin was contemplating the ultimate
sacrifice. Once he was leg-shackled, the house on
Hyde Park Corner would be lived in at last.

How his father had raged when he heard that his
countess had left the valuable property neighboring
the Duke of Wellington's home, as well as the bulk
of her vast fortune to her son. It was not that the
earl needed the money, for he was warm enough in
the pockets. It infuriated his parsimonious soul to
find that the money that he believed should have
been his from the start had once more eluded his
grasp. His son had long been out of his pocket, but
now Corvin would live in style without begging for
every groat from that nipfarthing old man or living

on his expectations at the mercy of the cent-percenters.

Worse still in the Earl's eyes, Emmaline's share of the wealth was beyond his touch. The late Countess had ensured that Emmaline's inheritance would be her daughter's alone. Although Corvin would manage the girl's funds until her marriage, not even Emmaline's husband would be able to lay his hand upon a penny. As it was, the Earl had grumbled about the will and had even sought to break it, but Mama had done it up right and tight. Custody of Emmaline, though, could not be changed. That right was unquestionably Sinclair's.

Corvin wondered if petty revenge had caused the old man to choose Morton House from the list of possibilities that Corvin had prepared? Since Corvin had offered to pay Emmaline's costs, it might very well be that his father had deliberately picked the school with the highest fees in the country. Well, it seemed that the old fool had done his daughter an unexpected good turn.

"How would you like to take a quick trip to Madame Robard, Em? The hour is still early."

Her eyes were alight with pleasure. "Could we, really?"

Corvin nodded. Nothing like a few fripperies to pull a woman out of the dismals. "One special gown and a few new dresses, I think, something more suitable for school," he said, trying to hide his distaste at her apparel.

"Do you not like what I am wearing?" Her expression was bland.

Corvin decided to tell the truth. "Not particularly."

"Then you have good taste. I cannot stand it. It was one of *her* castoffs."

"Have you nothing better of your own?"

"The gowns that Mama bought me are too small.

She said that it did not pay to purchase new clothes for me since I am growing so quickly, so she had her abigail alter some of her old ones to fit.''

Corvin tried to keep the anger from his voice as he said, ''Then we shall have to outfit you from top to bottom, young lady. We may require a few more such expeditions before we have rigged you out properly.''

What had become of the substantial clothing allotment that he had apportioned for Emmaline? On to Norah's back, he would wager. The new Countess was probably finding that marriage to Sinclair was not such an easy lot as she had supposed. One had to appease a mistress to keep her. Now that Sinclair had her as a wife, he could begin to practice his usual credo of economy.

Corvin was surprised to find himself enjoying himself hugely during the visit to the modiste. Emmaline's undisguised delight as fabric after fabric was brought for her consideration was a refreshing change from the avaricious calculation of the women whose attire he had purchased in the past. Madame Robard herself served them, and as always, she was the soul of discretion, pretending that she had never seen the Viscount before, yet subtly deducing his desires before steering Emmaline toward the choices that he favored. In this way, Corvin was able to seemingly defer to his sister's taste which, to his relief, seemed unaffected by her doxy stepmama. On the whole they emerged from the shop satisfied with their purchases.

Madame had promised to have all the garments finished by the week's end. By the time he had shepherded Emmaline to purchase accessories, the day was nearly gone.

''Thank you, Daniel,'' Emmaline said, as Corvin took up the reins of the carriage. ''Everything is just perfect. It will be wonderful to own some garments

that do not make me look like Haymarket ware."
She flushed as her stomach rumbled loudly.

"Hungry, Em?" Corvin asked. "I declare myself
famished."

"I have not eaten since breakfast," Emmaline admitted.

"Perhaps a detour to Gunther's would be in order?" Corvin suggested

"Gunther's?" Emmaline asked, her face lit with
excitement. Then she looked down at herself dubi-
ously. "I should have to remove my mantle. It
would embarrass you to be seen with me."

Corvin was deeply touched by her concern on his
behalf. "Perhaps you could wear that shawl that we
just purchased?" he suggested.

Emmaline clapped her hands. "Do you really
think it would do? What about the cerise hat? Then
we can be sure that no one will glance below my
neck; their attention will be fixed upon my head."

With the shawl in place and the eye-catching hat
upon her head, Emmaline was every inch the respectable young miss as the waiter deferentially
served their order.

"Thank you, Daniel!" Emmaline's eyes were
sparkling with delight as the pastries and chocolate
were placed before her.

As she enjoyed her treat, Corvin glanced dis-
creetly at his pocket watch and groaned inwardly.
He had all but promised to pay a call at Derwent
House. Elizabeth Derwent was a charming girl, a
paragon of respectability and superior sensibility,
just what Emmaline required to guide her across the
shoals of social acceptance. With Elizabeth as his
wife, Corvin had no doubt that the tarnished Sinclair name could be restored to virtue. Still, he hesitated to make the final pledge; a long-time
bachelor's cowardice, no doubt.

As Corvin turned the horses' heads toward Bond

Street, he had little fear that Elizabeth would be offended at his absence once he explained that Emmaline had needed him. The detour to the modiste had provided a necessary lift to the girl's spirits. Indeed, the change in his sister's mood was nothing short of marvelous. Mrs. Courtney had been proven correct; a little attention was causing Emmaline to blossom. For a barren disappointed stick of a woman, the schoolmistress had displayed a surprising amount of common sense and concern. Still, Corvin could not help but think that Emmaline required far more than any stranger, however caring, could give. Emmaline needed a home.

As he listened to the child's lively chatter, Corvin was convinced that marriage would alleviate a multitude of problems. The Earl could have no objection to Emmaline coming to live with a married brother. It would rid the old miser of responsibility for her bed and board. Certainly, Norah would be glad to wash her hands of the chit. As for Elizabeth, Corvin had no doubt that she would welcome his sister to their household. Miss Derwent would make an excellent wife and a striking countess with her alabaster skin and lustrous dark hair that was almost the same mahogany color as the mysterious morning rider's.

Corvin felt his curiosity stirring once more. He had never returned to Hyde Park to see her. The aching return of sobriety had made him realize that drink had probably distorted his mind. The late hours of his busy social schedule had precluded any dawn excursions to determine whether the woman was a bottle-produced fantasy. Yet, real or not, thoughts of the morning rider seemed to now invade his waking hours as well as his nights.

In Corvin's recurring dream, he rode a racing black stallion, but no matter how swift his pace, the woman on the bay was always just ahead of him.

He would shout, beg her to slow down so that he could see her face. Somehow, he knew that she was afraid and Corvin would wake with a feeling of profound sadness. Ludicrous! Corvin promised himself that he would be at Hyde Park in the morning, if only to convince himself of his own foolishness. It was doubtful that the rider would return and even if she did, the aura of mystery that had enthralled him was probably the result of a fuddled surfeit of imagination.

The afternoon was gone and the last caller had long departed Derwent House. The ormolu clock declared that the acceptable hour for social visits had passed. Lady Derwent eyed her daughter's increasing agitation with dismay.

"Perhaps you should go up and rest, Elizabeth," she suggested soothingly. "Perhaps Lord Corvin will be at Almack's tonight and you will see him there."

"He is not coming! I cannot credit it! Corvin is not going to call." Elizabeth Derwent threw the embroidery frame to the floor, not caring as the yarns scattered in a colorful tangle.

"Elizabeth, calm yourself," Lady Derwent urged as she picked up the frame and examined the delicate needlework. "Exquisite! Shall I have Molly set in a few more stitches this evening? Lord Dorsey was most admiring."

Elizabeth waved her hand. "As you wish. Oh what is the use, Mama! Let Molly finish it for all I care! It is for Corvin that I waited all afternoon, holding that wretched frame. As for Dorsey, he was intrigued with the embroidery because of the species of flower or some such. The man is a science-mad bore!" the beauty said as she paced angrily by the window.

"So, too, is the Duke of Belvent," Lady Derwent remarked.

"That is entirely different, Mama. Dorsey is a mere baron," Elizabeth explained, as if speaking to a dullard. "I refused a drive with Lord Dorsey so that I would be at home when Corvin came by. Oh! I am so furious!" A look in the mirror confirmed that anger had only enhanced her looks. The wood brown curls framed her reddened cheeks like a dark halo and her green eyes sparkled with a menacing gleam.

"You just declared that Dorsey bores you," her mother said.

"I vow, Mama, you are so countrified in your ways. Lord Dorsey is heavy in the purse and well enough to look upon. It would be foolish to let Lord Corvin think that I am already in his pocket and have no other suitors. He spends entirely too much time upon that wretched sister of his. I vow sisters are a curse!" Elizabeth hissed.

"Now, Lizzy, Lord Corvin did mention that he was going to bring his sister to Morton House this morning. I am sure that any delay was unavoidable."

"Mama, I have told you repeatedly never to call me Lizzy!" Lady Derwent's eyes dropped beneath her daughter's scornful look. "Morton House! An appropriate place for the wretched creature. I doubt that they can reform Emmaline's hardened character. After all, they have done nothing for my mouse of a sister."

"Actually, I am well pleased with Catherine's progress," Lady Derwent said as she bent to pick up the silks.

"Why could you not have named me Catherine? After all, I was born first?" Elizabeth asked with a pout, then ran to check the window once more, but the carriage that she had heard simply drove past. "The Duke of Belvent would take notice of me if I were an heiress like my little mouse of a sister.

Strawberry leaves and coronets! If only that old biddy had left her fortune to me.''

"You were named after my own dear mama!" Lady Derwent said.

Elizabeth let the curtain drop and turned in surprise at her mother's vehement tone.

"Though I must confess that Catherine is far more like your grandmama in her sweet temperament. You, daughter, are the absolute image of your papa,'' Lady Derwent said as she left the room, slamming the door behind her.

Elizabeth watched her mother's retreat in surprise, then concluded that she, too, had been disappointed by Corvin's defection and had not been trying to defend his inexcusable absence from Elizabeth's court.

Elizabeth wandered about the room wondering what had gone awry. Corvin had clearly been enchanted with her charms. He had danced twice with her last Wednesday at Almack's, a marked attention. They had driven together in the park several times and met at numerous parties and routs.

Had she erred in her judgment? She wondered. Elizabeth had supposed that the man, whom Brummel had styled "Saint Corvin" for his peculiar sense of moral rectitude, was looking for a model of propriety. Her guesses had never been wrong before, for she possessed an innate sense of what a man wanted to see and the ability to become the quintessence of that image. Until Corvin became involved in his sister's schooling everything had gone according to Elizabeth's expectations.

Elizabeth smiled slowly. Emmaline might just be the key to Corvin's affections. It would be easy to befriend the child and the Viscount would surely appreciate her efforts to comfort a poor motherless girl.

* * *

Evening had fallen by the time Lord Corvin reined in his team inside the enclosed courtyard of St. Clair Abbey. Emmaline's curly head stirred sleepily against his shoulder and Corvin found himself loath to wake the girl and return her to the nightmare his former home had become. The unused wings were shrouded in Gothic darkness and there was nary a candle in the window to show that the place was inhabited. Since the Earl's economies extended to the outdoor staff, Corvin was not surprised when no servant came out to meet them and take charge of the horses.

Emmaline sat up with a start and looked at her brother with sleep-clouded eyes.

"We are here," she said in mournful tones.

Corvin nodded. "Not for long, Em. Remember, not much longer."

"So, I shall," Emmaline promised, giving him a kiss on the cheek. "And I shall remember today as well, Daniel. I had a delightful time."

Corvin sent her inside while he reluctantly instructed his tiger to walk the horses. Indeed, the Viscount would not have set foot in the door but for the matter he needed to settle with his father's doxy wife.

Corvin found Norah, Countess of Sinclair, in the room that she had made her lair. The Egyptian style had gone out of fashion, but he had to admit that the Nile green of the furnishings suited her well. She reclined indolently upon a divan carved to resemble a crocodile.

"So, Corvin, were you terribly surprised when they refused to take the chit?" Norah asked, her beringed hand reached for another comfit. She popped it in her mouth and sucked noisily. "I am not. After all, the girl has driven off six governesses and I cannot blame the poor women. She is one of the most ungrateful, rag-mannered children that I have ever had the misfortune to deal with.''

Corvin's eyes were dark chips of ice. ''Is she? Well, then, you should be relieved to have her off your hands, Norah, since she will begin at Morton House next week. I would have her there tomorrow, except that the modiste needs time to complete her wardrobe.''

''There is no need for a seamstress,'' Norah snapped. ''She has ample clothes, Corvin. I suppose when a child has no one of taste to guide her . . .''

''If you mean to imply that she lacks taste, Norah, one cannot choose one's stepmama. That error is no fault of hers.''

Norah's face flushed as she rose. Corvin noticed that her lithe figure had become somewhat more Rubeunesque since she no longer had to inveigle for marriage.

''I shall tell your father of this!'' she threatened; her second chin quivered with fury. ''How dare you insult the Countess of Sinclair. Leave me, this instant.''

''Do tell my dear father, if you wish, Norah. While you are about it, ask him also when he intends to repay the sizeable sum that I gave him for Emmaline's wardrobe since you so thriftily clothed her in your own cast-offs. I begin to see the wonderful qualities that attracted my cheese-paring sire to your side.''

Norah's face paled and Corvin could see the outlines of the rouge that painted her cheeks. She pushed back a titian ringlet that had fallen before her eyes. ''You wouldn't?'' she asked fearfully.

Corvin's look was impassive. ''I most certainly would. After all, it is as Father says, 'you've got to watch the pennies or you'll lose pounds.' You know how he is about financial matters. Since the money was never used, it is only fair that it go back to me.

By all rights, Sinclair should be providing for Emmaline's needs."

Norah gave a snort. "His wife's by-blow. Why
should he?" She stepped back as Corvin advanced
toward her and grabbed her by the shoulders.

"Get your hands off of me," she hissed, trying to
writhe from his grasp.

"Let me make something absolutely clear, you
trumped-up strumpet," Corvin's words were whispered but distinct. "My sister is a Stanton. Heaven
help her, she is as much Sinclair's daughter as I am
his son. If you were a man, I would call you out for
what you have just said. Do not dare to repeat that
scurrilous rumor again, or I will make you suffer. I
swear it."

"Will you?" Her laugh was coarse and her look,
calculating. She wrapped her arms around him and
pressed her body against his. "How? Tell me and
perhaps I might agree."

He pushed away. "Those tactics might work with
Sinclair, but not with me, Norah. I am not a boy
anymore, to be caught by such brazen strategies,"
he told her, his disgust patent.

She looked at him, appreciation in her eyes as she
spoke. "Yes, you are a man, indeed. Those years
away have hardened you, made you strong. Do you
wish to use that strength to hurt me? I mean you no
ill. Why are you so cold to me, Corvin?" she asked
in a voice made for darkness, husky and sensuous
as velvet. It was still a siren's voice calling the un-
wary to forbidden delight.

She had tried to seduce him once, many years ago.
His father, against all decency, had brought his trol-
lop to his ancestral home. Norah had been foxed, or
else she would not have dared to enter Corvin's
chambers. When he had refused her, Norah had
tried to intimidate him, threatened to scream and

accuse him to his father. Before she could make good her threat, she had crumpled to a drunken heap.

He had hauled Norah's unconscious body through St. Clair Abbey fearing discovery and disgrace with every creak of the floorboards in those dark halls. Early the next morning, Corvin had fled to purchase his commission, never to spend another night since under his father's roof.

As Norah clung to him, Corvin wondered which had humiliated her more, his rejection, or her eventual resting place on that wretched night. He had placed her upon the dung heap behind the stable. In any case, she had never forgiven him and certainly, he had not forgotten how she had driven him from his home. The dreams engendered on that horrible night had plagued Corvin for years.

Corvin shrugged her arms from him with disgust. "Remember, Countess. My father will not live forever, and one day, I will be Earl of Sinclair. I have no doubt that Father will provide for your subsistence in his usual generous way, but were I you, I would make sure of my widow's jointure before I provoked the heir," he said, sweeping her a mocking bow just as the comfit dish flew above him.

"It must be a comfort to know that my entire family shares my regard for you, Stepmama. Cousin Felix, who would inherit in the event of my untimely demise even has a pet name for you, 'Nore the Wh . . .' " But the last syllable was swallowed as Corvin beat a hasty retreat before a flying wine glass.

Another crockery piece went soaring into the hall as Corvin pulled the door shut behind him. The Viscount noticed the awed stare of the footman with a tray of cakes in hand, who waited beside the entry.

"If that is for her ladyship, I would suggest that you stand aside as you open the door," Corvin suggested coolly. The shattering thud of china on wood emphasized the prudence of the advice.

"Thank you, milford." The servant's face was impassive but there was the suspicion of a twinkle in his eye.

Corvin grinned, savoring the minor victory although he knew that Norah would even the score somehow. His smile vanished as his father's portly form appeared at the top of the stair. From his unpowdered, periwigged pate to his high silver-buckled shoes Lord Sinclair was a relic of another era. The Earl had been rotund since youth and Corvin doubted that his father had purchased a new suit of clothing in years.

"Corvin, were they willing to take the chit off our hands?"

Corvin's face became a mask of reserve and he nodded towards the servant. "The hallway is scarcely the place to discuss these matters, sir," he suggested coolly.

The older man harrumphed. "The library then."

The waiting footman threw open the door then closed it behind them.

"Well, Corvin?" Lord Sinclair settled himself in a chair before the fire as if he could be warmed by the empty grate. Even at the height of summer the abbey's thick stone walls retained the chill.

"Emmaline is to start at Morton House next week," Corvin said suppressing a shiver.

"Surprised they took her in, considering her mother's reputation, but then they'll probably take in anyone willing to pay their outrageous fees. Took in Abernathy's daughter."

Corvin's smile was cold as his suspicion was confirmed. His father had indeed chosen Morton House because of the unusual expense. "She and her friend Lucille Putnum made the catches of the Season last year," the Viscount commented.

"Aye, true enough, but I doubt Emmaline will be any credit to 'em. From what Norah tells me, t'will be lucky if Morton House emerges with its reputation intact.'' Lord Sinclair pulled a snuffbox from his pocket and took a pinch. He offered none to his son.

''Really . . .'' Any one of Corvin's friends would have recognized the contained fury behind that drawled word.

Sinclair inhaled deeply so not a grain fell to the floor, then sneezed and wiped his nose on his sleeve. Oblivious of his son's growing anger, he proceeded with his diatribe. ''Those governesses ought to have taken a cane to her backside. One did, in fact, but Norah told me that the chit took the birch she used and broke it in two. The gel said she would put poison in that Friday-faced woman's tea if she ever tried to beat her again. I can tell you, that governess was gone by the day's end! Imagine, threatening murder.''

Corvin gave his sister a silent ''Hoorah!''

''Child has the morals of an alley cat,'' the Earl continued. ''But what can you expect knowing her mama? Norah says that the gel hangs about the stables, talking to the help. Put a stop to that, I did, but you can't watch a chit all the time.''

''Did it ever occur to you, sir, that the child is lonely?'' Corvin asked, pacing the floor in an effort to keep his teeth from chattering. Even if Morton House had been a dungeon, it would have been a far better place for the girl than St. Clair Abbey. The house had deteriorated greatly since he had left for the Spanish Peninsula. The ancient tapestries that had graced the library for centuries were dull with dust. The furnishings were worn and shabby with lack of care. Apparently, Norah's skills did not extend to housewifery.

''Chit's own fault. Not a respectable family in miles that has called since the gel came to the abbey.'' Lord Sinclair picked up his snuffbox from the table, shut it with a snap, and placed it in his pocket.

Corvin knew that his father's installation of a doxy as his countess was the cause of St. Clair Abbey's social isolation, but he bit back the angry retort. Argument would only hurt Emmaline's position, since reason and logic were useless once his father had clasped an idea to his bosom. If Sinclair chose, he could refuse to allow Emmaline to leave home. For his sister's sake, Corvin held his peace. By Monday, Emmaline would be well beyond the reach of his father's petty economies and the Cyprian Countess' spite. Using his restive team as an excuse, Corvin hastily took his leave, knowing that in his present weary state it would take but little to tax his temper to its limits.

As he took the carriage reins from his tiger, Corvin permitted himself a small smile of satisfaction. It was gratifying that matters seemed to be sorting out so well. Emmaline was to be settled in school. He had all but fixed his interest upon a veritable paragon of virtue who would help him recoup the tarnished Sinclair name. At last, the tangle of his life was beginning to assume a semblance of order and he could settle down to the stable existance he had always craved.

The light of the carriage lamps provided only poor illumination of the road ahead and the Viscount's smile faded as he realized that it would likely be hours before he reached his pillow. Although London was not far in terms of miles, the numerous ruts and obstacles that waited in the darkness would require slow, careful going lest he be forced to spend the night at the abbey.

"Must be getting on in years," Corvin mumbled. "Only past nine of the clock and I am longing for my bed." Sleep would be welcome indeed, but the Viscount found himself wondering just how restful his slumber would be, for he had little doubt that the dark-haired woman of mystery would ride through his dreams once more, destroying repose in the throes of fantasy. Corvin pursed his lips as he considered. Was there any way that he might control the wanderings of his mind once he closed his eyes?

A confrontation with reality was definitely in order. Doubtless, his drunken mind had invested the rider with an attraction that a clear view could easily dispel, since no real woman could ever so thoroughly capture his imagination. Corvin resolved once more to visit Hyde Park in the morning. If she was a habitual rider, then it would be relatively easy to exorcise the female phantasm who was cutting up his hard won peace.

Three

◄◄◄◄◄◄◄◄◄◄◄◄

THE DAY began as one of those late rare summer mornings. The leaves of the trees were bejewelled with the droplets of an early shower as the sun rose. Amidst a chorus of crickets, Guin reined in her horse so that she might gaze on the lush greenery. In all her months of early morning riding, Guin had yet to meet a soul and she knew that, for the while, Hyde Park was hers.

As the horse moved restively against her restraining hand, the schoolmistress patted Bombay's chestnut mane with affection. Doubtless, if his former owner were ever to see the animal again, he would regret selling the creature at a cat's-meat price. Although Bombay's coat would be permanently marred as a result of the carriage accident that had injured him, Guin's patient care had returned the horse to health. He would never be the showy animal he once was, but in heart, muscle and sinew, he was a prime piece of horseflesh.

Bombay pawed the dewy ground, eager for his run, and she let him have his head. No groom followed her, for she could not afford the luxury of stabling two animals. Guin thought the early hour protection enough. The ton did not rise to claim the park before noon and the footpads of London were doubtless dreaming in their beds after a hard night's work. Guin had found by experience that only honest folk were abroad just after dawn. Those men and women were far too busy to take notice of a shabbily dressed lone horsewoman.

She glanced at the elbow of her jacket with a rueful smile. It was a relic of richer days, the height of fashion years before, with its frogged fastenings and braid epaulets. The military air of elegance had long since vanished as the velvet grew threadbare. The fabric of the divided emerald skirt was held together with minute stitches that masked mended tears. The costume was comfortable and practical both sidesaddle and astride, but Guin knew it was barely serviceable.

Still, she hesitated to buy a new one. The schoolmistress felt remorse enough at the expense that Bombay caused. Since she handled many of the stable chores herself, Guin paid no groom, but every bag of oats seemed a bite out of their precious savings. When Guin's guilt overwhelmed her and the joy that Bombay gave seemed to cost too dear, she could always comfort herself that she had, at least, economized on the expense of the habit.

Guin and Bombay gathered speed. The morning was far too beautiful for thoughts of accounts. These moments of freedom when she was not the stern Mrs. Courtney, the dutiful niece or the mistress of Morton House were precious to her. For an all too short time, she was simply Guin and felt seventeen inside. Bombay was her Pegasus, soaring over fallen trees and hedges as if he truly had wings. Ten years fell to the earth below and Guin laughed with the sheer joy of being in flight. The sound echoed through the meadow and startled a flock of geese as they waddled through the dewy field. She slowed the horse to a walk and dismounted.

When she judged that Bombay had cooled sufficiently, Guin led him to a still pool near the bank and let him drink. As the animal slaked his thirst, she stared into the water, the spell broken. She was seven-and-twenty and the promises of seventeen were never to be reclaimed. There were the beginnings of wrinkles upon the once-smooth forehead of the outrageous girl who had once dreamed of love and a family of her own. Guin reconciled herself to the fact that her affection was destined to be spent in dribs and drabs on girls who would be hers for a short time, then go out into the world and forget her existence.

The knot at the nape of her neck had come loose during the ride. Absently, Guin released the pins and combed through her hair's length with her fingers in preparation for binding it up more securely. Her sole remaining claim to vanity cascaded down her back to her waist. Alfred had claimed that her mahogany mane was the one beauty that she possessed.

Alfred. He had been in her thoughts too often of late. What a pity Alfred Marshall had not died with his comrades in Spain, for he had always been a soldier, first and foremost. A glorious end on the battlefield would have suited him far better than one shot on a cold, drizzly morning and bleeding his life away on the damp ground. Guin had awoken to find herself Marshall's widow and whispers of Borne's notorious daughter were once more being bandied about with the morning chocolate.

The schoolmistress patted Bombay's neck and the horse lifted its head and nickered companionably. She drew comfort from the animal's unquestioning affection as her thoughts went unavoidably back to her late husband. She had made every effort to block those terrible times from her mind, but it was becoming increasingly difficult to ignore the questions of the past. Perhaps it was because her life had finally progressed beyond a simple quest for survival and she had the leisure to think once more beyond the next day.

Bombay raised his head once more and whinnied. Guin pulled the watch from her bodice. It was time for Elaine Guinivere Morgaine Marshall to become Mrs. Courtney again. As she reached back to gather up her hair, her spine prickled with a strange sensation, like a chill but far more disturbing. She had had that feeling often lately, as if someone were watching. Guin sighed. She must be getting eccentric as well as old to be experiencing such flights of fancy.

With a twist of her hand, Guin began to secure the pins using the rippling pool as her mirror. The calming water reflected a shadowed image that stood on the bank behind her. It was the figure of a man.

Guin spoke to Bombay with forced nonchalance as she fixed the pins into the twist. She kept her eyes on the image in the water as she plucked a clump of grass.

"A mouthful for you, my sweet." She walked to the horse's side; then in a swift motion, she was astride.

The animal sensed her fear and wheeled round instantly. He reared, nearly unseating her as he flailed the air with his hooves, threatening the unknown enemy that had troubled his mistress.

"Wait!" the watcher called. "I did not mean . . ."

But the rest of his words were lost as she thundered past him. Guin did not dare to look back, but as she considered it, she realized that the face in the pool had looked decidedly familiar. The thought was most disturbing.

The sunlight streaming in from the huge windows reflected upon the gold-banded china and illuminated the two men who were immersed in conversation at the linen covered table. Ives, Lord Corvin's majordomo, hovered in the background, attempting to anticipate their every need, be it coffee, chocolate or a fresh cravat; to this end he watched the breakfasting pair with intense concentration.

"It was the most amazing thing, Hop," Lord Corvin said. "Since I found that she came each morning, I would watch her from the copse. The woman is a veritable Diana! At first, I thought that she was out to kill herself and that great brute of an animal. But what I thought recklessness was just the confidence of consummate skill. I swear, I have never seen the like, even at Astley's Amphitheatre. Just when I think the lady is about to come a cropper." The Viscount demonstrated with a wave of his fork. "She is up in the air, over the obstacle. T'was like a centaur, Hop, an amazingly beautiful female centaur."

"And you say that she is always shabbily dressed, with no groom?" Michael Hopley asked, eyeing the abundant display upon the sideboard with undoubted appreciation. "Certainly an unaccompanied woman with a worn and faded habit is at odds with the type of horse that you describe. I would wager that a stallion like that would fetch a small fortune at Tattersall's."

"So I thought, until I found out when she began to walk the horse. His left flank is badly maimed, most of the coat scraped away," Corvin said, shaking his head. "The question remains. Who is she? Hop, she is the most magnificent woman I have ever seen and her hair, I vow it must have been down to her waist. T'was the color of polished wood, deep and rich."

"And how did you view her hair, pray tell? Does your 'Lady of the Morning' ride round with her hair falling loose like a gypsy?" Hopley picked up a fork and impaled a rasher.

"It had fallen loose and she was grooming it with

her fingers by the riverbank. I had finally decided to try and introduce myself. A mistake; I startled her. Before I could ask her name, she was atop that steed of hers and gone.''

''I say Corvin, it sounds like one of those Greek myths that I was forced to break my tongue over in school. Beautiful nymph by the riverbank, spied by lustful Greek god.'' Hopley lifted a silver cover and sniffed at the dish of kippered herring then heaped several upon his plate beside the mound of eggs and rashers. He eyed the tray of sliced ham appreciatively and finding no room on his plate, accepted another dish from Ives.

''You would make an excellent Greek god,'' Hopley said, turning his attention from the edibles momentarily to favor his friend with a glance. As usual, the Viscount was attired in the height of fashion, buff trousers, snowy linen and Hessians that showed no trace of a morning tramp in the park. ''Then she vanished and you haven't seen your Lady of the Morning since?''

Corvin shook his head as he helped himself to a slice of the ham. ''No. I have returned every morning. I suspect that I scared her off.''

''Lustful Greek gods are notorious for frightening off the nymphs,'' he declared as he added another rasher to the towering heap upon his dish. Then, seemingly deciding that he had accumulated sufficient victuals for a first helping, Hopley sat himself down to begin addressing himself to his meal.

Lord Corvin was silent as he watched his young friend eat. Despite his enormous appetite, Hopley was almost as thin as his purse. His uncle, Lord Farndale, was a very wealthy man, but he kept his twenty-one-year-old nephew perpetually in need of the ready. Not that it was necessary to keep Hopley on a short leash, for Corvin had never met a more mature young man than Michael. Indeed, Hop sometimes made Corvin feel as if he was the younger of the two.

Amazingly enough, Michael managed to live fairly well despite his empty pockets. He never borrowed money, refusing to fall into the common trap of living upon his expectations. Still, despite his economy, Hopley maintained his place in society by dint of being something of a professional guest, rarely dining at his own expense. The hostesses of the ton were grateful to know that Michael Hopley could always be called upon to make the numbers even. His biting wit had enlivened many a dull evening and his unfailing kindness to the shy young ladies who hid in the corners or lacked partners in the dance were much approved.

Being a practical fellow, he had decided not to rely entirely upon the chances of his uncle's early death or his perpetual welcome at the tables of polite society. Although Hopley's intention to enter the clergy seemed somewhat incongruous with his worldly outlook, Corvin had no doubt that Hop would succeed in his career of saving souls. There was an essential goodness to Michael that caused people to trust him, confide in him. Certainly, Pastor Hop could have any living in Corvin's control for the asking.

Apparently, Hopley had been chewing on his friend's problem. "Seems to me that she will be back, once she's sure that you ain't on the lookout for her no more," he said as he devoured his last piece of toast. "Any human being who gets up at that hour just to ride must love it so much that they will not want to go without it for long. Likely, she's just gone to some other park, St. James or Kensington."

Corvin's fork dropped to his plate with a clatter. "You are right, Hop! I shall try Kensington tomorrow morning," he declared.

"Wouldn't bother were I you," Hopley stated as he got up to the sideboard once more. "She will be back at Hyde Park soon enough."

"Why do you say that?"

"From your description of her, I would hazard that she's poor. Shabbily dressed, no groom, marred mount, it all adds up to no funds. It is likely that she is employed somewhere nearby, a governess most likely and the early hours are the only time she can get away from her charges."

"Surely any respectable woman would be accompanied?"

"There speaks a wealthy man! What groom would stir himself at that hour for a mere employee, Corvin? And how many employers would trouble themselves to provide one? I daresay that your lady somehow managed to get a loan of her horse and that was all she could get."

"And what if she is not respectable?"

"Hoping that, ain't you, Corvin?" Hopley asked with a grin, then bit into a pastry. He spoke as he chewed. "Tell me, my friend; what woman in the Cyprian line of work would get up with the dairy maids?" Hopley took a sip of coffee and sighed. "Ah, no one makes a cup of coffee like Ives."

Corvin's man accepted the compliment with a nod and refilled Hopley's cup.

"So, you think that she is not a Bird of Paradise?" Corvin asked.

"If she were under someone's protection, would the beauty that you describe be content with threadbare clothing, a badly blemished mount, and no groom to protect her in case some stranger came creeping up upon her unawares like you did?"

"I had not thought of that," Corvin mumbled. "I must have frightened the poor girl out of her wits. She must have thought . . ." He felt his face reddening. Hopley was right. Even if she had been a lightskirt, she might have feared that he would take advantage of her defenselessness.

Hopley spread some jam on another slice of toast. "Don't be too hard on yourself, Corvin. 'Tis hard for a man to see the world as women do. My mother used to say that if she could get the Deity to grant one wish, t'would be that men would bear children too."

"An unusual thought."

"Not really. Think how the world would change if men had to bear the same consequences for love as women. The Catholic brothers would have more men with a vocation than they could count." Hopley grinned. "Any more of those pastries, Ives?"

"Why do you think that she will come back to Hyde?"

"Probably the most convenient to wherever she lives. People whose time isn't their own tend to value what precious freedom they have, I have found." Hopley put down his cup and frowned as he took a pastry from the plate that Ives proffered.

"Something wrong with the coffee, Hop?" Corvin asked.

"No, not at all."

Ives' face relaxed.

Hopley hesitated. "I do not know if I should mention this, Corvin. I know that it might sound like I am a preaching Hannah More."

"Surely, you are fond of Hannah More?"

"There is a great deal that is positive in what she has to say, but it has always seemed to me that she feels that there is one Heaven for the rich and well-born and another for the poor, and that the poor will find it harder to get to theirs."

"And you, I take it, have a more egalitarian view of Heaven?"

Hopley accepted another pastry. "I do. That is

why I feel that I should mention a thought that just occurred to me."

"You might as well, Hop. It will come out eventually, anyway. You realize that if you inherit Farndale you will have great difficulty in ridding yourself of that conscience of yours and buckling down to a life of serious dissipation as a good peer with an easy route to heaven ought."

Hopley did not smile. "If the Lady of the Morning is not in the muslin line, what do you intend to do?" he asked.

"I am merely curious, that is all, Hop."

Hopley chewed silently at his pastry.

"She may be married," Corvin said, motioning for Ives to pour him another cup of coffee. "I have never pursued a married woman. But although they style me a 'saint' for it, my scruples have never been so tested. She is the most tempting morsel I have met in my life."

Hopley raised his eyebrows with mute eloquence.

Corvin reached for the sugar bowl. "And if she is not married and just a respectable young woman down on her luck? I could help her, Hop. Offer her a way out of poverty."

Hopley wiped at the corner of his wryly twisted lips.

"Damn! I am not out to seduce an innocent, Hop. So there is no need to glare judgment at me as if I am some impious future parishioner," Corvin said, setting down his cup with a clatter. Coffee sloshed over the edge onto his trousers. "Now see what you have caused."

"Me? Have I said a word?" Hopley asked as he stood up to brush the crumbs off his jacket. "Will you be eating that last bit?"

"No," Corvin said as Ives dabbed at the stain with a damp towel. "I find that I have suddenly lost my appetite."

"It will not go to waste." Hopley grinned as he picked up his plate once more. "I shall take care of it. Tell me, how is Emmaline faring?"

Corvin frowned. "Stop fussing at me, Ives," he commanded. "I will change before I leave, then you may continue your salvage attempt."

The Viscount watched his friend glean the last bits of food from the sideboard. "Emmaline is doing as well as can be expected. Mrs. Courtney has written frequently to keep me informed of her progress. Remarkable woman! A keen mind and a rather dry wit! I confess, I almost find myself looking forward to her notes," Corvin said.

"Ah, the redoubtable Mrs. Courtney, the paper ogre of Morton House."

"You know of Morton House?"

"As it happens, my third cousin, Doro Quigley, is a pupil there."

"So, you have a black lamb of your own in the family," Corvin said with a chuckle.

"Actually, Doro is a fine young lady, a bit unusual perhaps, but that's to be expected. Talented people have more quirks than us ordinary folk. You know that portrait of me in my lodgings?"

Corvin spread some jam upon his toast. "The saint with the face of a sinner? Do not tell me that your cousin did that."

"She did. In fact, I sat for her nearly three years ago, that would put her at about thirteen when the painting was done. Salt, please?"

"Remarkable," Corvin said as he passed the salt cellar.

"Isn't it?" Hopley grinned with pride. "It's Doro that tells me about the place. Apparently Mrs. Haven is a well-meaning but scatter-brained sort of soul. It is Mrs. Courtney who is the real power at the school. A spine made of steel."

"I can well believe it. The deceptive quality of appearance never ceases to amaze me. When I met that crow of a schoolmistress she reminded me of a nanny that I once had, a most miserable dried-up spinster of a woman. However, Mrs. Courtney actually seems most concerned with Emmaline.''

''Well, the schoolmistress is not a spinster after all. From what Doro tells, Mr. Courtney died at Waterloo.''

''Too many did.'' Corvin was silent for a moment, remembering. ''Too many. Why are we discussing such gloomy places as schools and battlefields on such a glorious morning, Hop?''

Hopley consulted his pocket watch. ''Afternoon actually. Half past twelve already.''

''Nearly time for luncheon,'' Corvin observed drily.

Hopley gave a contented belch. ''Why so it is!''

Corvin could not help but laugh. ''My mother once sketched me a picture of a python that she had seen in South America. It had just devoured a small goat. Damme if you don't look just like that drawing of hers.''

''I think that I am insulted.''

''Don't be. It was a very dignified python. I will attempt to mollify you by asking you to dinner tonight at Vauxhall.''

''I declare, Corvin, you do know how to placate a man. But I had thought that you were promised to Almack's tonight?''

''How did you know?''

''Corvin, you are not such an innocent to think that your actions lately have gone unnoticed. The matchmaking mama's are all mapping out strategies worthy of Wellington himself. They know that you have been at Almack's these three Wednesday's past. They know who you danced with, how many times, if you smiled, if you frowned, whether you preferred orgeat or lemonade. In short, my friend, you have become a prime object of matrimonial intrigue. It has been noted that you have driven in the park thrice with Elizabeth Derwent.''

''Did I?''

Hopley gave a solemn nod. ''Then went twice around the floor with her at Clemdale's ball.''

''Indeed? When do we plan to announce the engagement?''

''It is no laughing matter, Corvin. Are you on the lookout for a wife, or not? They are laying odds on you at Boodle's, you know? Two to one that you will be leg-shackled by the holidays. Miss Derwent is the favorite.'' Hopley had the look of a man who was considering if it was wise to say more. As he took his hat from Ives, he spoke. ''If it is a wife that you are seeking, perhaps you would be well advised to forget about this enigmatic woman.''

Corvin suppressed a twinge of annoyance at the unwanted advice. Hopley meant well and he had to admit, the young man had a point. Perhaps some illusions were best left shrouded in mystery. ''We shall see, my friend, but I would advise you not to place your money just yet. Vauxhall tonight. There will be plenty of time to get to Almack's later in the evening.''

The bustle of bedtime had finally ended and the halls of Morton House were silent save the quiet tread of servants going about their final evening duties. In the parlor, Guin and her aunt sat in the comfortable chairs near the empty fireplace.

''I just do not know how to reach her, Aunt Hermione,'' Guin said, cupping her chin in her hands as she stared at the clock on the mantle. '' 'Tis as if the child is surrounded by a stone wall.''

''As long as she stays within and does not bother anybody, Guin. I would be well content,'' the older

woman said, her mob-capped head nodding saga-
ciously.

"This biddableness worries me. If she would pout
or whine or pull a tantrum, I would understand, but
for the past few days, Emmaline has done just as
she was told."

"Why Guin, when Fortune gives you exactly what
you hope for, do you persist in questioning Her
gifts?" Mrs. Haven asked with an exasperated sigh.

"Because I know the signs, Aunt Hermione,"
Guin explained as she rose nervously from her chair.
"The child is up to something and I am almost sure
it is not one of the usual school-girl conspiracies.
Emmaline has not made any effort to befriend the
other girls, even though they have made overtures.
Why she barely speaks to Cat, and they share a
room."

"Give the child some time, she has barely been
here a few weeks," the older woman urged.

"If only I could find a way to reach Emmaline,"
Guin said, pacing back and forth before the hearth.
"I look at her and see myself, more's the pity. She
is so desperately lonely, but she does not trust people enough to let them get close to her." The schoolmistress leaned her head against the mantlepiece
and closed her eyes.

"Guin, you are wearing yourself out for naught,
dear. Emmaline will come round. You will see."

"I hope so. I hope so."

"Go to bed, Guin. It has been a long day. That
upheavel with Celeste has given you a case of the
dismals."

"I must say that I admire her inventiveness. I
never forbade her to use statues for models," Guin
said with a laugh.

Mrs. Haven smiled. "I particularly liked the fellow who was throwing the . . . what was it called?"

"I believe it was a discus."

"Reminded me of a young man I once knew, before my husband of course. He looked exactly like that."

"Really, Aunt? How did you know?"

"Imagination, child," Mrs. Haven said with a pert smile. "Strictly imagination. Well, while you may not have the sense to retire, I do. Good night dear." The door closed softly behind her.

Although she was tired, Guin knew that she was too uneasy for sleep. She flexed her shoulders to ease her cramped back. Lack of exercise these past few days was finally taking its toll, both in her health and temperament. Surely enough time had passed for the stranger to realize that she would not return. How vain of her to think that he would actually come back to wait for her in Hyde Park at such an absurd hour, but caution had prevented her from riding there again.

Guin clutched her shawl around her and crossed the room to the window. The late August night held the promise of autumn cool and the floor beyond the Axminster carpet radiated a chill that penetrated her worn slippers. From the street outside, she could hear the continuous clatter of carriage wheels going to a rout or ball somewhere close by. She doused the light and stood by a crack in the curtain trying to guess where the crush would be. She could picture the guests alighting one by one into the clear moonlit night. There would be strains of music spilling out into the surrounding street. Elegantly liveried footmen would announce the guests and usher them into the whirl of dancing men and women, a constantly shifting rainbow of color. Beneath the flow of music there would be eddies of talk and laughter, the excitement and gossiping speculation that was the life's breath of the ton.

The steady tic-tic of the mantle clock sent her thoughts questing back through time. How morose she was becoming. But her concern for Emmaline made comparisons unavoidable and Guin examined the circumstances of her past in the hope that she could find some clue that would help her with the girl.

Through the years, Guin had steadfastly shouldered the fault of her fall from social grace, allowing Caroline Lamb no blame in the matter. But now, Guin was no longer sure that Caro's motives had been entirely innocent. Surely, she had known that her wild schemes would push a young girl beyond the pale, yet Caro had urged Guin on in the most outrageous excesses, perhaps in an effort to divert the eyes of society from her own shocking behavior.

A cynical thought indeed, but Guin was honest enough to admit that it might be closer to the truth than she had heretofore acknowledged. There had been those who had tried to warn her, but in her youthful arrogance she had ignored them all. No one had ever been able to lead her. Distance and time had brought the realization that she and Caro were kindred spirits, lonely, free souls who had ignored the constraints of society to their own ruination. Nonetheless, Guin was convinced that with or without Caro, she would have destroyed herself eventually. Would that it had only been sooner, before she had brought Alfred down with her.

She was roused from her reverie by a tap at the door.

"Mrs. Courtney?" the maid called softly, poking her head into the room.

"What is it, Jane?" the schoolmistress asked.

"I was just checking the windows, madame, for Mr. Perkins says t'will rain by morning. I noticed that there was somethin' strange-like about Lady Emmaline's bed. The girl's gone."

"Oh no!" Guin started toward the stair and took two steps at a time in her haste.

Jane followed, talking as she ran to keep up with her mistress. "Just like Miss Lucy, Mrs. Courtney, pillows and blankets stuffed 'unner the quilt.'"

Guin burst into Emmaline's room and opened the drawers. She searched every girlish hiding place that she could think of while Cat snored away in the bed by the wall.

"I tried to rouse her, Mrs. Courtney. 'T'would be easier to wake the dead.''

"I doubt that she knows anything," Guin said as she rifled through the wardrobe. "If Cat were her accomplice in this, she certainly wouldn't be sawing her way through the night. Here it is! No young girl would ever throw away anything as precious as a billet doux."

She pulled the note from the rolled stockings. It was disappointingly brief:

Vauxhall Gardens, our spot near the Dark Walk, my darling. Eleven o'clock. I will be waiting. M.

"Bless me!" said Jane. "What kind o' man would send a lone girl to that rowdy place."

"A scoundrel, Jane, I fear. Only a scoundrel," Guin said, glancing at her watch. It was just wanting half past ten. They had missed her only barely. Damn! Guin slammed the wardrobe door shut.

"Mrs. Courtney, what is going on?" a sleepy voice from the corner demanded.

"Do you know anything about Emmaline's plans for the evening?"

Cat rubbed her eyes and took in the disarrayed state of the room.

"She has gone?"

Guin crumpled the note in her hand. "Just so! Cat, do you know who she is to meet at Vauxhall tonight?"

"Vauxhall? I'm sorry Mrs. Courtney. She does not say much to me, not much at all."

"I am sorry we disturbed you, Cat. Go back to sleep, dear. We shall take care of the matter."

Cat settled back in bed and Guin closed the door behind her.

"Tell Perkins that I wish him to meet me in the front parlor in ten minutes. Send a footman to seek a hackney carriage; then meet me up in the attic, Jane. I think that I can put my hands on that old costume of mine and with any luck, an old domino of my husband's. We haven't a moment to spare."

With her ear to the closed door, Cat heard Mrs. Courtney's instructions. As soon as the sound of footsteps on the stair faded, the girl slipped slowly out to the room next door.

"You are up and dressed! How did you know?" Cat asked as she watched Doro struggle into a pair of breeches.

"We are going to assist Mrs. C.," Eddy declared, presenting her back to her friend. "Help with these buttons."

"Mrs. C. had a chat with Mrs. H. regarding Emmaline. Mrs. H. had gone to bed," Doro explained as she pulled a shawl of black silk from a drawer and tossed it to Eddy. "We were almost asleep when Eddy heard Jane say that Emmaline had flown. The only question is where did the lass go? Can you make yourself useful, Cat, get us some glue while I start making a domino for Eddy? I think I have a scrap of pasteboard."

"They thought that I was sleeping, but I heard her read the note from Emmaline's beau. Vauxhall Gardens, a spot near the Dark Walk is where Emmaline will be, and I'm coming with you," Cat announced.

"No time, Cat," Eddy said, straightening the front of her gown. "Those pants are too short for you,

Doro. For pity's sake, you must have gained some
inches since the theatricals.''

"No one will ken, Eddy. Get those things for us,
Cat.''

"I still have that domino that I used for my part
in the highwayman sketch that we performed.''

"Just the thing!'' Doro buttoned the shirt. "Now,
Eddy, if you have the copy that we made of the key
to the kitchen door, we shall be on our way.''

The lantern of the boat mingled with the moonlight upon the wavering darkness of the Thames.
Guin swallowed several times, trying to calm the
rising terror that she felt as the ferryman pulled at
the oars. She closed her eyes tightly as the queasy
feeling intensified, telling herself that it was but a
short ride and would be over soon. The schoolmistress focused her thoughts upon Emmaline, praying
that the girl was too unfamiliar with Vauxhall to
come by way of the less congested water gate or else
Guin had undergone the torture of a boat ride for
naught. Since the end of August was at hand and
Vauxhall was soon due to close for the season, there
were bound to be large crowds at the famed pleasure garden. Guin hoped that admission through the
more popular main entrance would be slowed sufficiently to delay Emmaline. At last, the ordeal by
water was over and the boatman rowed back to the
opposite shore to seek new passengers.

Guin whispered some last minute instructions
while Perkins fumbled with his mask. "Remember,
when we find Miss Emmaline, I will draw her escort
off while you whisk her away. I doubt that she'll
recognize either of us in these rigs.''

Guin was wearing a Greek toga, crafted so beautifully that it made her seem as if she had been
dressed by a sculptor not a seamstress. The folds of
white fabric were caught above the left shoulder with

a trumpery brooch shaped like a serpent's head. A ribbon crossed at the breasts, molding the cloth, then letting it loose below in a gauzy flow to the heels of silken sandals. The drapery outlined her form as she moved, revealing nothing, but suggesting a great deal. Her hair hung loose down her back like a silken train of darkest brown. A mask of stiffened black fabric suspended below a wreath of gilded leaves completed the picture of the Greek goddess. The costume, and the harlequin's garb that Perkins wore so uncomfortably were among the pieces of clothing that she had been unable to sell. Their moth-eaten state was almost undetectable in the darkness

"Remember, Perkins, you get yourself away as quickly as possible and do not worry about me. We shall meet at Morton House as arranged."

"Begging pardon, madame, but what if the blackguard raises an alarm?"

"Not likely. He is meeting her clandestinely. The last thing he would want is to cause a scene." She adjusted her mask. "What do you think, Perkins? Anyone likely to recognize me?"

Perkins gazed at his mistress and shook his head. "No, madame. You are not at all yourself."

Guin chuckled at Perkin's awestricken face. Clearly the man was amazed at the transformation. In truth, she was not a little surprised herself. They paid their admissions and headed as swiftly as they could up the Grand Walk, searching the crowds for Emmaline.

"Jane says to tell you that she'll likely be wearing a bright yellow dress," Perkins whispered. "One of those from Madame Robard. Says it's missing from her wardrobe."

Guin nodded and breathed a sigh of relief. The unique color and style of the dress would make it easy for them to pick her out of a crowd. Lucky for them that the girl wanted to please her suitor to the point of ignoring discretion.

"There," the schoolmistress said, lengthening her stride. "She is just beyond the Grove. Come." It was difficult to move through the heavy crowds.

"The Dark Walk. She must be headed there," Guin declared.

"Aye, I'd fancy a dark walk with you, Goddess." A hand grabbed at her elbow. The dandy's breath was redolent with liquor. His look devoured her.

Guin felt a twinge of familiar fear, but managed to keep her voice steady as she said in her best classroom tones. "Sir, you are disguised. Unhand me before my escort takes exception."

Her attacker laughed. "Escort?"

The schoolmistress was dismayed to find that Perkins was an ocean of people away. Putting duty to the fore, she took stock of her situation. Emmaline was passing out of view. Guin had to move quickly. Silken sandals were far too light to be an effective weapon no matter how hard she brought them down on that Hessian covered instep. Moreover, the scene ensuing any such resistance would inevitably cause delay.

She recalled a trick that one of the stable lads upon her father's estate had taught her years ago. It would work rather well, particularly since the bosky gentleman had precious little balance left. She moved toward him, enduring his hot breath as she placed herself into proper position. Then with a sweep of her right foot, she pulled his supporting leg out from under him, adding a little shove at his elbow. They both toppled, but her landing was considerably softer than his, since he cushioned her fall. His hold on her had not loosened as she had hoped, so, she brought her knee up. The drunkard's attention was immediately redirected, his vise-like grip released.

A hand helped her up. She could see the apology in Perkins' eyes behind the mask.

"Out of here, fast," she hissed. "La!" she laughed loudly. "I vow! One glass of wine and some men cannot even stay on their feet." While the crowd's laughing attention was directed at the prostrate man, the pair made their escape.

"I think we are followed, madame," Perkins observed. They hurried to conceal themselves behind some bushes. All they could see, from their crouching position was two pair of feet and to their dismay, the wearers sat down at a bench before them.

"Is the chit here?" a female voice asked.

"She is. I have seen her," a male voice answered.

"Then why aren't you wooing your lady-love?" the woman questioned with a bark of coarse laughter.

"A few moments alone will do the job far better than all the tender words in the world. My man, Crum, has been watching her since her arrival. By now, she will be waiting for me in our little bower. Shortly, Crum will put a bit of a scare into our little lady and by the time I arrive, she will be so frightened that I will seem a veritable knight in shining armor. I will rout the villain. She will throw herself in my arms. Then, you need only do your part."

The sneering voice was uncomfortably familiar to Guin. Unfortunately, the only view she had was a pair of boots. The soles were in need of patching and the worn leather, while immaculately shined, had clearly seen better days. The heel swung perilously close to the tip of her nose as the woman in the expensive kid slippers said, "I'll be there with Farquar and the rest. Do you think a quarter hour is sufficient?"

"More than enough. Clever of you to bring Farquar along. He has the loosest tongue in the ton. Just the witness we need. Our little heiress will be so lovesick that she will be begging me to make her mine."

"And marriage will be her only option, I know. Spare me your braggadocio."

His voice took on a caressing note. "Surely, my love, you know that it is not braggadocio which makes me so sure of my charms with the ladies."

Kid Slippers' chortle was husky as she declared, "I will not inflate your already exaggerated opinion of yourself, my love. But I must warn you, I have seen her brother. He is in the gardens this evening."

"Better and better," Worn Boots said. "Contrive to entangle him in your party. That way, we can wrap it up and put a ribbon upon it right then and there. I am sure that Corvin can procure a special license forthwith. Then we can proceed straight to the church and wed that lovely fortune. So convenient that it is hers upon marriage. No settlements, nasty things those! Why my first wife's father, the mushroom cit, tied her fortune up in knots when we ran off to Gretna. I got barely a penny, but I was young then." Worn Boots sighed.

"And not getting any younger," Kid Slippers stated as she got to her feet. "We cannot be found together. No one must suspect that we are in league." Boots and Slippers embraced. Then they hurried off in opposite directions.

"We must follow the fellow with the worn boots, Perkins," Guin said as they rose from hiding. She hastily brushed the leaves and dirt from her gown. "I believe I know his identity. Emmaline is in great danger."

"Aye, he's our man, no mistaking it, the black-guard!"

They hurried after him.

Doro paid the price of admission with a flourish and swaggered into the gardens in her best imitation of a young buck out for an illicit night on the town. Her representation was excellent, since she had a pair of older brothers who considered themselves top-of-the-trees, and the girls were not remarked upon as they made their way toward the Dark Walks.

"Awfully gloomy," Eddy commented as she re-adjusted her domino. She jumped back as she heard a rustle from the bushes beside them. There was a murmur of voices, a giggle and the girls hurried away from the site.

"Lucky you're masked, Eddy," Doro commented. "I would judge from the color of those ears of yours that you are as red as a beet. That is why things are awfully dark, goose. Did you imagine that people come here just for the ham and the orchestra?" They walked arm in arm down the path.

"However will we find them, Doro?" Eddy asked. "Surely you don't intend to look under every hedge in the place."

"Emmaline is distinctly dressed, Eddy. Smart of Cat to think of checking the wardrobe; that yellow dress is a veritable beacon."

"Please, someone help me!" The voice came from a path nearby.

"It is Emmaline!" Eddy exclaimed. "I'd swear it." The girls followed the voices.

"Come, my lovely, give us a little kiss now," the masked man coaxed, pulling the struggling girl to him.

"Unhand the girl, you villain," Doro commanded in her deepest voice as she stepped forward.

The startled assailant let Emmaline fall in a heap. When he saw her champion, he began to bellow with laughter. "Well, well, bless me! Yer nanny know that yev snuck out o' the nursery, lad? Get on wiv you and leave a man to 'is pleasure," he declared.

"Please, do not leave me at his mercy," Emmaline

begged, tears flowing down her cheeks. "He is not my escort, believe me."

"Get away, pride an' joy. Afore you an' your ladybird regret it," the masked man warned.

"I shall distract him, Eddy. You get Emmaline away," Doro whispered. "I warn you, sir," she said aloud. "I am accounted quite handy with my fives." She clenched her fists and began to mince and weave, in imitation of her brothers' representations of prize fighters.

The villain chortled. "Well, if it ain't Gentleman Jackson 'isself! Do well, ye would to fly after that smart wench. Take to yer 'eels, boy, else I'll knock orf yer loaf o'bread so's ye won't 'ave need of an 'at no more."

"We shall see whose head gets knocked off," Doro replied. "Come on now!" She jabbed at the air as Eddy circled back and pulled Emmaline away. Doro did a ridiculous dance and Emmaline's assailant grabbed at his sides as he roared with laughter. Doro edged into a retreat and all would have been well had the man not chanced to look behind him and notice that his quarry had disappeared.

He rushed toward Doro with a bellow.

"Run for it, girls!" she shrieked and was about to follow her own advice when she tripped up on a tree root.

Eddy and Emmaline were back at the pathway when they heard Doro's cry. "We must go back and help Doro," Eddy said.

Emmaline's look was incredulous. "That was Doro?"

"No time for explanations, come on!"

The villain held Doro up by the collar. Her hat had fallen and a stream of red hair came spilling down her back.

"Well, me pretty maid. Where is the little lady,

ay? I kind o' fancied 'er, though yer a sweet piece yersel'.''

"Unhand the girl, you blackguard!" A voice rang out.

"Cor, agin!" the assailant mumbled, blanching when he saw his challenger. " 'e'll 'ave me 'ide sure, on this un." He obeyed the command, turned tail and fled.

Doro scrambled to her feet. "Thank you, sir," she said gratefully as she rubbed at her sore neck. "That was close."

"Who in hell are you?" he asked

Her hero seemed somewhat dismayed. In fact, Doro thought, if this was Emmaline's amour, the girl was singularly lacking in taste. He was forty at the least, Doro judged. A painter's view saw blood-shot eyes, angry and calculating as a cent percent-er's, thin cruel lips and a paunch that was not quite concealed by heavy corseting. A sharp's face, Doro surmised.

"Thank heavens you have come, Mortimer!" Emmaline exclaimed, bursting from cover and throwing herself into his arms. "My friends have just saved me from the most terrible man."

"How brave of them!" Mortimer exclaimed. "But now that you are safe, I think it best that they go. It is unwise to further involve them in our troubles; do you not think so?"

There was a rustle from the bushes and a shriek. "Help, oh please, help me!" A woman's voice cried.

Emmaline trembled and clutched at Mortimer. "This is a terrible place. Another lady in distress. You must save her!"

"But I cannot leave you and your friends defense-less," the man protested.

The shriek came again, louder this time.

"We will be fine, sir," Eddy said. "Please, go to that poor woman's aid."

He grumbled and went to follow the sound.

A hand came down over Emmaline's mouth.

"Miss Edwina, do not scream," a familiar voice commanded.

Eddy closed her mouth obediently. "Perkins? For pity's sake! I must say I prefer your other livery, although I have always thought you had a bit of a harlequin in you. Where is Mrs. C.?"

"Playin' will-o'-the wisp, I'd venture. Thought it was the best way to draw his nibs off. Stop your kicking, Lady Emmaline, or I will be forced to knock you senseless. I have been instructed to keep my hand firm over your mouth until we are well away. Struggle will do you no good. If you would follow me, ladies."

Doro giggled. Perkins sounded as if he were ushering them into a drawing room.

Four

FROM THE supper box beside the Grove at the heart of Vauxhall, Lord Corvin could hear the sounds of the band tuning its instruments. He was particularly looking forward to the scheduled performance by a composer whose work he had long favored.

"It certainly will be a welcome change from the so-called 'musical evenings' that I have been attending of late," Corvin declared. "I vow, I am weary of ill-tuned pianofortes and indifferent sopranos."

"Like Elizabeth?" Hopley teased.

"I do admit that her voice is less than 'perfection,' although I would be the last to tell her so," Corvin admitted.

Hopley set down a well-cleaned chicken bone and gave a satisfied burp. "A delicious repast, Corvin. I believe that I shall take just another few slices of the ham. Fancy charging such outrageous prices for these pitiful shavings and two emaciated chickens."

"They say that the carver could cover an entire garden with the slices from just one ham. Still," Corvin said as he took a bite, "you must admit that it is quite tasty. Now, what shall we have for the final remove?"

"Corvin!"

Corvin's eyes narrowed as he identified the source of the voice. It was Jonathan Farquar and with him were his stepmother and several of her cicisbeos.

"Pray, Corvin. Come join us." Farquar urged, his tones insistent. "I am sure that Hop has not left a bit of gristle to gnaw on and as I mentioned to your stepmama, I wished to talk to you." He lowered his voice as he neared the table. "I find myself short on funds. For the right price, I might be persuaded to let Indian Dancer go."

"Very well." Corvin agreed, setting his port aside. He had coveted that horse for a long time. Indian Dancer would make an excellent addition to the stables at his Yorkshire estate. "Will you come along with us, Hop?"

"I think not," Hopley said, as he brushed a crumb from his lip. "I know how much you enjoy your stepmother's company. I would not want to be *de trop*. Besides." He rose from the table, a puzzled expression on his face. "I do believe that I see someone I know. If you would excuse me, Corvin? I shall see you at Almack's, later."

"Stay. I shall return for the sweet course."

"Another time, my friend," Hopley demurred.

"Meet me for breakfast," Corvin called, receiving a curt acceptance as the young man hurried off.

"Must be someone special," Farquar observed. "Never known Hop to leave when there's food to be had." As they discussed the sale of the horse, the two men strolled toward the Dark Walk.

"Well met, stepson," Lady Sinclair greeted Corvin with an extended hand.

The Viscount touched the tips of her fingers gingerly, as if he meant to wipe his hands clean afterwards. The eyes behind the mask glittered with malice and the spots of rouge were marked against her pallor, but she made no remark as the party proceeded.

Corvin and Farquar walked ahead of the rest. They had just arrived at a price for the horse when they heard a scream from nearby.

"Let me go!"

They turned the corner and there on the path before them was Sir Mortimer Septimus, shaking a masked woman garbed in a Greek toga. She clawed at him ineffectually.

"I do not know what you are talking about! Release me, at once!" Her tones were unmistakably those of a lady of quality.

"Lead me on, would you?" He raised his hand to strike.

She cringed before the threatened blow.

"I would not, Sir Mortimer, were I you," Corvin drawled.

"Not at all the thing, Septimus, to hit a lady," Farquar added.

"You mistake the matter, gentlemen." Sir Mortimer smoothed his hair with his upraised palm in a lame gesture. "This woman is a cutpurse. She has just attempted to relieve me of my wallet."

"How ridiculous!" The woman pushed herself away from Sir Mortimer. "I became separated from my party and this . . . this . . . person accosted me. When I refused his advances he attempted to force himself upon me."

Corvin's eyes widened as he got a full view of the woman. Somehow, she was familiar. As she reached up in an unconscious gesture to straighten the wreath in that magnificent head of hair, Corvin knew. It was his Lady of the Morning.

"I believe that you are mistaken, Sir Mortimer," he said in a firm tone. "I know the woman. She is no cutpurse."

Guin froze, identifying Lord Corvin's unmistakable tone of command. Although she could not guess how, the Viscount had recognized her. The schoolmistress' thoughts began to scurry like a squirrel in a cage. How was she to explain the presence of the proper Mrs. Courtney unescorted in Vauxhall Gardens? Or worse still, what if he believed that Sir Mortimer was her companion for the evening? She doubted that the roué's reputation had improved with the years.

Guin did not think that Mortimer had recalled her as yet. But if the Viscount unmasked her, the reprobate would surely remember the face of his friend Alfred's wife, the woman he, Mortimer, had attempted to seduce. Still, what did it matter anyway if Lord Corvin were to discover Emmaline's evening escapade? There seemed no escape from the inevitable. Guin's reputation and possibly, that of Morton House, was ruined.

The schoolmistress' only hope was that the Viscount would not wish to publicly expose her identity for Emmaline's sake. She moved from Sir Mortimer's reach.

"Thank you, milord." Guin addressed Lord Corvin with deliberate hauteur. "Let me assure you, that were I a cutpurse, I would certainly find myself a better class of victim." If she were due to pay for her crime, she might as well get in a few choice words of her own. She was about to try to sweep past the group when the Viscount caught hold of her hand. So, she was not about to get off as easily as she hoped.

"Allow me to escort you, Goddess. Your worshippers seem to tend toward the unruly," he said.

Farquar chuckled. "Just like you, Corvin. Both a prime piece of horseflesh and a goddess in one evening. Care to introduce us?"

"Perhaps another time, Farquar," Corvin said.

He offered his arm and since there seemed no choice Guin stepped into place beside him.

"I tell you that she is a thief!" Sir Mortimer fumed.

"Do you still have your purse, Septimus?" Corvin asked as he turned with a frown.

"Yes. No thanks to her."

"It would look rather foolish, don't you think, to call in the law when no crime has been committed—or has one?" he questioned. "This fellow did attack you, did he not?"

"Yes, he did," Guin answered vehemently. "Although I was a fool to walk unescorted, I did not seek that miscreant's attention."

"Being foolish is not of itself criminal," Corvin said. "However attacking a lady is a crime. Perhaps we should call in the law after all and let them decide? What do you think, Septimus?"

"Perhaps we should." Guin added her voice to his. "I know that I have nothing to hide."

Septimus blanched. "I have no wish to cause a scene. Perhaps I acted hastily," he said.

"Not a very handsome apology," Corvin drawled. "Is his penance acceptable, Goddess?"

"For my part, he can take the matter up with Hades! My only wish is to find my escort. The poor man must be terribly worried."

Sir Mortimer gave a grunt of disbelief but a look from Corvin quelled him. "Be grateful, Septimus, you have been spared the wrath of the goddess. However, beware of mine."

"Corvin? Farquar? Where are you?" a female voice called.

It was Kid Slippers! Guin would have waited to see who Sir Mortimer's accomplice was, but Corvin clearly had other ideas.

He nodded a farewell to Farquar. "I will send my man round tomorrow morning with instructions regarding Indian Dancer. Please give my apologies to the rest of the party, but I must see that our goddess finds her escort unmolested."

Farquar chuckled. "Some men have all the luck!"

What would she say to him? she wondered as they hurried away from the scene. Undoubtably, Emmaline would be withdrawn from Morton House. Guin rebuked herself from worrying only about her own reputation. Septimus was an evil man and he was out to seduce the girl for her fortune. All those years ago, when she had refused to succumb to his blandishments, he had deliberately destroyed any fondness that Alfred might have had for her. Mortimer was constantly at hand, pointing out her faults, playing up her past misdeeds, whispering in her husband's ear, insinuating until Alfred had loathed her and been ready to believe any tale.

Guin vowed to keep him from destroying Emmaline, but how would she stop a girl who thought herself deeply in love? Would Corvin believe her if she told him of the plot against his sister? There seemed to be no choice. If Emmaline were taken from her care then someone would have to watch over her. However, Corvin had explained to her during the interview that he did not live at St. Clair Abbey. There seemed no solution to the conundrum.

Guin shivered. The evening had grown cooler and Perkins had her shawl. It seemed that the only warm spot on her body was where Viscount Corvin held her arm. Her trepidation grew as he led her farther and farther from the main garden. She summoned the remnants of her courage.

"Milord, is the Grand Walk not in the other direction?" she asked.

He smiled. "It is. Do you still worry about your 'escort'?"

His inflection on the last word made it clear that he did not believe that she had one. Guin inhaled sharply. The look in his eyes was unmistakable. Ahead was a small isolated grove. Was that his game, then? He had recognized her as his sister's schoolmistress. Did he think that she would be willing to exchange her favors for his silence? Although the path was empty of any hope of rescue, she pulled her arm away abruptly.

"So, it is clear to me now that I have exchanged one dilemma for another. Whatever you may believe, milord, I am not a doxy and will not be treated as one. You claimed my acquaintance, sirrah, but if you think that I am a lightskirt then you know me not at all!" To Guin's dismay, her voice broke. It was so unfair, all the work of years would be destroyed by an unhappy little girl, and now, she would be forced to protect herself from the attentions of Emmaline's amorous brother. The tensions of the evening broke through the floodgates of her control. Tears welled in her eyes as she turned to flee. If the Viscount wished to rebuke her, he knew where to find her, but she would be damned if she would allow herself to be used so.

His hand gripped her wrist.

"Let me go!" Guin kicked at his shin, but the satin slippers were incapable of making the blow tell. "I will scream, milord. Perhaps my next rescuer will not be a brute!"

"Peace, exquisite Goddess! Peace! I mean you no harm." Viscount Corvin took hold of her fist just before it made contact with his jaw.

"Will you stop spouting that goddess nonsense!" Guin tried to squirm from his hold but was powerless as his hand moved toward her mask. He had both her hands firmly clasped in one of his own. He seemed to tower above her. Although her height was average, her head came barely past the Viscount's shoulder. He removed the mask and she glared at him through a blur of tears.

"You are crying," he said, surprised to see the moisture that glistened on her lashes.

"How very observant of you, milord. Perhaps I am a trifle overset. It is not every day that I have the pleasure of being molested by two men." Guin emitted an ear-piercing shriek. "Thief! Thief!"

His hand came down to cover her mouth. Teeth clamped into his flesh.

"Vixen! I do not mean to hurt you, I swear. I only wanted to find out who you are." The Viscount put the bleeding finger into his mouth.

He had not recognized her! Guin spoke warily. "You claimed to know me, milord. Or was that merely a ploy to seize the bone from the dog who had it?"

"I have met you before, in a manner of speaking; a week ago in Hyde Park. I startled you."

"Was that you then? You frightened me half out of my mind. Perhaps if my wits had not been wanting, I would have run you down," she said as she tried to twist away, but he held her fast.

"I wanted to apologize."

She eyed her imprisoned wrists significantly. "I might be able to take you seriously if you released me."

"Only if you promise not to run away. It is far too dangerous for a lone woman here, especially a beautiful one." His voice was a caress.

"So I find," Guin declared, feeling as though she had gone from the frying pan to the fire. Apparently, he did not recognize her as the proper Mrs. Courtney. The chance still remained that he would discover her identity, but the more immediate problem was the man's intentions, clearly less than honorable. She would need some powerful means to keep him at bay. "I will give you my word, milord, not to run, if you will give me your oath as a Stanton that you will not touch me without leave."

He was startled. "You have the advantage of me, Goddess. You know who I am."

"Quite the contrary. It appears that the advantage is entirely yours," Guin snapped. "After all, 'tis I who is being forcibly detained. Now do you give your word as a Stanton or do I start shrieking again? You cannot cover my mouth and keep hold of my hands.''

"You would lose that bet," he said with a grin and his mouth came down to cover hers.

Corvin was an attractive man and his expertise was far beyond anything in Guin's experience. Yet, the knowledge that she was being used against her will destroyed any pleasure that she might have felt. She was a block of ice, cold, unresponsive, waiting for him to remove his lips from her mouth so she might scream. Guin had no illusions about what could happen. She might shout herself hoarse and even were someone to hear they would think it part of the usual play in these pleasure gardens.

Corvin's eyes opened at last. Clearly he was startled by her expression.

"Are you quite done?" she asked in a choked voice.

He nodded, his face a picture of puzzlement.

"Thief! Thief!" The best Guin could manage was almost a sob. "Help me, oh what's the use . . . ?" Her shoulders shook silently while the tears streamed down her cheeks.

"Do not cry, Goddess. Please, you need not have any fear that I will do you harm; it is just that you are so beautiful. Here." He pulled a piece of snowy linen from his pocket and began to wipe at her face. "The dye from your mask ran and you have the look of an African zebra. Please, stop crying," he said moving closer, longing to gather her into his arms.

She stepped back and turned to flee, but the ties to her sandals came loose. Guin landed in a distraught heap. The Viscount towered menacingly over her and she raised her hands above her head in an attempt to shield herself.

"Do not run again, Goddess. I shall not touch you

unless you wish it, I swear, word of a Stanton," he declared. "Now give me your pledge that you will not run into the night alone."

Guin searched his face.

"No Stanton has ever broken his sworn oath," he said softly.

The look of desire that Guin had feared had been replaced by concern. "You have my word, milord," she agreed reluctantly, refusing the hand that he offered as she got herself to her feet and brushed the dirt from her gown.

"As . . . ?" He was fishing.

"As a goddess, of course," Guin told him while she chafed her wrist. It would be bruised by morning, no doubt of it.

"Did I hurt you?" the Viscount said anxiously.

"Why would you ever think that, milord? I have gotten quite used to being manhandled this evening. I vow, it is veritably water off a duck's back."

"You quite rightfully named me a brute."

His apologetic look did not mollify her. "No, milord, you are no brute. You are merely like many a male of our class, an arrogant, self-centered rogue who thinks that every woman who catches his eye will fall gratefully at his feet, but never a brute."

"Well you have fallen at my feet, certainly, but I do not see any signs of gratitude."

Guin looked at him in surprise. He was roasting her.

"I suppose that I do deserve a set down," Corvin continued. "I honestly did wish to apologize though for sneaking up on you unawares the other day. You looked so lovely there as you sat by the waterside."

"I accept your apology, milord, along with all the Spanish coin. Now, should we not be getting back?"

Corvin heard the plea in her voice. Despite the oath that she had extorted, she was clearly afraid of him. When he had tried to help her up, the woman's defensive posture had confirmed that her reluctance was not the flirtatious play of a Cyprian adding spice to the chase, but genuine terror. She had thought that he was about to strike her.

It was a puzzle, indeed. When Corvin had recognized her as his Lady of the Morning, alone at Vauxhall, he had thought her a lightskirt and fair prey. Now he recognized that she was no experienced demimondaine. Most of the fashionable impures who affected genteel ways quickly reverted to their low origins in stress or anger. Only a lady of quality would have thought to seek a gentleman's pledge to protect her person and only a lady would think it worth anything.

"I gave my word," he reminded her softly.

"Now it is I that must apologize, milord. I did not doubt you," she lied taking the dirty handkerchief that he offered once more and dabbing at her nose. "There now, I am usually not such a watering pot, but it has been an eventful evening."

She had left a smudgy trail where the linen had touched. "Your face is still dirty. Will you let me?" he asked, watching the conflict in her eyes. "Surely you do not want to go back to your escort looking like that?"

Corvin was somewhat shocked when she nodded and handed him the cloth. He cleaned the dirt away gently, forcing his hand not to linger on those magnificent high cheekbones. He could feel her trembling, compelling herself not to flinch. "There now, good as new," he said, displaying the dirty handkerchief. "You had best wait till the mask dries a bit before you put it on once more."

"I have ruined your handkerchief," she said.

There was a tremor in her voice and Corvin felt a stirring of pity. She had suffered a great deal this evening, but if the goddess was a lady, why had she been without escort? Septimus had said that she had led him on. What had that meant? Obviously, if she were a novice seeking a patron in the muslin trade, her judgment was singularly lacking, for the man was a loose screw and empty of pocket beside. She was an enigma, this goddess. A Cyprian would have continued to secure his sympathy, while playing the fearful damsel and kept the knowledge of his identity secret.

"It is no bother at all," Corvin assured her. "I have another just like it."

She gave him a weak smile. "Thank you, milord."

"Ah, much better. Since you do not wish me to call you Goddess, do you have a name?" he asked, deliberately keeping his tone light and teasing.

"Goddess will do fine for this evening, milord," she said, shaking her head. "It may seem rude of me, milord, but I would as soon no one knew about tonight's escapades."

Another possibility occurred to Corvin. What if she was an impoverished gentlewoman on a night's lark that had gone wrong? Her gown was of good quality, its elegance clearly the labor of a first rate modiste, yet up close, it was obvious that the moths had been at work and there was an unmistakable camphor smell. Her fingers were long and shapely, the hands smooth, not those of a woman who toiled. In the moonlight, he noticed the gleam of gold. A wedding band.

"Shall we search for your husband?" Corvin said, a dull ache rising in his breast. So, the tale of an escort was likely true. "Unless the man is a fool, he is probably tearing the place apart looking. I will help you find him."

Guin seized upon his false assumption. "No, do not trouble yourself, milord. We had words. If you would just accompany me so that I might get a carriage at the gate, I would be grateful."

"Have you eaten yet?" he asked, his voice unintentionally harsh as he contemplated a man careless enough to drive such a woman to venture unaccompanied at Vauxhall or to let her ride in Hyde Park alone at dawn. He would wager that the lout was responsible for the fear in her eyes. The woman had been brutalized, of that he had little doubt.

"I am not hungry, milord; just weary and wishing for home. I will just put on my mask and go."

She seemed incredibly sad. He hated her husband, sight unseen, for causing her such sorrow and pain. Any man who was craven enough to abuse a woman was no man at all in Corvin's estimation.

"Very well," Corvin offered his arm and after a brief hesitation, she took it. They walked in silence toward the music and crowds. Corvin wished that she had not masked herself once more so that he might read the expressions on her face.

Elsewhere in Vauxhall, Michael Hopley was dodging through the crowd upon the Grand Walk.

"Where do you think you're going, Ian, my lad?" Hopley said, as he reached his object at last. Grabbing the boy firmly by the nape of his jacket, the young man whirled him around. However the face was not the one that Hopley had expected.

"Doro!" he whispered.

"Play along, Michael," Doro said in a undertone. "Unless you want a scandal that will bring Uncle Farndale down upon all our heads."

Hopley forced his visage into a pleasant expression and said, "Well, well, Ian, playing truant from Oxford, I see." He murmured between clenched teeth. "What is going on here, Doro?"

"Explanations later," she whispered. "We were just leaving, Hop. Will you walk with us?" Doro said aloud. She offered her arm to a dark-haired girl in a dress of cherry red, who responded with a simpering giggle in perfect imitation of a young tart.

"Will you hurry?" said a harlequin with a masked young girl in reluctant tow. He pulled up with a start when he saw Hopley. "Bless me!"

"Yes, definitely," Hopley said, his mouth set into a grim line. "I definitely think that you will need all the blessings you can get before this night is over, Perkins."

"I beg you, sir," the harlequin-costumed butler whispered. "For your cousin's sake, do nothing to draw attention to us."

"I am not a fool, fellow. Let us get to a carriage quickly. That ginger mop of Doro's is threatening to spill out of the hat."

They got to the gate.

"Over here," a voice called.

Ordinarily, Hopley would have thought that they were being met by a blonde-haired boy, but his perceptions had been sharpened. It was a girl in boy's clothing that was shepherding them to a waiting cab. Within minutes the party was safely ensconced in the hackney and on their way to Green Street.

"Well, I am waiting for an explanation." Hopley surveyed the quintet of faces, masked and unmasked.

"Thanks Cat," Doro said with a smile. "That was good thinking."

"I was hoping that you would exit by the main gate. Didn't want to miss all the fun," Cat declared, grinning broadly.

"He shall think I deserted him!" The girl in the yellow gown began to wail. "Oh why didn't I scream and yell and kick? At least he would have realized that I was being taken away against my will."

"For pity's sake, don't be a fool, Emmaline," Doro's companion said.

Hopley recognized the girl who spoke as Doro's friend Eddy. Emmaline? Was that Corvin's sister beneath the domino?

"You may be a lovesick idiot, but surely you would have gained nothing by causing a scene and exposing yourself to scandal. Especially for that man," Eddy wrinkled her nose eloquently. "Why, he is a snake if I ever saw one and an ancient reptile at that."

Hopley groaned. The last thing he needed was to be caught in the middle of a schoolgirl's disgrace. With his limited prospects, he hung barely onto the fringes of acceptability. Any hint of scandal and he could see his table being cleared. There would be no more invitations to dine if he was tainted by rumor. He cleared his throat to ask for an explanation, but could not get a word in.

"You do not know him, Eddy. He has been maligned, I tell you. He is so kind, so good to me. He loves me," Emmaline declared defiantly.

There was a derisive noise from Eddy. Hopley looked on, appalled, as the thwarted lover's defenses crumbled and she began to bawl.

"Ah, our Eddy is always quick with a kind and soothing word," Doro remarked to her cousin by way of sarcastic explanation. "Hush, dear. If he truly loves you then he will find a way to be with you," Doro crooned, casting Eddy a quelling look as she soothed Emmaline.

"Where is Mrs. C.?" Cat asked.

"She told me to see you back to Morton House. She will take care of herself, she said," Perkins explained.

"No one will bother her, I'm sure," Eddy commented with a laugh.

"I would not be so *sanguin*," Doro disagreed with a frown. "There is a lot more to Mrs. C. than meets the eye. She makes herself ugly so that no one will see what is really beneath."

Perkins nodded. "I must admit that the thought of her alone in that place worries me."

"I cannot pretend that I understand what is going on here," Hopley said, "but no respectable woman should be left unattended at Vauxhall. I will escort the ladies home, Perkins, so that you may go back for your mistress."

The harlequin-costumed butler's face broke out in a grateful smile. "Bless you, sir," he said. "I am afraid that she might come to grief."

"With this squeeze of traffic we have only gone a short way," Cat said. "You should be back in a matter of minutes, Perkins."

"Now! I want a full explanation, Doro," Hopley demanded, settling back against the seat as Perkins shut the door behind him.

"On one condition, Michael. I claim my favor first."

"Doro!" The word was menacing.

"You owe me, cousin, and I claim it now."

"I was only fourteen, Doro, when I put that frog in Uncle's humidor," he protested, but he could see from that stubborn look that she would stand firm. "What do you want?"

"Your promise that nothing that I tell you will be revealed to a soul."

"Very well, my promise, Doro. Now we are quits."

Doro grinned. "I always knew that the whipping I took for you would be of use. As you are so fond of saying, Pastor Hop, nothing is without purpose."

Hopley had the distinct feeling that he would regret his vow.

The famed fireworks at Vauxhall had begun, but Corvin did not lift his eyes to the sky. He looked at her, glimpsing the traces of her first true smile of the evening as the wonder of light and sound exploded overhead. He heard the sharp intake of her breath as a shower of silver sparks lit the skies in a glittering rain. Then, the thunder from above ceased and the moonlight filtered weakly through the haze left by the explosives. Her eyes met his, igniting a desire within him that was almost an ache, but it was a pain that he would have to deal with. Corvin had given his oath and he would not break it, no matter how great his urge to take this unknown woman into his arms once more.

She was married, he reminded himself. Married. How she trembled. Was she, too, sharing this unexplainable longing for a stranger's embrace or was it merely the effect of the night's magic? The moon shone full upon her, imbuing her with a mystical light as if she were truly conjured up by some marvelous sorcery. The fullness of her lips, the glory of her hair and those gem-like eyes that seemed cut from a perfect summer sky all tempted him to madness. Only the awareness of his word kept him at his distance.

Corvin's senses were so heightened that he immediately perceived the abrupt change in her demeanor, despite the mask covering the upper part of her face. He followed the direction of her gaze and saw a harlequin coming towards them.

"Your husband?"

"He is a very jealous man, milord," she said. "You had best go. I thank you for your help."

"I will trouble you no more, Goddess. My apologies. But remember, if you ever need my assistance, call upon me," Corvin said, hurrying away to avoid being seen. Once around the bend, he doubled back and secreted himself behind a large oak. If the oaf raised a hand against her, then heaven help him, be he husband or no.

"Madame!" the harlequin called. "Thank Heaven, madame. I had all but lost hope of finding you."

"I had told you that I would take care of myself," she said in annoyed tones. "Why are you here?"

"All that you asked has been done, madame, but if you will forgive me, I just could not leave you here alone, unprotected, despite your orders. Milady would have my head, if she knew of this night's work. It would be my position if your aunt ever found out."

"Then she will not know, will she?" The goddess' voice held a mischievous grin.

"I hope not!" the harlequin said. "Anything could have happened, madame. I shudder to think."

"But nothing did happen. I am quite safe. Now, let us hurry home." She gave a last look around her, gave her arm to the harlequin and vanished into the darkness.

"So that is our jealous husband. 'Madame,' he called her," Corvin murmured to himself as he strolled back to his box. "A servant as her escort and she deliberately let me think that she has a husband. Now, it was not her husband's wrath that our harlequin was worried about. It was milady, the aunt. I would wager that there is no husband. A widow? Perhaps. The ways of goddesses are most mysterious. Just attempting to quell a somewhat amorous boor, and very nearly succeeding, too. Well, Daniel, you gave your word not to touch her, but only if she doesn't give you leave. I will just have to change her mind. It is Hyde Park in the morning and if she does not put in an appearance within the next few days, then I shall begin a search. A most intriguing mystery."

Perkins explained his return to Vauxhall on the way home. Guin devoutly prayed that Mr. Hopley had gone on his way after safely delivering the girls to Morton House, but her supplications were un-answered. The anxious, angry young man was wait-ing in the parlor. His eyes opened in disbelief as he saw the schoolmistress turned goddess and Guin groaned.

"Mrs. Courtney?" Uncertainty made Hopley's greeting to a question.

"Yes, it is Mrs. Courtney," Guin said, seating herself with a sigh. "Do sit down, Mr. Hopley. Pac-ing the floor can be tiring, I know. Perkins, I will trouble you for some brandy, if you please. Then you may send the staff to bed and retire yourself, with my thanks."

She sat for a moment looking at Doro's cousin. No doubt Doro had told him the whole, for when Guin had been present as chaperone during the young man's visits, the two had been thick as thieves.

Perkins returned with amazing speed. Indeed, the butler was a trifle breathless when he entered with the brandy and glasses. As he set the tray down, he glanced at Mr. Hopley significantly.

"You need not worry, Perkins," Guin told the faithful servant. "Our young friend here is to be trusted, I'm sure."

"Begging your pardon, madame, sir—but the mis-tress will have my head."

"Perkins, if she hears anything about this night's work, it will be both our heads. Have some brandy yourself. You deserve it. Thank you once more for coming back to my rescue."

The harlequin bowed stiffly. "It was my duty, ma-dame."

Guin took a sip of the amber liquid as the door closed softly. Normally, she kept well away from liquor, but she felt a need for courage and comfort. It burned down her throat, spreading a warm glow that radiated from the pit of her stomach.

"Well, Mrs. Courtney?"

"Well, indeed, Mr. Hopley. No doubt Doro has told you all about this evening's fiasco. I doubt that anything that I might say would enlighten you further. However, I would like to thank you for your escort of the girls. Perkins saved me from a rather awkward situation. Had it not been for your help, he could not have returned."

"I am glad to be of service, Mrs. Courtney," Hopley said, his earnest face reflecting his concern. "You must allow that it was only luck that brought me on the spot. It could have been a disaster with the reputations of all four young women totally in ruins. How could you be so lax as to allow such a thing to happen?"

"Four?"

"Cat was waiting at the gate," Hopley stated, then took a taste of the brandy.

"Dear Heaven!" Guin exclaimed, closing her eyes for a moment as she contemplated the disaster that might have been. She was exhausted. All she wished to do was fall into bed and rest. Now, to be rebuked by a puppy for events that had been no fault of hers was the outside of enough.

"If Doro told you everything, Mr. Hopley," Guin said, trying to keep a teacher's rein on her patience. "You know that I had absolutely no idea of their plans. Insofar as I knew, they were all left sleeping in their beds. What would you have suggested? That I bar the rooms? Chain them up? Who would dream that they would embark on such a perilous scheme?"

"As you did?" he asked. "You took a great risk for young Emmaline, madame, staking your own reputation, that of the school. Those girls love you, you know, think the world of you and I am beginning to see why. I am sorry if I seem angry, but you should not have taken such a chance."

His gentle smile defused her smoldering anger. "There was no time, Mr. Hopley, to call upon help. Emmaline would have been hopelessly compromised," Guin said, slumping back wearily in the chair. "And she may yet be ruined, sir, should word get out of what happened tonight."

"Not from me," Hopley promised. "I have already given my solemn oath to Doro, Mrs. Courtney, and I give it to you as well, though it puts me in a deuce of a bind."

"How?"

Hopley toyed with his empty glass. "Well, her brother is a good friend of mine. I should hate to conceal anything so important from him. If that out and outer, Septimus is out to snag Emmaline, Corvin ought to protect her."

He was Lord Corvin's friend. Guin reached for the decanter. She barely managed to keep her hand from trembling as she poured for Mr. Hopley, then for herself, ignoring the young man's surprised look. "That is my dilemma, too," she explained. "If he hears of Emmaline's rendezvous, I have no doubt that the Viscount will remove her from the school. Then, there is no choice but to send her back to St. Clair Abbey, where, I am told, no one really cares for her. It will only be a matter of time before she is in that cad's arms again. Even were I to tell her that Septimus and his mistress are planning to ensnare her, she would believe it a lie."

Hopley frowned. "His mistress as well?"

"Perkins and I chanced to overhear them," Guin explained. "They hoped to compromise Emmaline before witnesses."

"That is ill news, indeed. But I believe you are right. Morton House is the best place for her. Sending her back to St. Clair Abbey would only drive her to Septimus. I will keep your secret, Mrs. Courtney, though it will be difficult."

A thought struck Guin. "Perhaps, Mr. Hopley, you might be able to warn the Viscount in some oblique way? Tell him that you have heard that a fortune-hunter is bent on pursuing his sister?"

"It might work," Hopley agreed, then swallowed the last of his brandy. "I am still allowed to concoct a story or two, for I have not taken the collar yet. But, if I might be allowed to make a recommendation." He took the decanter from her reach. "You are clearly not a habitual toper, Ma'am and if you don't get some food in your stomach, you will have the devil of a head tomorrow."

"I do believe Cook left some ham in the pantry," Guin said, rising unsteadily to her feet. "And there may be a few cakes. Would you care to join me? I will wager you that Perkins is still awake belowstairs, waiting for the sound of your feet going out the door."

"Just the thing." Hopley's grin was engaging as he offered his arm. "I hope there's enough food to go around. I must confess that all this adventure has made me prodigiously hungry."

Five

CORVIN YAWNED as he glanced at his watch once
more. After the encounter with the goddess at
Vauxhall the previous night, rest had entirely eluded
him. When at last he closed his eyes, she had ridden
through his dreams, no longer an ethereal entity,
but a woman of form, of fire. The longing to see her
once more was a palpable force that had driven him
to Hyde Park, to wait, to hope against hope that she
would return. Only she could answer the questions
that plagued him.

Now, as a light drizzle began to fall, Corvin realized that she would not come. There were already a
few early-rising riders pounding along the near-
empty pathways. Feeling more than a little ridiculous, the Viscount emerged from his hiding place in
the bushes.

"Pounce on me would ye'." A startled old woman
raised her umbrella and began beating the Viscount
over the head. "It's gettin' so's a decent woman
cannot even take a morning constitutional without
being set upon. Footman! Footman!" she called.

Corvin glanced below his shielding arm to see an
elderly servant advancing with all the menace of a
toothless hound. There would be no chance for explanations, nor seemingly, any good if they were
made. He ran to the copse where his horse was tethered.

His mood was not lightened in the least when he returned home for breakfast and found an anxious looking Hopley waiting for him.

"I had almost thought that I misheard your invitation at Vauxhall last night. Ives said that he expected you back over an hour ago. You are drenched."

"Am I?" Corvin questioned with mild sarcasm. "No, Hop, you heard me aright and feed you I shall, as soon as I am rid of these wet clothes."

Ives hurried to assist his master and in a few minutes, Corvin returned, attired in a red and blue figured-silk robe.

"What took you out into the rain at so early an hour?" Hopley asked. "I hope that nothing is amiss?"

"Nothing, except a whimsical notion that my mysterious lady would return," Corvin said.

"Are we to that again?" Hopley sighed, taking the plate that Ives proffered. "Any fool could see that it was bidding fair to rain this morning. At least that shows that your Lady of the Morning has enough sense to stay out of the wet. More than I can say for you."

"Love can do strange things to a man," Corvin said as he sat down and sipped at his coffee, savoring its warmth.

"Love? Do not abuse the word," Hopley said, shaking his head. "A woman you have seen only a few times and then at a distance, never spoken to; someone you know absolutely nothing about and you call it love? A misnomer. Lust, perhaps, certainly not love."

"You do not believe in love at first sight, Hop?" Corvin asked lightly. Perhaps it was the weather that kept her away? Corvin thought, or simple fatigue, for he was well nigh exhausted himself. It was a logical explanation since there was nothing else to keep her away from the park now. The goddess knew enough about him to think herself safe from "Saint Corvin," the man who never dallied with other men's wives. "I had always thought that all young men are romantic at heart, Hop," Corvin commented as he rose to stare out the window at the downpour.

"Initial attraction? Lust? Oh, I believe in them; but love? The way people use the word these days, you would think love is as common as any weed to be plucked by the roadside and just as casually tossed away. Love is not something that is easily found. It is a gift not given to many."

Corvin turned and smiled at his young friend's serious face. "And how do you come to know so much about love?" he asked.

"I have seen it, Corvin. My parents were in love with each other till the day they died. It may seem heretical of me, but I have always counted it a blessing that that coaching accident took them both. I do not know how they could have survived one without the other." Hopley spoke softly, his eyes misting in memory.

Corvin was moved by the profound sadness in his friend's expression. "I envy you, Hop," he said frankly. "With that example before you, you are bound to know love when you find it. I fear that Emmaline and I have only our parents to follow, a poor model to pattern ourselves upon if ever there was one."

"Actually Corvin," Hopley began. "I did want to speak to you about Emmaline. Last night, at Vauxhall, I saw an old friend of mine."

From the way that his friend looked down at his plate and pushed his eggs about, Corvin could guess that Hop was uncomfortable with what he wished to say. "Is that why you left so abruptly?" Corvin asked, attempting to draw the young man out.

Hopley nodded and put his fork down. "It was fortunate, indeed that I saw this er . . . fellow. He had noticed you in the supper box with me and finding that I was well-acquainted with you, Corvin, told me something that disturbed me greatly about Sir Mortimer Septimus."

"A strange coincidence. I met the bounder last night myself under rather unusual circumstances."

"It seems Septimus is on the lookout for an heiress," Hopley said, at last.

"When has he not been?" Corvin asked. "He will have considerable difficulty catching one though. His reputation is hardly savory and most of society's hostesses have barred him from their ballrooms."

"I realize that," Hopley said, tugging at his shirtcollar as if it had abruptly become too tight. "Yet, there are still some places where the man is accepted."

"Few," Corvin said with a grim smile. "He has always had a reputation as a scoundrel."

Hopley flushed then stammered, "Th . . . This is deuced difficult to tell you, Corvin, but my friend has heard the rumor that Mortimer has set his sights on your sister."

"The Devil, you say!" Corvin exploded. "Even Septimus would not have such gall!"

"I only repeat what I heard," Hopley said, moving his bacon to lay neatly beside the mound of egg. "Your sister is a considerable heiress."

"Yes, but the money will not be entirely in her control until she is twenty-one. If she marries beforehand, I may release it at my discretion."

"And her husband may not touch it?" Hopley asked.

"No, that part of my mother's will is quite specific. Emmaline's money is entirely her own. The solicitors have assured my father that the will is unbreakable."

Hopley whistled. "Septimus would not know that."

"No one does, beside the men of law, my father and myself. It is not the sort of thing one bruits about," Corvin explained, paring himself a slice of cheese as he considered. "I think, Hop, that it might be prudent to set a man to watch Septimus and make sure that he stays clear of Emmaline. The man is more of a villain than anyone suspects. Last night, after you left me at Vauxhall, I caught him assaulting a young woman."

"A lady of the evening?" Hopley ventured.

"No, actually, it was my Lady of the Morning, Hop. She had lost her escort and Septimus thought to try his luck with her."

"So you met her at last," Hopley said, picking up his fork once more. "You came to her rescue?"

Corvin nodded. "We came upon her struggling against him."

"I hope you dealt the rogue a facer!" Hopley said.

"You are a rather bloodthirsty fellow for a soon-to-be man of the cloth," Corvin declared with wry amusement. "And I do know more about her than you think. She is definitely a woman of quality." Corvin could not keep the excitement from his voice. "Well-bred and I would venture to say of some respectable family. She is so incredibly beautiful, Hop, more lovely than I remembered."

"Better and better," Hopley said, then lit into his curried eggs with enthusiasm.

"I think that you were right about her, Hop. She's no common Cyprian. She must be some impoverished gentlewoman, for I can think of no other explanation for her behavior. Her gown was excellent, but had seen better days," he said, shaking his head as Ives offered to refill his cup.

"Shall I warn 'Perfection' Derwent that she must

look over her shoulder?'' Hopley asked, buttering a fresh roll. ''This sounds quite serious.''

''The deuce of it all, Hop, is that I do not even know her name.''

''How is that?'' Hopley asked, before he took a bite.

''She would not reveal her identity,'' Corvin said. ''That is why it is so essential, you see, that she returns to her morning rides.''

''I am afraid I do not see at all,'' Hopley said in puzzlement. ''Surely, no lady of breeding would consent to meet you at that hour in the park.''

''She did not. Tried to put me off in fact, make me believe that she was married.''

''She must know who you are, if she realizes that you have a reputation for leaving other men's wives alone,'' Hopley remarked, his brow furrowing in thought.

''She does know who I am. It was all very strange, Hop, and at the moment, the only thing that I am sure of, is that I must see her again.''

''Strange, indeed,'' the young man agreed, as he observed the Viscount's unusual demeanor. Never before had Hopley seen the ever-calm and collected Corvin in so exhilarated a state. ''Corvin, what are you about? She obviously has no wish to see you. Can you not just leave it alone?'' he advised in concern.

''I cannot, Hop,'' Corvin protested. ''Perhaps it is the mystery of it all that intrigues me. I just want to talk to her, to find out more about her.''

''I must confess that I am beginning to be bewildered. You court one woman while you frantically search for another. Upon which of these ladies am I to wish you happy, the would-be wife, the might-be mistress, or both?'' Hopley asked, raising his coffee cup in a mock toast.

Corvin considered the question seriously and was

disturbed to find himself more than a little confused. "I am not so sure, Hopley. It may seem ridiculous, and I swear, if you ever repeat this to a soul, you shall never eat at my table again. I feel something when I am near her, something strange as if some inner voice were saying, 'Here she is, the one you have waited for.' "

"Divine voices?" Hopley declared with patent amusement. "You have missed your calling Corvin. It should be you going down to Oxford. Again, you have failed to mention about which woman the voice whispers."

"Fate," Corvin mused aloud, ignoring his friend's teasing tone. "Mama used to say that the Arabs call it 'kismet.' Call it whatever you wish, Hop. I have to find her again and, somehow, I know that I will." He smiled at his friend who was staring at him in open-mouthed wonder. "I did not mean to put you off your feed. Try the salmon. Ives had the recipe from Careme."

Obediently, Hop took a forkfull and began to chew. "You are well and truly on the hook, Corvin," he commented.

"You may be right, Hop. She will return to the park, probably tomorrow. After all, it was rather late last night when the harlequin took her home."

"Harlequin?" Hopley asked, pausing in mid-chew.

"A servant, I think although the goddess tried to convince me that the fellow was her husband. A bouncer if there ever was one."

Hopley began to cough uncontrollably. His face reddened as he strangled on the mouthful of salmon. Both Ives and Corvin pounded on the young man's back until at last he came back to his normal color.

"Sorry," Hopley choked as he tried to speak and accepted a glass of wine from the anxious Ives. "Something was . . . difficult to swallow."

* * *

Meanwhile, at Morton House, the exhausted schoolmistress rubbed her bleary eyes, longing for her bed even though it was but ten in the morning. Regretfully, it had been necessary to insist that the girls rise at the usual hour since it was vital that nothing appear amiss. As she paused just outside the open door of the classroom, Aunt Hermione's voice wafted into the hall. The lesson was in deportment, Guin recalled.

"Now, Eddy, I am Lady Jersey and we have just been introduced. What do you say to me?" Mrs. Haven asked.

Eddy was hesitant, her weariness apparent in her voice. "How do you do, ma'am."

"Why you must be from the Colonies," said Mrs. Haven, easily assuming the lofty tones of the Almack's patroness. Although her words were harmless enough every syllable implied immense condescension as if she stated outright that the young miss before her was the most gauche of provincials.

"They are not Colonies anymore, for pity's sake," Eddy replied crossly.

"Edwina!" Mrs. Haven scolded in her own voice. "You are ruined. Banished from Almack's and all chance of social success. You have just contradicted a patroness. If Lady Jersey—and by the by, always say, 'milady.' If Lady Jersey says to you that the moon is made of cheese and the stars of sugar plums, you must charmingly agree and compliment the woman on her scientific acumen. Emmaline, can you show us how to go on here?"

"Good evening, Lady Jersey. That gown must be Robard's work, it is so exquisite! I vow, I do not know why Lady Crombie does not follow your lead. She looked absolutely wretched yesterday, but do not tell her that I said so, please, milady. She would be well advised to patronise your modiste."

"Excellent!" Mrs. Haven approved.

"But why does such an insult serve?" Eddy asked plaintively. "Is Lady Crombie not Lady Jersey's bosom companion?"

"If you would but listen, Edwina, you would remember. Although the two are often together it does not make them friends. The combination of one's fair looks and the other's dark handsomeness makes for a striking contrast, as well they know. Nonetheless, the two women despise each other heartily, since they were at one time rivals for the Prince Regent's affections. There are few surer ways to the Patroness of Almack's heart than to compliment her looks and disparage Lady Crombie."

There was a tittering sound.

"It is no laughing matter, I assure you, ladies. However, I must caution you all that such malicious tactics are not used lightly. You can be sure that Lady Jersey will repeat it to Lady Crombie, for the patroness earned the sobriquet 'Silence,' by dint of having the loosest jawbox of any woman alive. Remember too, that Lady Crombie is the Earl of Templar's only child, a most powerful enemy in her own right and you must learn to choose whose favor you would be wise to curry. Now, Catherine, you have just danced with the most odious young man. He has stepped on your toes, torn your hem, stuttered and stumbled his way through the dance."

"If he has not been familiar, I must treat him as though he were a prince among men," Cat repeated the familiar lesson. "Smile; reassure him that he was a most pleasant partner. Any awkwardness is my fault."

"Very good, Catherine. Remember girls, be kind to everyone you meet, from the most gangly looking youth, to the most graceless girl who is left behind on the chairs. You never know who their brothers or cousins may be, and graciousness will never go amiss," Mrs. Haven reminded them. "Now Edwina, let us try again." Once more Mrs. Haven was "Silence" Jersey. "Do you not have the terror of Indians?"

"There are none in Philadelphia, milady. The most formidable terror I have confronted yet is yourself," Edwina replied.

The class dissolved into laughter and Mrs. Haven banged vainly upon the desk until some semblance of control was regained. "Edwina, I assume you wish to remain a spinster and be alone for the rest of your days, for I vow that is what will happen if you continue to make light of these lessons. Those first impressions that you make will be the most important of your life. The opinions of these proud, vain women will decide your fate in the ton. Gain their approbation and you will succeed, but should they look at you askance, nothing, not birth, not wealth, not beauty will save you, gel."

"Yes, Mrs. Haven."

To Guin's surprise, Eddy sounded chastened.

"Now, for our next class, I would like you to tell Lady Jersey something about life in America. Make it sound exciting; put some Indians in perhaps," Mrs. Haven suggested.

"But life in Philadelphia is dull as ditchwater, Mrs. Haven," the girl protested.

"Use your imagination, child. She will not know, I assure you. Most of the ton's knowledge of geography don't go beyond Pall Mall."

There was a scuffle of feet and Guin retreated down the hall as the girls went on to their next lesson.

Aunt Hermione was gathering up some papers from the desk.

"I had them writing invitations," she said waving

the sheaf at her niece. "I vow, some hostesses these days do not know how to word a proper one. Why, when I was a girl, it was an art to persuade a reluctant guest, but now? Bah! These young women could not even write a decent billet-doux."

Guin shook her head. "Please, Aunt, do not include that in your curriculum, I beg you. We have enough troubles as it is."

"Sinclair's gel. She seems to have settled down a bit after last night's uproar," Aunt Hermione stated, eyeing Guin archly.

"You know?" Guin felt her face go red.

The older woman frowned. "I may be old, Guin, but I ain't deaf. I had to threaten it out of Perkins. Feared that I'd turn him out after all these years he has been with me, but he told me in the end."

"I had hoped to spare you the worry," Guin mumbled.

"Spare yourself the scolding you mean," her aunt said, crossing to close the classroom door. "How could you be so foolish, gel? First, Vauxhall, then entertaining a man alone in the middle of the night?"

"The man is going to be a vicar," Guin protested.

"Wears breeches don't he?" Aunt Hermione snorted and shook her head. "What is below the collar is the same as any other man. How could you be such a fool?"

"You need not worry about Mr. Hopley. I vow, if I ever were obliged to ward the man off, all I need do is throw food at him. He finished near half a ham, and a plate of currant buns besides. As for Emmaline, I could not leave her to Sir Mortimer Septimus' mercies."

"Septimus?" Mrs. Haven asked, sitting down abruptly in her chair. "Septimus, you say? Did he recognize you?"

"No, not at all. I was masked," Guin said reassuringly. "It has been years."

The woman's eyes were clouded with worry as she looked up at her niece. "He could ruin us, dear. Destroy everything."

Guin gave her aunt a reassuring hug. "I doubt that we will see him again, Aunt Hermione. I have instructed the staff to accept whatever bribes he offers, as doubtless he will try to correspond with Emmaline, but his notes will come to me first. I cannot pretend that I enjoy spying on the child, but I must know what that devil is up to," she said with a frown.

"I beg you, Guin. Send Emmaline home. Let her family deal with the problem. I have a feeling in these bones of mine, child. A terrible feeling. No good will come of this," Mrs. Haven said, her expression beseeching as she wrung Guin's hand.

"I am sorry, Aunt," Guin declared softly, "but I cannot. Septimus must not be allowed to win this time. I will not run away again."

Those brave words, however, were not proof against the doubts that assailed the schoolmistress that night as she sought sleep. Although every bone in her body seemed to ache with exhaustion, Guin punched at her pillow and sighed when she acknowledged at last that her dilemma would allow no peace. Worse still it seemed that every time Guin closed her eyes, Lord Corvin's face appeared to haunt the darkness with his mocking smile. The memory of the feel of his embrace, the moist touch of his lips made relaxation impossible. In dreams, he would be beside her, murmuring words that Guin knew, even in the midst of her night's fantasies, were likely lies. She shook her head at her foolishness and buried her face in the pillow.

Stupid! Stupid! Stupid! The schoolmistress castigated herself. Corvin would never be interested in the woman he thought Guin to be for anything more than a casual affaire de couer and not even that anymore, she reminded herself relentlessly. He believed that she was married and that would certainly protect her from his attentions. All the Stantons had their peculiarities and apparently Lord Corvin's was his refusal to dally with married women. He despised adultery, it seemed. No wonder, with parents like his. At least, she comforted herself with the thought, she could go riding without fear once more.

Guin sighed and pulled on her wrapper, deciding to seek a book. Perhaps reading would distract her thoughts from Emmaline's brother. She lit a candle and made her way down to the library. After some consideration, she pulled *Childe Harolde* from the shelf and began to immerse herself in Byron's epic. She might despise the man, but his poetry was beyond himself. There was nothing petty or pouting about his words, although she could detect the traces of the self-centered man she had known.

Time had given Guin enough perspective to see Byron's side of his affair with Caroline Lamb. Caro had been relentless in her pursuit, hounding the poet until cruelty was almost his only recourse. Still, Guin could not help but wonder if Byron had been using Caroline Lamb as a rung in his climb to social standing. Certainly, it had enhanced his fame to have the daughter by marriage of the prestigious Lady Melbourne as his inamorata. How many men could have a blatant liaison to a married woman and be a friend and confidante with the cuckolded man's mother? But in the end, not even the poet's much vaunted charm could save him from the condemnation of society. All those lives, destroyed for a glance, a word, a touch.

As for her own marriage, that had gone wrong from the start. When her father, at last, had come out of his books long enough to realize that his daughter's reputation was in tatters, he desperately sought for any suitor that would take this family embarrassment off his hands. Alfred Marshall had been a younger son of a noble but impoverished family. Although Alfred had found that she was not the damaged goods that he had expected, he was constantly accusing her of trying to imitate her mentor, Caro. Guin had tried desperately to please him, wearing less attractive clothing when they went out in public, behaving circumspectly, but then he would call her a drab mouse. He would condemn her for rebelliousness, demanding nothing less than the total subjugation of her soul and she had failed him, unable to make herself into the dutiful wife he desired.

The memories were too powerful. Guin shut the book and stared into the pool of darkness beyond the candlelight. Music. Guin heard the distant strains and for a moment was unsure whether the sound was a product of her imagination. She opened the library door and listened.

Her candle threw flickering shadows as she walked down the drafty hall toward the music room. Guin had insisted that the room be placed at the far end of the house, lest the sounds of practice disturb the other classes in session. Was Miss Kodaski awake and playing? It was not the music mistress' habit to practice alone at late hours, and although Maria Kodaski was a tolerable violinist, the pianoforte was her favored instrument. The strains vibrated on the night air, like the sound of muffled crying, intense and bitter in a burst of staccato anger. No, it was surely not Maria who wrenched such raw emotion from those strings.

Guin opened the door a crack and held her breath. It was Emmaline, holding the instrument beneath her chin, while she caressed the strings like a lover.

The girl's lawn nightgown floated about her as she brought the bow down, drawing an eerie whine from the bowels of the polished wood. The music seemed to possess her and Guin watched bewitched, as Emmaline played on.

The melody was one that Guin had never heard before. When she saw no music on the stand, the schoolmistress realized with a start that Emmaline was improvising, speaking the deepest feelings of her soul through the instrument in her hand. A single candle sputtered and died on the table, but Emmaline did not stop. The music reflected the child's desolation, the search for something that eluded her grasp. The bow came to a screeching halt.

Emmaline had noticed the flicker of the candle in the doorway, and the dreaming look in her eyes had been replaced by the usual sullen defiance.

"That was beautiful, Emmaline."

"You needn't try to cozen me, Mrs. Courtney. I've been warned about this caterwauling of mine, but I thought that no one would hear back here, so far away from everything," she said in flat tones.

"I am not trying to flatter you, Emmaline. I am merely stating a fact. You may dislike me, but have you ever known me to lie?"

The girl shook her head. "No, I shall say that for you," Emmaline agreed.

A grudging admission, Guin thought, but at least it contained no overt hostility. "Why did you not tell Miss Kodaski that you played the violin?" she asked.

"Why bother. After last week's escapade at Vauxhall, I would be a fool to expect any special treatment around here. Besides, the violin isn't a proper lady's instrument like the pianoforte. It looks ridiculous tucked up under your chin, not pretty and delicate like a lady at the harp. Besides, I'm not any good anyway."

"Nonsense," Guin said. "I may not be able to play a note, but I know an excellent musician when I hear one. Under whom did you study?"

The girl was still wary. "Oh, I had lessons here and there, when Mama remembered. One of Mama's . . . friends gave me my violin. It was made by an Italian, a man named Guarnieri, and the sound it made . . ." she said, eyeing the instrument in her hand with a look akin to pity. "It was the most beautiful thing I ever owned."

Guin was almost afraid to ask the obvious question. "What happened to it?"

Emmaline turned to face the window, her figure silhouetted by the moonlight. There was no need to see her face. The pain in her voice was a bleeding wound.

"*She* took it," Emmaline declared, her voice close to breaking.

There was no need to ask who Emmaline was referring to, the pronoun was a word of hatred. Viscount Corvin had told Guin something of the new Countess' treatment of her stepdaughter.

"*She* said that a violin was no fit instrument for a lady, as if *she* knows what the word 'lady' means. *She* threw it on the fire."

The raw agony in the girl's voice was almost unbearable. Guin could see by Emmaline's trembling shoulders that she was reliving the moment when her instrument was consumed by the flames.

"Did you tell your father?" Guin asked.

Emmaline's laugh was tinged with hysteria as she faced Guin once more. "Tell, Papa! What good would that have done? He will do anything to please her as long as it will cost him no money. But I cannot blame him for preferring her to me." Emmaline declared in matter-of-fact tones, belied by the depths of pain and desolation in her eyes. "I am not his daughter, after all."

"Why do you say that?" Guin asked.

Emmaline looked at the schoolmistress with a wizened mockery of a smile. "I know. All one needs to do is count nine months. *She* told me. I felt like such a fool, Mrs. Courtney, it seems like I was the only one in the world who didn't know."

"It still may not be true, Emmaline," Guin said softly. "Babies have been known to be premature. From what I know about your stepmama, my dear, she can be a cruel woman."

"Why would she lie?" the girl asked, her face clouded in recollection. "At first, she tried to turn me up sweet, told me to call her, 'Mama,' but I couldn't Mrs. Courtney. There will always be just one 'Mama' for me and I tried to explain. She was so angry. Her face got all red and she told me that then, I could not call the Earl my papa, because he was not and never would be. That my real father was one of my mama's amours."

Guin felt a catch in her throat. In order to consolidate her position of power with the Earl, it seemed that his new countess was seeking to undermine all his other familial relationships, alienating him from both son and daughter. The Viscount could take care of himself, but the deliberate destruction of a young girl was almost too cruel to be believed. One by one, the Countess had maliciously knocked the underpinnings of Emmaline's life away. It was no wonder that the child was teetering on the brink of disaster.

The silent tears coursed down the girl's cheeks and she turned her face away, unwilling to let another see her pain. Tentatively, Guin reached out to touch the shaking shoulders. The streaming eyes focused on her, questioning, fearful of rejection. Guin gathered the girl in her arms and let her weep, letting her own tears fall in silence. She crooned a dimly remembered formula from the misty days of her own childhood. ''There, there, it will be all right. It will be all right.''

Strange, the power of comfort in those words. Memories arose of a lilac-scented woman with hair as dark as Guin's own, the image a reflection of her face. ''It will be all right, Emmaline. I promise,'' she whispered. She was not sure if she could fulfill that promise, but at least Guin now knew how to begin.

Six

ONCE THE key to Emmaline had been found, the rest seemed to follow naturally. The girl's musical gift had required a far better teacher than Miss Kodaski. So, Guin had penned a note to an old friend, Bronwyn Geoffry, who had also followed the drum across the Peninsula. Bronwyn had lost her husband at Waterloo and the last Guin had heard, the officer's widow was eking out a precarious living giving music lessons and selling her exquisite embroidery. Guin was glad that she had found a pupil worthy of Bronwyn's considerable talent, and Bronwyn's compassionate nature was just the thing for Emmaline. Their mutual love of the violin had drawn them together from the start. A mere three weeks of Bronwyn's patient tutelage had changed Emmaline almost beyond recognition. The girl had begun to blossom.

Even though the surreptitious notes from Sir Mortimer Septimus had resumed, Guin believed it was far wiser to allow the correspondence to continue. While she had her misgivings about intercepting and reading Emmaline's personal letters, it was Guin's only means of monitoring the situation. Thus far, he had confined his importuning maunderings to the type of drivel calculated to turn a young girl's head. It was the schoolmistress' hope that Emmaline, diverted by her music and growing friendships with the other girls, would lose interest in the roué.

Despite her elation at Emmaline's progress, Guin felt a peculiar sense of restlessness, a tension that found release only in her early dawn rides. In the weeks since her encounter with Lord Corvin at Vauxhall, the schoolmistress had ridden daily to the more distant St. James Park so that she might totally avoid the possibility of another meeting with the Viscount. However, on one particularly grey morning the threat of rain was implicit and a trip to St. James seemed a sure route to a drenching. If she were to ride at all today, Guin decided, it would have to be in nearby Hyde Park.

In the concealment of a leafy copse by the water, Corvin glanced up at the darkening sky, all but ready to return to his rooms. There was little hope that she would come, only a fool would be out in this weather. A fool. Corvin did not hesitate to so designate himself, for there was no other explanation for his behavior these past weeks, rising almost daily at dawn, skulking about the park in the vain hope of meeting a woman who clearly wanted no part of him. Yet, as the days passed and she failed to show again and again, the mysterious goddess seemed to increasingly occupy his thoughts. Certainly, she dominated his dreams.

Guin hesitated once she reached the Grosvenor Gate to the park. Bombay snorted restively, as if deriding his rider for her ridiculous fears. It was highly unlikely that Lord Corvin was waiting, Guin convinced herself once more. He thought that she was married. Guin glanced down at her wedding ring. The dull gold had once seemed the heaviest of shackles, now it protected her, creating a veritable fortress against the Viscount Corvin.

''Men who trifle with other men's wives, I cannot

abide them, Mrs. Courtney. They are responsible for a great deal of harm," he had said.

Guin could not recollect how the discussion had come to the subject. Certainly it was a strange statement from a member of the first circles of the ton. His frank evaluation of his sister and by extension, himself, during that interview had turned her initial dislike of the man into a real respect. In his concern for Emmaline, Corvin had revealed information that had never been told to another soul, Guin would wager. His simple description of the horrendous condition of his family had awakened a sympathy and compassion within her that she had never felt for any man. Yet, despite those feelings it was entirely ridiculous to feel a tinge of regret that he believed her married, and silly indeed, to wish away his scruples. Guin tried to turn her attention elsewhere, deciding that the Viscount had occupied entirely too many of her thoughts these weeks.

The Serpentine reflected the dull leaden look of the sky and for a moment, she wondered if she would be wiser turning home. A toss of Bombay's head reminded Guin of his impatience to be off. She gave in to the horse's demand gladly, eager to clear the conflicting feelings that cluttered her head. They rode parallel to the shore thundering down the empty pathways in a manner that would have been reckless at any other hour. The sky above darkened ominously, but Guin was too busy managing the fresh animal to notice the growing storm until a flash of lightning cut the clouds above her, followed by a drumroll of thunder. Another bolt struck a tree on the path ahead, filling the air with a peculiar acrid smell. There was a roar, a flash of dazzling light. Bombay's nostrils quivered, his ears twitched in fear as he reared and pawed at the air.

It was a horrifying tableau; the great animal upright against the stormy sky, jagged bolts flashing in the background. The rider slid to a helpless heap on the ground beside the terrified horse. Corvin was transfixed in fear as he saw the hooves hit the ground once more, barely inches away from the crumpled form. Then, with a fearsome shriek, the horse careered away from the smoldering tree. The woman did not move.

Corvin ran and knelt beside her, searching for signs of life. The pulse at her throat beat steadily, although her breathing was so shallow that he had feared the worst. Competent from years of battle-field experience, he felt her limbs. Seemingly, there were no bones broken. There was a long scratch on her cheek and he wiped the smear of dirt away gently with his handkerchief.

The long lashes fluttered open.

"You," she murmured.

"It seems that I am forever cleaning this face of yours," he said. How amazingly blue her eyes were. He noticed that the color was returning to her cheeks.

"My mother used to say the same, when I was little." She tried to sit up, but closed her eyes and lay back once more. "I shall be fine," she whispered, almost as if she was trying to convince herself. "Just had the wind knocked out of me, that is all."

"Let us hope so. It appears that nothing is broken," he said, running an expert hand along her left arm.

Her eyes flew open once more. Their look was accusing. "Your oath!"

"Wouldn't apply if you were dead, Goddess, and that is what I thought, so help me. You took a terrible fall." He reluctantly let go of her hand. "There, my word is in force once more, but," he said, "I will ask your permission to help you to your feet. Do you think you can stand?"

She nodded. "I shall try."

He grasped under her arm and she rose slowly. But as soon as he let go, she blanched and began to sway. He caught her in his arms.

"You will let me carry you," he commanded. "If I violate my oath it is your silly fault, Goddess, but I will be damned if I let you fall face in the mud for some absurd standard of propriety."

"Very well," she agreed with words that were almost a sigh.

Corvin lifted her with a grunt of effort. A pity his goddess wasn't some insubstantial bit of ether, but a very well built, solid being of female flesh. Still, there were definitely some compensations to substance. No incorporeal being could nestle so comfortably in the hollow at neck and shoulder. A spirit would not smell so sweetly of lavender or have hair that rubbed like silk against his cheek.

"Damn!" Corvin cursed as a drop of rain hit the bridge of his nose. All at once, the clouds burst. His load grew heavier with each step as the sheets of rain soaked the full skirts of her riding costume. Corvin was so busy trying to avoid slipping on the now muddy path that he almost failed to notice the charming effect that the water had on the fabric of his goddess' garments. Most definitely corporeal. Corvin nearly missed his footing and for a second his load dipped precariously before he regained his balance.

"I think I can walk now," she said, her eyes opened once more, their expression anxious.

"Nonsense," Corvin grunted. "You are light as a feather."

"Of what leaden bird? Please, milord, let me try."

"We are nearly there," he said, hoping that the phrase hadn't sounded too much like the prayer it was. Corvin vowed to visit Jackson's parlor more regularly; London life was making him soft. Luckily, the copse where Windrunner was tethered was closer than he had hoped. The thick leafy canopy had sheltered the horse from the worst of the downpour.

"Can you stand?" he asked, noting that she was still somewhat pale, but her eyes were focusing normally once more.

She nodded. "I think so."

He set her gently on her feet. "We will have to ride pillion, I am afraid. Lean against Windrunner if you need to and I shall take you up."

"There is no need really." Tendrils of hair curled to frame her wet face. "I have troubled you far too much already. I am feeling much more the thing." Her voice trembled and he could see the fear in her eyes.

"I would be a poor excuse for a gentleman, if I did not see you home."

"No!" She backed away from him. "You cannot! I mean . . ." Her face blanched.

Corvin stepped toward her, ready to support her if she should fall once more. "Your jealous husband might misinterpret?" Corvin watched her face.

"Exactly!"

Her expression as she seized the excuse confirmed Corvin's certitude that there was no husband. She was a terrible liar. Corvin swung himself into the saddle and pulled the protesting goddess up before him.

"Where are you taking me?" she asked.

Her voice had dropped to a weak whimper. She sank back against him and he grasped her tightly to keep her from slipping. She had fainted once more.

Guin heard the crackle of flames and smelled the magnificent scent of brewing coffee. It had been a dream, she concluded, snuggling beneath the covers, savoring the slippery smoothness against her bare skin. Silk! The feel was unmistakable. She sniffed. Bay rum! Did dreams have scent and touch? Guin wondered as she debated whether or not to open her eyes. She peered out from beneath the curtain of half-opened lids and groaned.

A mob-capped woman was leaning over her. "She be wakin', I think, milord. Truth is, I was beginning to fear that I made a mistake, tellin' you not to call a leech. A dreadful bump, it is. Poor, poor lamb."

Guin winced as a hand touched the lump on her head.

"I'll be bringing up one of me possets in a minute. Never you worry, milord, she'll be right as rain in no time."

Guin heard the sound of a door clicking shut.

"A poor choice of expression, don't you think, Goddess?" Corvin asked.

A shiver shook Guin when she realized that the source of that deep voice was startlingly close. There was no hiding behind sleep anymore and she opened her eyes to see Corvin, kneeling at her side. The dark hairs of his chest curled above the closure of his figured dressing gown, blue Chinese dragons chased each other across a background of burgundy silk. Her eyes dropped beneath his concerned scrutiny and Guin felt her cheeks go warm.

"No need to worry, Goddess. I kept my word you know," Corvin said as she pulled the covers up beneath her chin. "Mrs. Truesberry, my tartar of a landlady, got you out of your wet things and for some reason, she brushed aside my offers of help and banished me to my rooms. You are wearing one of my robes until your own clothes dry, so you must excuse the poor fit."

Guin realized that he was trying to reassure her, but there was something in his tone that had an opposite effect on her. She felt hot all over, her mouth dry and her palms clammy.

Corvin could see the fear and confusion chasing across her face and reluctantly moved to a chair near the divan. ''Something to drink, Goddess?'' he asked as he poured a glass of wine from a decanter on a nearby table. He tried to keep from staring at her starkly pale face, framed amidst the glorious mantle of her hair.

''No, thank you. How long have I been unconscious, milord?'' Guin asked, watching the wine swirl in his glass, reflecting like some ruby gem.

''It is just past ten of the morning.''

Guin tried to calculate, but the fascinating play of firelight brought out bluish gleams in Corvin's hair and burnished the silk robe with its glow, making it difficult to concentrate. She found it hard to decide whether it was the fall or his Lordship's proximity that so befuddled her thoughts.

She was nearly three hours overdue, and Bombay had probably run straight back to his stable. They would be searching for her, or would they? She had left the stable door open and it was entirely possible that the horse had found his own way to the stall. As she thought of poor Bombay, soaked to the bone and frightened, Guin prayed that the beast would not take sick. Since Guin took care of the grooming chores herself, it was unlikely that anyone had gone to the stables looking for her. She recalled that she had reserved the morning for progress reports, letters to parents and the like. With any luck at all, no one would miss her unless she failed to join Aunt Hermione and the deportment class after luncheon. Guin's lip curled in a smile—ironic that the lesson for the day was polite flirtation.

''A smile. Much better, Goddess,'' Corvin said, taking a sip of wine. ''You looked as if you thought that I would eat you. Can you share your amusing thought?''

''I think, milord, that I had best be on my way as

soon as possible. If your Mrs. Truesberry would be so kind as to return my clothes?" She clutched the voluminous folds of the robe around her, the male scent of him growing stronger as Guin hugged the silk closer. It was a match to the one Corvin wore, she realized, but the colors of blue and burgundy were reversed.

"I doubt that they are dry," Corvin ventured, concerned by the increase in her pallor as she moved. He tried to effect a casual tone despite his growing worry. "And I find myself wondering whether you are fit to move. You sustained a bad blow, Goddess. Perhaps I did wrong not to summon a physician?"

"I am fine," Guin lied. "I am truly sorry to have caused you all this trouble, milord, but there is no need to distress yourself any further on my behalf. If you will just get me my clothes?" she pleaded, dismayed at the waspish tone of her voice. There was a look in Lord Corvin's eyes that definitely boded trouble. His scruples might usually exclude married women from his list of those eligible for dalliance, but men had a peculiar talent for overcoming such reservations at their convenience.

"I did not rescue you, Goddess, to cast you out into the rain once more," Corvin declared, wondering what he could do to calm her. The rapid rise and fall of her bosom and the almost frenetic way she cast her eyes hither and thither put him in mind of a trapped creature. Corvin was sure now that she was no Cyprian, for no demimondaine would lose so golden an opportunity for seduction. His orderly mind searched for some category in which to place her, he could find none.

"Will you stop calling me Goddess," Guin all but shouted at him, feeling ashamed of her loss of control as she did so. Her agitation grew as she acknowledged a curious feeling of fascination with the man who sat watching her with such obvious admiration. She tried to collect herself, but her head was throbbing. Every bone in her body was beginning to feel sore and worse, her heart was racing wildly. Although it would be foolish beyond permission to go out into the deluge that drummed on the window pane, it would be more foolhardy still to remain with this man. What was it Caro had said about Byron? "Mad, bad and dangerous to know." Corvin might be neither mad nor truly bad, but he was most definitely dangerous and should he recognize her as Mrs. Courtney of Morton House, he could destroy everything she had worked for.

"How can I call you anything else?" Corvin asked, trying to keep his voice light. "If you could see the effect of fireglow on that hair of yours, you would not deny the appellation. But if you will give me another name, I'll use it even though it might not suit you half so well."

"Elaine," Guin said, scarcely believing as she said it. It had been years since anyone had called her that and it was impermissibly foolish to give him a clue to her identity. Still, she had sensed that he would easily detect a lie.

"The Fair Elaine." Corvin said, raising his glass in salute. As he tipped down the remainder of his wine, a strange surge of elation filled him. Although a mere given name was hardly a token of trust, it was a beginning. "I like Goddess better, but Elaine does become you. The wife of Galahad was she or something like that?"

"Yes, she too was *married*," Guin reminded him. To her dismay, Corvin rose from his chair. She clutched the robe tightly about her and scrambled to her feet. There was a poker near the hearth and she grabbed it.

"Ferocious Fair Elaine, I gave my oath, remember?" he asked, raising his hands, palms open, in a gesture of peace as he slowly backed away. "Sit down."

"Forgive me, milord, but a word is a somewhat fragile thing, especially in such an unusual situation," Guin asserted fearfully. The iron rod was heavy and it was a strain to hold it aloft. "And if you have no intentions toward me, then how was it that you happened to be in Hyde Park this morning?"

Corvin searched for a reasonable explanation and could find none. How could he justify returning to Hyde Park, morning after morning, to seek a woman who obviously wanted nothing to do with him? It was something that he was hard put to understand himself. "You are not the only one who enjoys an occasional early ride, Godd . . . Elaine," he said, knowing as he spoke that it was a flimsy falsehood. "And if my intentions toward you were less than honorable, then pray, why would I require my landlady's assistance in disrobing you when I could have had that pleasure myself?"

Why, indeed? Although she knew that his explanation was weak, Guin's hand wavered and she began to feel a trifle foolish. Lord Corvin had, thus far, acted the perfect gentleman, yet she was treating him as if he were a rake bent on rapine. Her cheeks flushed as she realized that she did not fear Corvin so much as her own reactions of the man. Moreover, even if his designs were upon her person, there was little she could do to fight him. She caught a glimpse of herself in the mirror above the mantle. Her face was haggard and scratched; an egg-sized bruise was splotched vividly across her forehead; hair tangled wildly like Medusa's. A poker dangled from one drooping arm while the other clutched the tent of a robe at her bosom. Despite an overwhelming feeling of weariness, Guin could not help bursting into laughter.

"Are you alright, Goddess?" Corvin asked, wondering what had caused this sudden change in her demeanor.

The Viscount's brow furrowed in an expression of worry. Obviously, Corvin feared that she was in the throes of hysteria—a candidate for Bedlam. She attempted to explain. "You would be desperate indeed to want that . . . ha . . . ha . . . harpy . . ." Guin stammered, pointing at the mirror as she was rocked by yet another giggle.

Corvin's tension relaxed as understanding dawned. "Thinking that you are not at your most seductive now, are you? You are wrong, but you may still depend on me to keep my word," he declared, while he dabbed at the smear of mud on his face. "You must admit that I am somewhat sloppily attired for the seducer's role. Ives wanted to clean me up, but I would not allow him to help me. Not until I made sure that you had regained consciousness. While Mrs. Truesberry took care of you, I had barely time to change out of my wet things."

The laughter vanished abruptly as the two of them stared together at their reflection; it seemed that they dared not look at each other for fear that they might be forced to acknowledge this strange affinity between them.

Although Guin's fears of Corvin were dispelled, something else charged the atmosphere. Turning away at last, not trusting herself to speak, Guin put the poker back in its place. Despite the traces of dirt, he was more attractive to her than he ever had been and there was something in his voice, something that she dared not put a name to. What would it be like, Guin wondered, to touch that cheek and wipe the smear of dirt away? She might believe him, but could she put faith in her own power to resist the strong attraction that she felt for the man?

"Thank you, milord. I am grateful for all your

care," she said, with a catch in her voice, deliberately averting her gaze from his face as she made her way back to the divan.

Corvin too, felt as if some almost imperceptible change had occurred and, waiting until she had seated herself, spoke once more. "I wish you to know why I was in Hyde Park. I have been there every morning since that night at Vauxhall. I had to see you again. I had to make sure that you were taken care of . . . I was afraid and I was right to be. Riding alone like that, neck or nothing."

The fact that he cared for her well-being caused a surge of pleasure that Guin quickly dampened. He had no claim upon her. Here was another man, a stranger, who thought that he had the right to rebuke her. "I can take care of myself. I always have," Guin said.

"And if you had been taking care of yourself today?" Corvin asked, the very thought of what could have happened to her lending unintentional harshness to his tones.

It seemed to Guin that, through some trick of the firelight, his brown eyes had flame in them and the intensity of his gaze caused a frisson of fear.

"You would have drowned in the mud or perhaps some Samaritan, who would have made you pay dearly for his kindness, would have found you?" he continued to question her, chilled to his very marrow as he realized that he might have lost her and never known.

"And you?" Guin asked, as she realized with wonder that this anger was for her sake. "What do you want, milord?"

"I am not sure," Corvin whispered, as he once more attempted to answer the question that he had asked himself so often in these past few weeks. "Heaven help me, I do not know, but when I first saw you, I knew only that I had to see you again. I have to see you again, Elaine.''

They stared at each other, the crackle of flame the only sound in the room. Corvin knelt beside the divan and raised his fingers tentatively toward her, as if to touch her cheek.

All of Guin's senses were thrown into chaos. Not since Alfred had died had a man touched her with her consent. All the old terror came to the fore. Her husband, too, had been gentle at first.

''Milord, please . . .'' What was she pleading for? Guin's temples seemed to be squeezed in a vise as an abrupt stab of pain caused her to close her eyes.

''Elaine?'' The name spoke a volume of concern. Corvin hovered beside her, only the force of his oath preventing him from gathering her into his arms. Even if he could have held her, Corvin realized, such remedies might not answer. The woman's face had told him far more than she knew. The Viscount silently cursed the brute whose treatment had caused the naked fear that he had seen in her eyes.

A rap at the door announced Mrs. Truesberry. As th woman set the tray down before Guin, the steaming bowl sent delicious promising wafts of scent.

''Poor lamb. Your head, I would wager. Drink this, dearie,'' she urged, putting the cup to Guin's lips. ''T'will take the ache away.''

''Will it make me sleep?'' Some sneaking suspicion made Guin ask.

''Aye, dearie, but it's sleep you need to heal you. Now drink,'' Mrs. Truesberry commanded, offering the potion once more.

''No, although I thank you just the same,'' Guin said, trying to focus on the kindly woman's face, but shimmers of light danced before Guin's eyes, as if she were looking at sunshine upon water. Her own voice seemed to gain a tinny echo as she spoke. ''I must go home, please. I must go home.''

"Bless me, milord. You must convince her to take the draught. She's in terrible pain, she is," Mrs. Truesberry said. "We'll send word to your people, lamb. Won't we, milord, so they won't worry? Drink, dearie."

"No," Guin refused, shaking her head although the motion made it ache all the more. She heard her own words as if from a distance. "I will go home, now. Please get me my clothes, Mrs. Truesberry."

The landlady looked anxiously at Lord Corvin.

Although he knew that it would be absurd to let Elaine leave, forcing her to stay against her will would only increase her agitation. Corvin nodded his permission and Mrs. Truesberry bustled away, a look of patent disapproval upon her face.

"If you will find me a carriage," Guin heard herself say.

"I will take you home myself," Corvin insisted. Surely she did not believe that he would allow her to travel alone in such a state.

"No," Guin told him, trying to quell the queasy feeling in the pit of her stomach.

"Under the circumstances . . ." Corvin spoke soothingly, trying to calm her unmistakable panic.

She drew a breath. "You do not understand. Please, milord. Remember my husband is a jealous man."

"I cannot simply set you in a cab, not ill as you are. How will I know that you will be taken care of? I will come with you," Corvin declared, about to tell her that he knew that her jealous husband was a sham.

"No!" Guin tried to think of some way to make him see reason, but there was too much pain for the process of thought.

Without so much as a warning knock, the door burst open. "What's this Ives tells me of an accident?" Michael Hopley asked, stopping short as he realized that Corvin was not alone. "I say!" With a reddening face, the young man took in Corvin and . . . Mrs. Courtney? It was beyond belief. Hopley would have spoken but her eyes begged him to be silent.

"Hop, meet the Fair Elaine," Corvin said, his gaze locked upon the woman's wan face as he spoke. "Perhaps you can help me convince her to stay and rest as she ought. The lady insists that she must go home, ill as she is, and she will allow no one to accompany her."

Guin was relieved to realize that Corvin had not perceived Hopley's look of startled recognition. "Him," Guin said, feeling much like a drowning woman who has seen a means of rescue. "He shall escort me, but he must swear not to reveal where I go, my circumstances."

Corvin looked at his friend, puzzled that she would trust a stranger above himself. "Will you take her home, Hop?" Corvin asked, trying to suppress a twinge of jealousy.

"Please?" Guin begged.

"I will escort her, if she wishes," Hopley agreed, compelled by the depths of desperation in the woman's eyes.

Mrs. Truesberry bustled in with Guin's damp clothing and shooed the men away to seek a carriage. As she helped Guin into her chemise their eyes met. "He didn't see dearie," Mrs. Truesberry whispered. "For 'twas my own self that undressed you. He is a good man, a kind one."

Guin knew that Mrs. Truesberry too, understood the meaning of the tracery of healed scars on Guin's back. In that sisterhood, there was no difference between the gentry and the common folk.

At last, when Guin was fully dressed, the good woman pressed a bottle of her nostrum in Guin's hand. "Take it when ye' get home, child. Keep the

room dark, for the megrim that's comin' on is bound
to be a strong 'un and stay abed for a day or two.
Ye'll be right as rain.''

Guin forced a smile as Mrs. Truesberry squeezed
her hand.

''I unnerstand, dearie. It don't do for a lady of
quality to be stayin' alone with no gennelmun an'
yer quality, I know.'' She fastened the last button,
then summoned the men from the other room.

The two helped Guin down the stairs and into the
waiting carriage.

''How will I know that you are well?'' Corvin
asked as Hopley seated himself beside the wan
woman. ''Send me word through Hopley as soon as
you are fit and meet me in Hyde Park, I deserve
that, at the least. Promise me?''

Guin could not resist the plea. She nodded her
head weakly as Corvin closed the door.

The Viscount stood in the rain, watching until the
hackney turned the corner and disappeared from
view.

Hopley shivered as he huddled miserably in the
corner of the dank carriage. It seemed to him that
his world had abruptly turned upside-down. Within
the space of a few days his closest friend seemed a
fair way to falling in love with Emmaline's schoolmistress, but was courting another woman. Emmaline was meeting Mortimer Septimus in Vauxhall
Gardens and who knew elsewhere. Most worrisome
of all to Hopley, who had always prided himself on
his honesty, was the fact that he was now bound up
in a Gordian knot of oaths, constrained by promises
that tied him to a course of silent deception. If Corvin were to discover the extent of his duplicity, the
young man feared that he would never be forgiven.

Hopley was shaken from his orgy of self-pity by
the sight of a trail of tears slipping down Mrs. Court-

ney's face, all the more eloquent because of the silence as they slipped down her cheek. He realized abruptly that his sufferings were not as great as he thought them to be.

Seven

←←←←←←←←←←←←

ALMOST TWO weeks after Guin's accident, Eddy stared out her bedroom window at the rain-washed street. "A miserable day, indeed," she remarked to the two girls who sat upon the bed. "I almost count Mrs. C. lucky to have missed the afternoon 'at home.'"

Doro glanced up from her outline of Emmaline's face. "I hardly think that it was worth being knocked down by a carriage so as to absent one's self, Eddy," she said in wry rebuke. "Mrs. C. spent nearly a week abed and the bruises that she received will be livid for some time."

"I think that I would have preferred an accident to what I suffered this afternoon," Emmaline said. "T'would have been far better than enduring Elizabeth's false friendship. I vow, if Daniel marries her I shall run away, for I could not bear living under the same roof with that conniving woman."

"For pity's sake, men can be the veriest fools at times," Eddy agreed. "I wonder how a girl as sweet and kind as Cat can have such a viper for a sister. It is interesting how offspring assort themselves. Did you know that spiders—"

"I do not," Emmaline asserted. "I have no wish to know about the breeding habits of spiders, Eddy, so please do not go off on one of your tangents."

"She is absolutely right, Eddy," Doro cut in to

forestall the beginning of another of Eddy's scientific lectures. "Elizabeth Derwent is the subject at hand."

Eddy made a moue of irritation then closed her eyes in a mode that her friends knew denoted fierce concentration. "Maybe Cat could do something?" Eddy suggested.

"She is far too loyal, you know that, Eddy," Doro said. "She would never do anything to ruin her sister's chances. That is why I made sure that she was occupied elsewhere."

"We *must* do something," Emmaline murmured, looking anxiously at her friends' faces. "She looks at me as if I were some sort of odd insect that would bite if it came too close." Her voice rose in imitation of Elizabeth's high-pitched tones. " 'My dearest Emmaline, you are such a sweet little thing, not at all what I expected. I had though that you would be a blowsy little tart.' " Emmaline concluded, her nose lifted in the air.

"Never say that Elizabeth was so vulgarly plain-spoken, for pity's sake."

Emmaline's lips tightened into an angry line as she spoke. "She did not say it, Eddy, but she implied it and there were quite a few other things that she did *not* say, ever so subtly. It is plain that she does not want me to be part of her household after she marries my brother and even if Daniel insists, I am sure that she will make life so miserable that I will wish myself back at St. Clair Abbey."

"Is she so sure then that your brother will declare himself?" Doro asked as she put aside her sketch-pad and scrutinized Emmaline's face closely.

"In her estimation, they only need to insert the notice in the *Gazette*, choose the church, and set the day."

"And your brother?" Doro inquired, picking up her pencil to shade in the area above the cheekbone.

"I do not know," Emmaline replied, her expression miserable. "He does not talk about his courtship, only asks me if I am happy here at Morton House and how I am progressing in my lessons. I am hesitant to ask for fear of the answer that I might get."

"Why do you not simply tell your brother how you feel?" Eddy asked.

"What right do I have to come between Corvin and the woman that he wishes to take to wife?" Emmaline asked as she rose to pace the room. "If there is one lesson that my mother taught me, it is not to meddle in the love affairs of others. One can never know what ties two people in love and it is unjust to interfere."

"It seems to me," Eddy said slowly, "that your axiom would be true only if two people *were* in love. However, in this equation, it is only your brother who may feel some true affection and it seems to me that you are not even sure of that."

"Whatever do you mean, Eddy?" Emmaline asked.

"Cat mentioned some time ago that Elizabeth originally had ambitions to become Duchess of Belvent. Algernon, the Duke of Belvent is a cousin of mine. I believe that Elizabeth would not even give your brother a second look if Algy beckoned."

"Do you say that Elizabeth does not even *care* for him?" Emmaline demanded angrily. "That scheming jade must not marry him! If I have to throw myself in front of the aisle as she walks to the altar, I will not allow it."

"Dramatic, but verra' impractical," Doro said, tapping her pencil on the sketch pad. "It seems to me there must be an easier way. If I recall, you say your cousin is totally absorbed by science, Eddy?"

Eddy nodded in agreement. "The study of gaseous matter is the only thing that Algy loves beyond money. He is a colleague of Sir Humphrey Davy's."

"Do you think that you could get him to come to one of Mrs. Courtney's afternoon gatherings?" Doro asked. "If we can get Elizabeth and the Duke together, we might find some means of piquing his interest."

"I do not know," Eddy frowned. "He is only concerned with gases; Algy rarely attends any social functions." She was silent for a moment, then shouted, "Eureka!"

"You what?" Emmaline asked.

"A Greek expression, Archimedes was said to have uttered it when he discovered—"

"Eddy!" Doro screeched, dropping her sketchpad in frustration. "Tell us!"

"I have been working upon an experiment in my laboratory, something that Algy would be quite interested in viewing. The duplicate of the apparatus that my father uses in his studies has been modified, you see I attached—"

"Eddy! For pity's sake!" Emmaline groaned.

Eddy grinned. "I think Algy would come to see it, if Mrs. C. would allow me to conduct an experiment. But I don't know if she will, after the sulfur fire-starting device," she added doubtfully.

"We will convince Mrs. C.!" Emmaline declared, grabbing Eddy and dancing her about the room. "As Mama used to say, 'Every journey begins with one step.' "

Guin sat at her escritoire and read the lines of Corvin's latest note once more.

"I must see you, Elaine," Corvin had written. "It has been nearly two weeks now and Hopley assures me that you are up and about once more. However, his declarations do not satisfy me and I remind you again of your pledge to me. If you do not meet me at Hyde Park corner this Thursday, you will leave

me with little choice. I needs must seek you out myself.''

Guin folded the missive carefully and placed it in
its nook with the three others that she had received.
There seemed no alternative; each of Corvin's suc-
cessive billets was more demanding than the last and
Guin began to believe that he would actually fulfill
his threat to pursue her. She would have to discourage his attentions. Strange to think, even as she contemplated her reply, Corvin was downstairs watching
his sister perform. Guin stared at the empty paper trying to find the words to convince him that she truly
did not wish to see him. Unfortunately, it was almost
as difficult to write the lie as to speak it.

The chatter of the girls as they ascended the stair
alerted Guin to the fact that the programme had
ended and she went to her bedroom window to
watch the parents depart. Guin did not even hear
the tap at the door as she watched Corvin hand Elizabeth Derwent into her carriage.

"I have the oddest thing to tell you, Guin," Aunt
Hermione declared as she entered the room. She
looked at her niece in consternation. "Come away
from that window, at once," she commanded.

"No one will notice me, Aunt," Guin protested,
letting the curtain drop.

"I vow child, sometimes you are the veriest fool,"
the older woman said crossly. "I have spent the afternoon excusing you to the parents with stories of
a terrible megrim and now you will make me into a
liar, all for a glimpse of Lord Corvin."

"I would never be so foolish. It is just that I
wished to see the demeanor of the parents, to know
if they enjoyed themselves," she declared lamely,
stepping away from the window.

"No, of course you have no interest at all in his
lordship," Aunt Hermione said acerbically, as she

sat herself down in the overstuffed chair by the bedside. "I know you too well, Guin. You have mooned over him like a schoolgirl since that interview, listening every time his name is mentioned, talking of him so fondly, running for a glimpse of him. I vow, I cannot understand why you put us at risk by your behavior."

How upset the woman would be if she knew the whole, Guin thought, guilty over the secrets she kept. She had told her aunt nothing of her encounter with Corvin at Vauxhall and Hopley had been given the credit for bringing her home after her so-called, "carriage accident." "I am not a foolish child anymore, Aunt, wishing for the moon, the stars and true love," Guin protested.

"We all have our dreams, Guin, to give us hope from day to day, but when one can no longer discern twixt dream and reality, therein lies danger."

"Do you think me so far gone?" Guin asked. "I know that Lord Corvin is far above my touch."

The older woman's eyes narrowed shrewdly. "No, I would not say you are gone beyond recall. Still, it is just as well that you get those windmills out of your head, gel, for I would not see you hurt. You were wise to play least in sight, especially with the remains of that bruise upon your forehead drawing attention to you. Corvin is far too young to recognize me as Lady Cathcart, so there is no problem there, but you? Well, gel, if he looks too close, he might see Guinivere Courtney is Elaine Borne."

"He was away upon the Peninsula," Guin declared.

"Can you be sure?" Aunt Hermione asked pointedly. "Even officers have leave."

Guin deliberately turned the subject. "Tell me about the programme. Did Eddy's experiment go well?" she asked.

"It was most impressive," Aunt Hermione said.

"I confess that I sat close to the doorway, if the need arose for a rapid exit, but thankfully there was no stench this time. On the whole, this afternoon went very well. It was quite a feather in our cap to have the illustrious Duke of Belvent as our guest. Edwina's cousin was quite attentive to a schoolgel's experiment, kept his eyes on that bubbling whatever-it-was for the duration. I must say, Elizabeth Derwent was quite put out about that. 'Twas clear that she would much rather have had the Duke look at her; but I am sure that I must be mistaken. That cat knows where the dish of cream is located."

"About what were you mistaken?" Guin's question was abstracted. Had her fascination with the Viscount become so obvious?

"Rumor has it that Miss Derwent is a favorite for becoming a viscountess. I can only conclude that Elizabeth Derwent must have been flirting with Belvent to rouse Lord Corvin's jealousy."

Guin tried to remain impassive. "Indeed," she said coolly.

The older woman nodded, unfooled by her niece's pretense. "T'would be just as well, Guin," she said gently. "If it is not la Derwent, t'will be another. Still, I am no longer as sanguine as I once was regarding which one she is after, Corvin or Belvent. I would be mightily surprised if His Grace is her true objective. He will be difficult quarry indeed," Aunt Hermione remarked. "I would not put it past her though, for she managed to corner His Grace after Emmaline's performance and Miss Derwent sounded almost like our Eddy. I nearly laughed aloud, let me tell you, to hear her spouting all those strange terms and the Duke looking at her as if he were regarding his Holy Grail. In fact, His Grace invited Miss Derwent and our gels to attend a demonstration of the effects of some stuff or other, to be given at the Royal

Institution. Apparently, Sir Humphrey Davy has given Belvent permission to use his apparatus.''

"That will be fascinating," Guin said, both disturbed and elated. If Corvin was seeking a wife, it was no business of hers, but she could not help but be glad if Elizabeth Derwent had turned her attentions to another man. Corvin deserved far better.

"I think not," Aunt Hermione said. "Lord Corvin is to come as well. I think that it would be best if I were to chaperone."

Guin nodded in agreement, swallowing her disappointment.

"The less you see of him in the future, the better, Guin, else you'll try your luck once too often," the older woman chided. "Septimus has seen you. Hopley knows of the girls' escapade at Vauxhall but has vowed to keep his mouth shut about that and the fact that you ride that brute of an animal without a groom for company. I can only be thankful that it was young Hopley who found you after Bombay threw you. It was clever of him to concoct that carriage accident story. I only pray we can trust his discretion."

Guin shifted uncomfortably, remembering the notes that Hopley had delivered at Corvin's request.

"You mentioned when you came in that you have something odd to tell me. What was it?" Guin could see by her aunt's expression that the older woman would have liked to say more, but she allowed herself to be diverted.

"It is the most strange thing, Guin," she said, lowering her voice. "I had gone upstairs to fetch that piece of fancywork that Dorothea has framed above her bed, so that I could show Lady Derwent a sample of our student's skills with the needle. Coming from the hearth, I could hear Elizabeth, as plain as day, gel, every blessed word of Bronwyn

Geoffry's too, for all that the music mistress don't speak above a whisper.''

Guin winced as she wrinkled her forehead in thought. ''That explains a great deal, actually. I have always wondered how the girls always seem to know exactly when we are about to surprise them with an inspection of the rooms, or how they found out about my plans that night at Vauxhall. Last night, they must have known that I was on my way up, for Jane swore that Emmaline and Cat were gone from their beds, and when I got there, the two were sawing away.''

''Shall I order the gels moved from the room?'' Aunt Hermione asked.

''Impossible. Every bed in the house is full,'' Guin said.

''Yes, that is true,'' the older woman agreed with a smile. ''We have actually had to turn eligible pupils away. The change in the Earl of Sinclair's gel is the talk of the ton.''

Guin considered. ''Perhaps we may be able to use this information to our advantage, Aunt. A direct channel to the ears of those girls who are in the forefront of any mischief, may have its use. In the meanwhile, any private discussions will take place in our bedchambers and I will make sure that the girls are away from their rooms if any interviews take place. In fact, I believe the girls are in their rooms now. Come down to the parlor with me and follow my lead.''

In the parlor, Guin posted herself by the hearth and beckoned her aunt to come near. ''Remember,'' the schoolmistress whispered, ''speak clearly and naturally.''

Her aunt grinned when she realized what her niece was about. ''It is a pity that your headache prevented you from witnessing Eddy's experiment and Emmaline's performance," the older woman said in conversational tones.

"I was so sorry to miss it, Mrs. Haven. I must confess that I had some trepidation about Eddy. I still get a whiff of sulfur every time I sit down upon the cushions in the parlor."

The woman's eyes danced as she said, "Sometime that gel shows a signal lack of consideration, ignoring all else for those experiments of hers. Why, Madame Vallée has told me that she pays no attention to art instruction and I can vouch for her lack of attendance in deportment."

"What would you suggest, Mrs. Haven?" Guin asked, smiling in encouragement.

"I say, bar her from her laboratory," Mrs. Haven declared, warming to her subject. "Shut it down and turn it back to a stillroom. Perhaps then she'll pay more attention to the things she really ought."

Guin shook her head. "Now, now, Mrs. Haven, let us not be hasty. Eddy has made considerable progress, but if she continues in her irresponsible behavior, I fear that we may have to do as you suggest," she said.

"Yes, she is a good-hearted child. It would be a shame to have to deprive her of something she enjoys so much," she agreed, sending Guin a broad wink. "Well, my dear, I will leave now to inspect the bedrooms. I trust that they will be in good order."

Both women looked up and smiled when they heard the scuffling of feet from the floor above. It was clear that their message had been received.

"I am glad to hear that you are feeling more the thing, Guin," Mrs. Haven said as she departed.

"I am fine, now, just fine," Guin assured her, although nothing could have been farther from the truth. The ache was gone, but thoughts of Corvin were constantly on her mind. Guin stood before the hearth and stared into the fire. She had no choice. She had to see him. Perhaps then, she could banish his specter from her thoughts.

The next morning, a light breeze blew off the Serpentine as Corvin tethered his horse in the shelter of the trees. In the growing light of dawn, he paused to unfold Elaine's note and read it once more, trying to find a trace of warmth in her words, but her message was as cold and formal as it had been upon the first reading. "Milord" this, "your lordship" that, she begged him once more, to take Hopley's word upon her well-being. Yet, Corvin was encouraged by her strong reluctance to meet him, taking it as a sign that she too, feared the strength of this strange bond between them.

As the sun rose higher, Corvin vowed to seek her out if she broke her word and did not come as promised. It would be easy enough, even though Hopley had kept to the letter of his oath, revealing nothing of Elaine's location or circumstances. A striking woman, who rode a monstrous marred horse, had a titled lady for an aunt, a harlequin for a servant and lived in the vicinity of Hyde Park, would not be difficult to locate.

Common sense would have dictated that Corvin follow Hop's advice and leave the matter alone and indeed, he had tried to banish Elaine's memory from his mind. Although he had filled his nights with routs and balls, he found himself looking for her even though he knew that she would not be there. More than once Elizabeth Derwent had chided him gently for his inattentiveness. And home alone in his rooms, the vision of Elaine standing before him, her hair glowing with firelight would haunt the darkness. The scent of her, the feel of her against him taunted him at the oddest times and even in the midst of company, Corvin found himself feeling a loneliness deeper than any he had experienced. It was the mystery, he told himself once more, the mystery that surrounded her was what tantalized him. If he were to find out about Elaine's background, see that she was a woman like all others, then he would be able to free himself of her and give Elizabeth all she deserved. Now, all he could give Miss Derwent was his respect, that other part of him which he had reserved to himself for so long, had somehow become bound with Elaine.

At the sound of hoofbeats Corvin's pulse started to pound like a hammer. Although he tried to steel himself for disappointment, he could not quell the rising excitement.

It was Elaine. Her face was pale and drawn and the shadows beneath her eyes told a story of sleepless nights, but her expression remained impassive. Corvin wondered what she was thinking, whether she too felt the tension that was almost a palpable thing between them. He reached out to offer his help at dismounting but dropped his hand when he saw the cold look in her eyes. She remained upon her horse, staring down upon him.

"Milord," she greeted him in tones that were as aloof as her demeanor. It was the only way to discourage him, she schooled herself. Do not let him know that your heart is racing.

"Elaine, thank you for coming," he said, his voice husky with unspoken emotion.

"Now you can ascertain for yourself. I am 'right as rain' again. I think it would have been far better had you taken Mr. Hopley's word for it," she said, making the words as chill and clipped as she could. From the look of puzzlement and hurt in his eyes, she knew that she was succeeding.

Corvin found himself taken aback by her hostility and wondered if the Elaine of the firelight had been the product of his imagination, for the woman before him seemed to be made entirely of ice.

"How could I be sure that you were not trying to simply put me off and Hopley helping you?" Corvin asked. "I swear, the boy has been attempting to discourage me."

"He is your friend, milord. Perhaps there is reason for you to be discouraged," she declared rebukingly, holding up the hand with her wedding ring upon it, like a magical talisman. The band gleamed dully in the morning sunlight. Let him be convinced, she prayed. "This should be ample reason for you to leave me in peace."

"You are not married," Corvin said, anxiously watching her face for reaction as he called her bluff. As he had hoped, the mask of reserve slipped. Elaine went pale and her fists clenched tight upon the reins.

"I had thought Hopley was a man of his word," she cried, devastated at the thought that she had been betrayed. "What is the world coming to, when one cannot trust the oath of a gentleman and one who is to join the church at that! How much else has he told you?" The schoolmistress scanned his face for some clue. If Corvin knew all then why was he toying with her so? She had never thought him capable of such cruelty.

"Hopley told me nothing," Corvin said, wondering once more just what the woman was hiding. "I have suspected all along that your excuse at Vauxhall was all a hum. You have just confirmed my suspicions. Why can you not trust me, Elaine?"

"Trust?" she questioned him with a bitter-edged laugh. Although she was relieved that Corvin was still in the dark, she was dismayed that she had been so easily duped. "You have just tricked me and you wish me to trust you?"

"You lied to me when you said you had a hus-

band," Corvin pointed out with what he thought
to be perfect logic. Even the angry sparks that her
eyes threw at him as she spat out her answer were
preferable to the aloofness that she had affected before.

"I am a widow, milord, and I did indeed have a
husband once. If I prevaricated it was but to protect
myself," she declared, feeling a growing sense of
helplessness now that she could no longer hide behind the wedding ring. "It appears that I was foolish to think that the sacred bonds of marriage would
protect me from your attentions. Despite my express
wishes you continue to seek me out, milord, and
send your friend on fool's errands."

"You came," he said simply. "You did not have
to."

"Did I not?" She blazed. "Did I not? Any idiot
could have realized that if I had not responded, you
would have tried to ferret me out. I had no choice.
Why do you continue to plague me?"

Corvin met her fury with equanimity. "Yes, I
would have sought you out; to the earth's end if
necessary, Elaine," he said, realizing that she spoke
the truth. He would have pumped Hopley for information and if that had not answered, he would indeed have initiated a search. Why *did* he continue to
plague her? Corvin attempted to answer her as honestly as he could. "I do not wish to spend the rest
of my life wondering where you are and why you
are so desperately unhappy."

"No. It cannot be true, milord," she said, looking
into the depths of his eyes, startled by what she saw
there. For a brief moment, she believed him. "You
know nothing of who I am, my station . . ." *Do not
be taken in*, some inner voice warned her. *Remember
fool, that he is courting Elizabeth Derwent as he tries to
cozen you. He is a man, like all men he seeks but one
thing.* "How clever of you, milord, 'earth's end' in-

deed. And for a moment I responded like a green girl.''

With a diplomat's sense, Corvin realized that he was losing her. ''No! It is not at all like that,'' he protested, at a loss to make her understand something that he himself could not fully comprehend. ''Do you believe in destiny?''

''Destiny, heaven, hell, the Church of England, judgment day and the Duke of Wellington, not necessarily in that order,'' she recited with the merest hint of laughter in her voice. ''But I cannot believe in you, milord, for that chestnut is old as Methusalah. Is your next line to be that we were 'fated to meet'?''

''Yes, dammit!'' he cursed, his frustration growing as he looked at her, so close but untouchable because of his sworn word. If only he could take her in his arms, hold her, then she would be forced to view him in seriousness. Corvin made one final appeal. ''Elaine, do you not feel it? This affinity between us? In all honesty, can you gainsay it?''

''No,'' she said, although she knew it would have served her better to deny it. The curious bond was too strong. His bewildered expression drew her sympathies and she tried to speak as gently as she could. ''I cannot. You are a very attractive man, milord. I will not deny that, but that is all it is, physical attraction; that and the fantasy that you have built upon what you do not know. Let me assure you, sir, I am nothing extraordinary.''

''Will you let me be the judge of that, Elaine?'' Corvin asked, his eyes dropping before her probing stare. Her assessment had come far too close to his own evaluation of the truth.

''Certainly not! I give no man the right to be my judge!''

Corvin was startled by the venom in her voice. A

chill gust blew, whipping tendrils of hair against her face and her eyes glistened with angry tears. "It is more than attraction, Elaine. Far more," he said softly, knowing that he had unwittingly touched some wound.

"Whatever you choose to style it," she told him, not bothering to contain her anger at his presumption. "Give it any name you like, but it can come to nothing, Lord Corvin, nothing but unhappiness for us both. We are too far apart, you and I."

"I think that you make the distance farther than it really is, Fair Elaine. Tell me, then, who you are and why you are so afraid to let me find out about you?" he asked, but her face was shuttered once more.

"Is this some new form of amusement?" she asked with a sneer. "Twenty questions or less until my soul is bared to satisfy your curiosity. Well I shall not play, although I am sure that you will find some other woman who will be delighted to join in your game."

"Listen to me," Corvin said, but he knew that she was far too angry to hear him.

"No I have heard enough. Do not await me here anymore, milord, since I shall not return; it is best that we not meet again," she told him, hoping that she would be far away once the tears began to fall, but before she could take up the reins, Corvin had stepped forward and caught hold of the bridle.

"I will not let you go this way, Elaine," he said, trying to ignore the look of fear upon her face. "I will follow you home. If you elude me, you know that I will find you."

She gripped her riding crop, sorely tempted to whip his restraining hand away and gallop, as fast and as far as Bombay could carry her. But her hand was stayed by the knowledge that Corvin could easily do as he threatened. She was totally at his mercy. "Why do you do this to me, milord?" she asked, her voice atremble. "If you truly care for me as you claim, you will let me leave in peace. I beg of you."

"I offer you an alternative, think upon what I have said and meet me here, two days hence," Corvin stated, making up his conditions as he went along. "Then, all I will ask of you is four meetings more, all in a public place. My oath to you stands. Let me talk to you, get to know you and you shall become better acquainted with me. Then, if you still feel the same, I will make no attempt to seek you out."

"Blackmail," she accused, trying to fight the overwhelming feeling of powerlessness. "And if I refuse those generous terms?"

As if sensing the upset of its mistress, her horse moved restively beneath Corvin's restraining hand. "Blackmail is a harsh word. I am simply trying to prevent you from throwing away what is between us. I will not allow it," he said, his threat implicit. He could hardly meet her eyes as they grew hard with disdain.

"There is nothing between us, *milord*, and shall never be," she spat the words, infusing his title with mock servility. "Still it seems that I must obey your demand, *milord*. Till Thursday. If you will but release my horse now, *milord*?"

Mutely, he obeyed, watching as she galloped like a Fury until she was out of sight. A numbness set in as the full ramifications of what he had just done became clear. Never before had he been the bullying sort, certainly not when it came to women, but the very thought of losing her had caused him to use tactics that he abhorred. Corvin could only hope that she would not hate him for his machinations. No matter what the name for his tumultuous feelings, there was no excuse for such manipulation.

Eight

T HE HOUR was unconscionably early. Indeed, most
of those habitués of the Royal Institution who
dabbled in science were still abed and dreaming
Wednesday morning away. A few dedicated souls
were surprised to hear voices emanating from the
lecture room at the august academy. However, upon
determining that young chits from the famed Morton School for Young Ladies were the source of the
chatter, they promptly scurried to the library or the
basements and wished the Duke of Belvent to perdition for bringing this female plague upon them.

Luckily, His Grace was supremely unaware of his
colleagues' maledictions. The Duke examined the
apparatus upon the platform with quiet efficiency,
making terse comments in response to Eddy's rapid
questions about the functions of the equipment and
her idol, Sir Humphrey Davy.

Although Belvent's answers were unintelligible to
her, Elizabeth Derwent, nonetheless, nodded and
occasionally inserted a question of her own.

Lord Corvin was considerably surprised at the apparent breadth of Elizabeth's understanding. He had
not suspected that Miss Derwent's interests extended to scientific investigation.

Neither, apparently, did His Grace, and his looks
became increasingly admiring, so much so that, to
Eddy's annoyance, he actually stopped his work and

answered Miss Derwent at length, his phrases becoming unnecessarily flowery.

Eddy winced as Doro jabbed her in the elbow.

"Let him talk to her, idiot!" Doro whispered as she ostensibly examined the device.

"I had forgotten," Eddy whispered in chagrin. "Is this not exciting?" Only Doro's long-suffering look and the threat of another poke forced Eddy off the platform and back to her seat.

"Remember what you are here for, Eddy," Emmaline cautioned in an undertone so that Cat, who was several seats beyond them, would not hear. "Have you given Elizabeth some more questions to ask?"

"Elizabeth thinks that I am so gullible, taken in by her sudden interest in science," Eddy said with a chuckle, as she made herself comfortable on the cushioned bench. "The woman has the most amazing skill, I must admit. Although initially, I had to feed her the pap like a babe, she actually sounds as if she knows what she is talking about, now. At least, Algy seems to think so," the girl noted, nodding toward the platform. "I have never seen him speak so earnestly to any female and look, his hand is actually resting atop hers." As Eddy spoke, His Grace flushed and withdrew his fingers abruptly. Miss Derwent turned a becoming shade of pink.

"I vow," Doro murmured, "I have never before seen anyone who can blush at will. 'Tis a talent indeed."

Emmaline glanced several rows behind her to where her brother had seated himself beside Mrs. Haven. "Daniel looks irritated," she reported. "He is frowning and Mrs. H. is in place."

"Lucky Mrs. C. could not come, she is far too canny by a half," Doro remarked. "It looks like we are off to a good start."

"Just you wait," Eddy said, rubbing her hands in anticipation. "Em, you know the questions?"

"Every one," Emmaline replied, offended. "There are not that many, you know?"

"For pity's sake, do not get angry, I just wanted to be safe since we cannot be sure how many that you will be able to put to Elizabeth. So remember, ask them exactly in the order that they were written; the most important are first. When we get the response we want, do not let her ramble on; continue to the next."

Emmaline nodded and turned her attention to the platform as Belvent began to speak, his voice echoing as his audience took but a few of the nine hundred seats in the semi-circular room.

"And now, young ladies, Lord Corvin," the Duke of Belvent addressed the audience, inclining his head to its sole male member. "I would like now, to demonstrate the peculiar effects of the substance nitrous oxide. This amazing gas was discovered by my good friend, Sir Humphrey Davy. If I might have a volunteer?"

Eddy held her breath. She had gone to great lengths to reassure Elizabeth that the gas had no ill effects and was, on the whole, a most enjoyable experience. Over and over, Eddy had emphasized how much her cousin, the Duke, admired those who did not fear the wondrous works of science. Unless her prompting bore fruit, all their planning was for naught.

As they had hoped, Elizabeth rose from her seat and walked gracefully up the stairs to the platform, looking like a veritable Athena in quest of scientific wisdom. Her walking dress of blue watered silk was a perfect compliment to her pale complexion and the light flush that colored her cheeks beneath the wide-brimmed bonnet completed a most delightful picture.

Eddy wondered if Algy realized how incredibly like a frog he looked, attired in a pea green waistcoat, with his mouth hanging open, as if Elizabeth Derwent were a fly that he longed to devour. His eyes were bulging in admiration and pleasure as he assisted her onto the platform.

There was a moment of silence before the Duke recovered himself. "Most brave of you, Miss Derwent. Although I assure you it is quite safe," he said.

"I know," Elizabeth agreed without a quaver. "I have always longed to experience the effects of nitrous oxide. I have read about Sir Humphrey Davy's bold experiments, but have never had the privilege of attending his lectures. Now, I am glad of it," she said, her wide with innocence, heavily lashed eyes turning upon the Duke with their full force. "For I am sure that I would not have felt half so safe as in your hands, Your Grace."

"How does she manage to look so worshipfully upon that toad?" Doro asked, stifling a giggle. "His Grace seems overwhelmed."

Emmaline glanced behind her and saw the almost imperceptible tightening around her brother's mouth that was a certain indication of displeasure. "Daniel is not quite overwhelmed yet, but he will be," she said with certainty.

"Pay attention," Eddy whispered through clenched teeth. "He has begun to administer the nitrous oxide."

"Now, Miss Derwent, inhale deeply," the Duke instructed. "Again."

All eyes were intent as Elizabeth closed her eyes and breathed the gas.

"As you will soon see," the Duke intoned. "The gas has a remarkable effect, producing a sense of profound relaxation, floating if you will. How do you feel, Miss Derwent?"

"Wonderful!" Elizabeth declared, her voice almost unrecognizable. The normally dulcet tones of the proper young lady had descended to a husky depth.

"I advised Elizabeth to breath deeply," Eddy whispered. "She should be ready about . . . now."

Doro rose upon cue. "Does the gas effect the way people act, Your Grace?" she asked.

"In a way," the Duke said with a condescending smile. "It is somewhat akin to being drunk, although you ladies would not know of that. There are those who will lose their inhibitions upon inhaling enough of it."

"Can people speak normally, and answer questions under the influence of the gas?" Doro asked.

"Of course," the Duke replied, nodding his head. "Only their answers might be different than what they ordinarily would be. People tend not to regard what they say."

"May I ask Elizabeth a question, Your Grace?" Emmaline requested.

"Certainly," the Duke consented.

"Elizabeth," Emmaline asked. "How do you really feel about me, Lady Emmaline?"

"You are not at all as bad as I expected," Miss Derwent replied, her tones were decidedly woozy, rising and falling like a rocking boat. She opened her eyes and attempted to focus. "For the daughter of a slut."

"Emmaline!" Mrs. Haven gasped, rising and starting down the aisle toward that young lady, but she tripped over an outstretched leg and landed in Cat's lap.

Doro glanced back to see Lord Corvin's expression. His face was thunderous.

"And do you like His Grace?" Emmaline continued quickly.

Elizabeth turned to look at the Duke dreamily.

"He is everything that I have ever wanted in a man," she said, regarding Belvent worshipfully.

The Duke regarded Elizabeth in wonder. No woman had ever regarded him with such obvious desire and due to the influence of the gas, he could credit that she spoke the truth.

"And Corvin?"

"This is the outside of enough Lady Emmaline!" Mrs. Haven cried, she had risen and was struggling to negotiate the sea of skirts between her and her objective.

"Yes, what about Corvin? I would be most interested," the Viscount inquired, leaning forward in his seat.

His eyes were dark with anger and his mouth was a tight line, chiseled into stone, but Elizabeth was far too befuddled to recognize her danger. "Oh, I like you well enough, milord, although you are a stuffy pompous ass, but I far prefer Algernon, for—"

Eddy would have liked to hear the continuation of the statement but she feared that it would not serve their purpose to have Elizabeth say more. "For shame!" Eddy shouted, jumping to her feet. "The lady trusted you, Your Grace, and you have allowed her to be taken advantage of." She turned upon Emmaline and pointed an accusing finger. "And you too, should be ashamed of yourself for destroying a scientific experiment in this manner. It is sacrilege! Yes, sacrilege!"

"On the contrary, Miss, I have found it most enlightening," Lord Corvin said, rising from his seat.

Elizabeth, wreathed in smiles, trilled, "Leaving so soon, Corvin? Are you not interested in science? I find it most intriguing, I vow. I feel soooo wonderful."

Corvin paused at the door and doffed his hat, giving her a stiff bow. "Then I shall leave you to further discoveries, Miss Derwent. I have just remembered a pressing engagement.''

Elizabeth waved cheerfully as Corvin shut the door behind him.

'' 'The daughter of a slut.' Makes me the son of a slut by extension,'' Corvin mumbled, as he hurried down the steps of the Royal Institution. ''Shouldn't have walked out that way though, Daniel, bad ton, no matter how outrageous the insult.'' As he reached the outdoors, the cool morning air was like a slap upon the face, bringing him to his senses once more.

Corvin's tiger jumped down to assist his master into the silver high-perch phaeton, but the Viscount waved him away.

''Take 'em home,'' Corvin ordered. ''I think myself in need of a walk.''

As the Royal Institution disappeared behind him, Corvin realized that his courtship of Elizabeth Derwent was over, yet all he felt upon its dissolution was a vague sense of anger. The revelation of Elizabeth's true feelings had caused him no true pain— no jealousy, no loss, just humiliation. The Viscount covered Albermarle Street quickly in long strides, heading in no particular direction except away.

''You are a blind fool, Daniel,''. Corvin told himself. Up until this morning, the courtship had been proceeding entirely as he had expected, calls at Derwent House, rides in the park in the afternoon, dances at the various balls and routs that they attended. Their acquaintance had moved on the inexorable wheels of common expectation to the brink of betrothal. Yet, now, when all his hopes had been dashed, Corvin felt nothing more than pique. No, that was untrue.

With each step, Corvin experienced a peculiar sense of elation, almost as if he was a prisoner whose

impending execution had been unexpectedly com-
muted. He was not going to marry Elizabeth Derwent! One by one he brought forth the mental list
of her faults that he had hitherto refused to acknowledge. All these characteristics, he now recognized, would have ultimately driven him to
distraction were he obliged to suffer them for the
prolonged duration of a marriage. Corvin shuddered inwardly. How close he had come to a life-
long disaster. Were it not for Emmaline's chance
question . . .

"Emmaline!" he muttered to himself. "Daniel,
you selfish beast, the poor child must be overset."
Corvin turned around, about to hurry back to the
Royal Institution when a strange thought struck him.
Chance? As the whole scene repeated itself once more
in Corvin's memory, the image of his sister's face as
she asked those ill-fated questions came to mind. That
deliberate, calculating look had held the expectation of
a specific result. It was too neat, Corvin realized; the
event had been entirely too well-ordered for the spon-
taneity of accident. It was suddenly clear that the minx
had known exactly what Elizabeth would say.

Corvin began to grin as he recognized that the entire incident had been masterfully orchestrated, from
the choice of participants, to the seating arrange-
ments for Emmaline. His sister had been safely ensconced within a crowd of girls, effectively
hampering Mrs. Haven's efforts to reach her and
prevent any more embarrassing questions. Somehow, Emmaline had known Elizabeth's true feelings
and with total disregard for discretion, had decided
to make them known to the entire world. Em ought
to have come to him, Corvin thought, but then how
can one confide in a pompous ass?

Corvin's wanderings had brought him instinctively homewards, past the shops of Picadilly,

through Green Park to the precincts of Hyde Park. The sun was showing shyly from behind a bank of clouds and despite the damp autumn chill that permeated the air, children threw balls with fervent vigor as if the brief break in the rainy weather required them to make up the time for all the play that they had missed.

Corvin could not help scanning the faces of the maids and nannies upon the benches, in the absurd hope that he might find Elaine there among the crows who cawed among themselves as they watched their charges. Most dropped their eyes at the gentleman's obvious scrutiny, a few met his gaze with indignation and some with admiration, but nowhere among them was the face that he sought.

Corvin shook his head and turned his thoughts inward once more. Tomorrow would be the first of the meetings that he had extorted from Elaine and he knew that, inevitably, she would be hostile, provoked by his coercive tactics. The one tie that bound them together, the physical attraction between them, could not be relied upon. It would be a challenge to woo her with words alone when so much more could be conveyed by the merest touch. His only advantage would be the element of surprise, Corvin thought with a smile, and he had his ambush well-prepared.

The breeze that ruffled the water clearly stated that autumn had arrived and the branches of the trees upon the riverbank sent a shower of leaves to float beside the strange boat that drifted upon the Serpentine.

The elegant craft was like nothing that Guin had ever seen and she wondered how Corvin had managed to produce this marvel in so short a time. Elaborately carved representations of folded wings painted gilt and white, projected from either side of the boat. The prow was a swan's head, the long wooden neck adorned with feathers to resemble the avian reality. Even the paddles were designed to simulate webbed feet.

Guin sat stiff-backed on her padded seat, refusing to relax against the comfortable-looking pile of silken cushions that Corvin had provided. No matter that the craft looked like some creation of a poet's fancy; the mere fact that she was upon the water kept her nerves upon edge.

Corvin's frustration mounted as one by one, his conversational gambits were checked. He had counted upon her being so enchanted by the boat that she might relax enough to let down her guard. For all his efforts, it seemed that nothing would pierce the wall of her hostility. Corvin had coerced her physical presence, but his every verbal foray was met with a monosyllabic reply.

"The weather is getting chilly," Corvin said. The sentence was the measure of his diminishing repertoire of openings for discussion. The topic of weather was the last resort of a man on the brink of locutory defeat. All his elaborate preparations were for naught.

"Yes, it is," she replied.

"Three words!" Corvin started to rise from his seat in mock elation. "Three words, all in a row! I vow, 'tis a record for the day. You distinctly said, 'Yes it is!' "

Although the boat rocked but slightly. A wave of terror engulfed Guin as recollection overwhelmed her.

"Nooooooo . . ." The scream traveled across the open water and echoed among the trees. Her hands gripped the sides in a convulsive gesture.

"Elaine?" Corvin called her name, grasping her shoulders as he tried to evoke some response from those unfocused eyes but she seemed lost in the depths of some internal terror. They drifted along for some moments before she started to come to herself once more and began to struggle from his grip.

As Guin fixed once more on the present, she realized that it was not Alfred grasping her, but Corvin. The shock and concern on his face made her want to thrust herself against him and envelop herself in those strong arms until the fear had all ebbed away. Instead, she tried to gather the shards of her shattered composure.

"I am sorry, milord, for my foolishness. You may release me now."

"It is I who should apologize for frightening you so," Corvin said, keeping his tones carefully neutral as he reluctantly released his hold. In her moments of horrifying silence, the Viscount realized that he had encountered much the same type of abrupt madness in his years as an officer. Many a seasoned soldier had been pushed into like hysteria by happenstance even though he might be a long away from the battlefield. A chance noise, the smell of gunpowder sent him beyond reality to relive a moment of terror. Corvin knew that he had to tread carefully lest he push her back into panic.

The loss of Corvin's touch had nearly destroyed her false air of assurance. Guin was grateful for his silence as he maneuvered the boat away from shore. The rhythmic dipping of the oars as they cut into the water was calming but it could not completely sooth the tumult within. Guin watched the bubbles of the wake behind them, trying to focus her attention on anything but the Viscount. Surely he would be revolted by her outré reaction? What did he think of her now? Her eyes were drawn to him despite her mortification. Careless of the chill, he had removed his jacket and she could see the ripple of muscle through the lawn fabric of his shirt, as he drew the oars back in seemingly effortless motion.

His apparent lack of anger gave her courage. She felt that she owed him an explanation of her seemingly irrational conduct.

"The reason that I screamed, milord, was because I feared that we would capsize," she told him, rushing the words out quickly before she lost her courage. "You see, I nearly drowned once by falling from a boat. Do you recall the Prince Regent's great fete several years ago? The one that celebrated the first victory over Napoleon?"

"I was on the Continent at the time, but I do recollect some of the accounts of the event. It was quite lavish." Corvin spoke slowly, encouraging her to continue.

Guin nodded. "Amazingly so, even for Prinny . . ." Her voice trailed off momentarily as her mind spanned the years, recalling every detail of the event as if it had occured only the previous day.

"My husband and a friend had secured a boat so that we would not have to stand among the crowds in the summer heat. We had an excellent view of the re-enactment of Nelson's victory. It was splendid. There were fourteen miniature ships-of-the-line. My husband said that they had been constructed to scale. Even the guns worked."

Guin looked out over the water seeing in her mind's eye the little puffs of powder as the mock battle was joined. "It was near sunset, and the battle with the make-believe French fleet had gone on for nearly an hour. The entertainment was seemingly over when one of the ships caught fire and drifted toward the French fleet, setting it ablaze. How the crowd had cheered, thinking it was but a part of the show!"

Guin frowned and closed her eyes as she recalled. "Suddenly, there was a tumult upon the shore. A young woman—I would guess that she was not much older than myself—had stripped herself naked and was trying to plunge herself into the water. Some were trying to stop her, but my husband and his friend had risen in the boat and along with many other men they cheered, urging her on," Guin said, painfully confronting that despairing face in her memory once more.

"We were close enough to see her eyes. They were haunted with such desperate madness. I shall never forget. My husband and his friend were foxed and they did not realize how terribly they were rocking the boat in their effort to get a better view. It finally capsized and we were all pitched overboard. They swam circles around me, laughing and swearing, but neither made a move to help me."

Her drawn face told Corvin a tale far more vivid than her matter-of-fact tones. In it he could read her sympathy for the madwoman, her boundless loathing of the men's actions and her fear as she thought herself drowning.

Guin had opened her eyes once more. She could see the growing disgust upon Corvin's face and would have stopped but the words seemed to tumble out of their own accord. "My skirts were dragging me down. I tried to swim, but the weight and the smell of that noisome water overwhelmed me. I went under, but unfortunately someone had seen me go under and dove in to fish me out."

"Unfortunately?" Corvin fixed upon the word, shocked by its implications.

"It would have been far better if they left me to drown, milord. Just as it would have been far kinder to allow that woman put a period to herself. Instead, I was spared and a group of black-clad women dragged the poor female off, to consign her to some madhouse, as I recall." She attempted a light tone. "And as the ladies' atonement for the madwoman's disgraceful disruption of Prinny's fair, the Countess of Spencer started a subscription for the statue of Wellington that is to be placed in Hyde Park.''

Corvin's face was thunderous, causing Guin to flinch within. His expression of revulsion ripped open the wounds that she had thought long healed. By inadvertently revealing that she had wished herself dead, she believed any regard that he had for her totally destroyed. Perhaps it was just as well, she thought dully. Surely, he would have no desire for her company now.

Corvin was shaken by the revelation of such callous brutality and the knowledge that there was surely more left untold if she had been driven to such depths of despair. Although Corvin was not a violent man by nature, he found himself almost sorry that her husband was dead, savoring the thought of killing the man that had done this to her. She had withdrawn to the farthest corner of her seat, almost cringing, as if anticipating some physical blow from him. Surely he had done nothing to justify such an expectation. Or had he? Corvin was abruptly struck by the realization that one did not have to physically assault to abuse. He, in his own way, had been cruel in his conduct.

''I am sorry, Elaine,'' he said. The simple words seemed insufficient to convey the depth of his contrition.

Corvin's gentle tone had startled Guin. She had been prepared for a rebuke. ''You could not have known that rocking the boat would send me into a frenzy,'' she said.

''You were driving me to distraction with your 'yes, milord,' 'no, milord,' 'surely, milord,' but that is no excuse. I ask your pardon for upsetting you. I would never do anything to hurt you, Elaine, I swear.'' He brushed his hair from his forehead in a frustrated gesture. ''But even more so, I owe you an apology for forcing you here. I realize now that I had no right to coerce you to come. That foul bargain was the only means that came to mind so that I might see you again. Do you understand?''

''I do, milord.'' Guin said, knowing, however much she tried to deny it, her compulsion was almost as great as his, but now it was at an end. ''I agree it would be best that we sever our acquaintance.''

''No, Elaine, you misunderstand.'' Corvin shook his head as he realized what she meant. She thought that he had taken her in contempt. ''I still wish to continue our meetings.''

''Why?'' she asked. ''What can you feel for me now that you know I am so weak a creature?''

''I have been drawn to other women before, Elaine,'' Corvin tried to explain, pulling the oars in and choosing his words slowly as he attempted to phrase something that seemed entirely irrational. ''But not in this way. Although you have said that we are strangers, I feel that I have known you before and even though it pains me to cause you grief, I still have no wish to release you from the devil's bargain that I have made. I ask no more than a chance to talk to you, as one friend to another if you wish for nothing else. If you will but grant me this favor, I swear that I will not cause you any further pain.''

The simple apology moved Guin far more effectively than any endearment. She could see that he was finding it difficult to speak. Men such as Corvin were unaccustomed to pleading, yet here he was begging for her indulgence. It would be so easy to drift with the sweet swells of emotion, to submerge herself and be overwhelmed by his obvious desire, but Guin knew that if she let go of reason she would surely drown.

As she looked at the open entreaty in his eyes, she knew untruths would be of no use. Guin had always suffered for being a poor liar. She could not tell him that she wanted it to end. Even had she been skilled at deception, this strange rapport with Corvin would have rendered the tactic transparent.

"You are making an oath that you will not be able to keep. We will both be hurt, milord, by indulging in this fairy tale," she declared with an all encompassing wave of her arms.

"Ah, but they always end happily, the ogre vanquished, the princess rescued," Corvin replied, his face breaking into a smile as he realized that he had won the first round. He took up the oars once more and began to steer the boat toward shore.

"Only for children, milord, for they believe that such outcomes are possible. I ceased to believe in such tales a long time ago."

Guin spent the week wondering what impulse had moved her to divulge so much to a stranger and worrying about her next meeting with the Viscount. The empathy that she had sensed within Corvin was his most dangerous weapon, the schoolmistress realized. Despite her growing feelings for him, Guin could ill-afford to think of the man as anything other than an adversary. He had already shown his ability to maneuver her into revelation and she vowed not to let him past her guard again. Her only hope was that he would keep his word and let her alone if she fulfilled the extorted promise.

On the day set for the second meeting, Guin rose earlier than usual, feeling an odd mixture of anticipation and dread. She told herself that she arranged her hair in a softer style than she customarily wore so that he would be less likely to recognize her as Mrs. Courtney. She promised herself that this time, she would remain adamant, let him do all the talking. "Remember, we do not go out of choice," she told Bombay as she saddled him. "If we fail to appear, he will surely seek us out."

Bombay whinnied loudly as if he too, was aware that his mistress was a poor liar, even when she lied to herself.

Corvin rode up beside her as soon as she and Bombay entered through the Park Gate. His face was alight with excitement.

"I have something to show you," he said. "Follow me."

To Guin's surprise, he led her out of the park. They left Mayfair entirely and rode rapidly past St. James Park, heading toward the Thames, through the near empty streets of Westminster. Guin's puzzlement grew as they passed haywains and produce wagons in increasing numbers. Did Corvin intend to leave London entirely? But all her questions were met with "just a few minutes more," until they reached Bridge Street and the foot of Westminster Bridge.

"Have we much farther to go?" Guin asked. "I must return soon."

"Just a bit further," he coaxed. When they were halfway across the bridge, Corvin slid from the back of his horse and motioned for her to dismount as well. "Turn round, now," he said, eyeing her face, feeling much like a child who has discovered a treasure and wonders if it is fit for grown-up enjoyment.

Obediently, Guin came about, her eyes widening in wonder at the sight before her.

> " 'This city now doth, like a garment wear
> The beauty of the morning; silent, bare,
> Ships, towers, domes, theatres and temples lie—' "

Corvin quoted the lines, wondering if she understood. She did not fail him and continued the passage:

" *'Open unto the fields, and to the sky;*
All bright and glittering in the smokeless air—'

"I had thought that the London Wordsworth saw on that day was entirely the product of a poet's imagination. Now I see that he did not speak entirely from his inner vision. I cannot count how many times I have passed this way, but the city never seemed quite like this," she said.

Spread before Guin was an impressive panorama. On her left, the houses of Parliament cast a massive reflection into the murky water. The early morning sun gilded the gothic towers of Westminster Abbey transforming the brooding shadows with light. The earthen palette of autumn foliage blended in a warm glow with the reds of brick buildings as the streets stirred. London was waking much as it had that day in 1802 when Wordsworth had stood upon this very bridge to compose his sonnet.

"I had never understood what the poet found so attractive, until I chanced to come here in early morning before the people of London had lit their morning fires. When one passes in the afternoons the end of the bridge is barely visible for all the smoke and haze," Corvin said, feeling the peculiar enjoyment that a giver receives when his present is truly appreciated.

"The horizon has surely changed somewhat over the years since the poem was written," Guin observed as she forced herself to step away from Corvin. Although he did not touch her, he was so close that the cloud of his breath in the frosty morning air touched her with its warmth. His look made her shiver. Guin tried to turn his attention and her own to the scenery. "With all the building that Nash has done, London has been transformed. I recall that

Lady Melbourne once said that Mayfair is scarcely recognizable from when she was a girl.'' Guin realized her slip and silenced herself. There was danger in speaking too much; best to let Corvin do the talking.

Corvin added the fact that she knew Lady Melbourne to the information that he had already compiled, but gave no sign that he had caught her indiscretion. "On the whole, I would say that there is a great deal of sense to what has been built so far. With peace at last, England can finally move forward. London needs to be far more than a great jumbling labyrinth. The nation of shopkeepers that Napoleon dismissed so contemptuously has the capacity to triumph where he failed. We can conquer the world, with commerce.''

Guin smiled as she said, "Strange, indeed, to hear one of the ton speak with such praise of the shop, milord.''

"The opinions of the ton have long ceased to hold much significance for me, Elaine. They fail to recognize that the world is changing far more rapidly than anyone realizes. The future is commerce and I have invested considerably in that future, although I do not noise it about.''

"Ah, then you do not dismiss the opinions of the ton entirely?'' Guin asked.

"Not for myself,'' Corvin asserted, somewhat sheepish at being caught in a contradiction. "For my sister mostly. There has to be one Sinclair who cares for propriety, if only on the surface. Bad enough that my sister will be condemned for her parents' follies. I have no doubt you have heard of my mother? Everyone has,'' Corvin said, scuffing the toe of his Hessian boot in the dust looking much like a shamed little boy. "She was quite notorious. One of the legends of the ton.''

The hurt in his eyes belied the deceptive lightness of his tone. The resemblance to Emmaline had never been more clear to Guin then at that moment. Both brother and sister had developed the same means of defense against the world's censure: a care-for-naught defiance that was a self-made mockery of their own worst pain.

"I cannot count the times I was forced to defend her honor with my fists at Eton," Corvin said, staring out over the rail of the bridge as a barge passed below. "It seems strange, does it not, to defend a harlot's honor?" he asked bitterly. "My father would berate me for tearing good clothing to defend the whore who was my mama."

Knowing the cruelty of schoolchildren from long experience, Guin could picture him as a boy, knowing that the taunts were undeniably true, yet fighting nonetheless. "Why did you defend her?" she asked softly and at once she was appalled by her own audacity.

Corvin hesitated. He had never asked himself that obvious question and sought a truthful answer. "A schoolboy's sense of chivalry, I suppose," Corvin said, then shook his head. "No, it was more than that. I think even then I knew that Mama's behavior was not her fault. My father had driven her to become what she was."

"Children understand far more than all of us realize," Guin said, surprised, nonetheless, that he did not totally condemn the Countess as so many did.

"Unfortunately, my parents' battles left little to the imagination, Elaine. They never bothered with a facade of hypocrisy. I think that it would have been preferable if they had. At least if they had remained together, I might have watched my sister grow. I managed to endure all those years at St. Clair Abbey. Mama might have tried." Corvin picked up a pebble and flung it into the river with all the force of his resentment.

Guin could see that he still carried that agony within him, the boy still aching for his mother. "Perhaps, leaving St. Clair Abbey was the only way that she could survive," Guin tried to explain, unable to keep the memories of her own pain from infecting her voice. "I am sorry, I should not speak when I know nothing of what happened. No one can truly comprehend what goes on in another's house."

"No, do not apologize, Elaine," he said. There was an intensity in her words, a wisdom in her eyes and somehow, he knew that she was speaking from her own pain. "I just do not understand your defense of her. Running is the coward's way out."

"Sometimes escape is the only means of survival, milord, and it is more cowardly to remain in unendurable security than to face the unknown," Guin declared. Although she knew that it would be far better to remain silent, she could not help but come to the woman's defense. "Surely, there are many who understand what your mama did. Your father's foibles are common knowledge. I consider the Countess a brave woman to risk the world's censure, for the world never forgives an erring female. Do you not realize? It would have been far easier to stay in England and live a liar's life than to face society alone."

Guin saw the growing annoyance in his eyes but she dared to continue. "Would you have wanted that for her, milord? To have her stay and watch her diminish day by day into a shadow as your father bullied the spirit from her? Would your sister have emerged from the existence that you endured whole and healthy?" Corvin's look took her measure and Guin quailed inwardly at her own temerity.

"I had never considered it quite that way," he said after a long silence. "I suppose that there may be some truth to what you say. I can still remember how they fought the few times that they were together. Emmaline's birth was the final blow to their marriage. You see my father was a younger son who had inherited the title after his older brother's death. Another boy would have been a surety against fate."

Corvin's face turned bleak as he recalled his father's fury and loathing. "How he railed against her! Cursed her! Accused her of returning to him only so that she could pass another man's by-blow off as a Stanton even though Emmaline has the Sinclair crescent on her shoulder. A sure sign of her sire if there is one. Then he struck her." The silence grew as he remembered the look of shock on his mother's face, the imprint of red upon her cheek, his rage at the unfairness of it all. When he spoke again, he could barely keep the quaver from his voice. "I think that was when my father realized that I was nearly a man grown. I flew at him, but I was still a stripling of fourteen and no match for his cane. He struck me blow after blow while Mama screamed. When I came to, Mama was holding me, wiping the blood from my face. That is how my snout came to be skewed like this," he said tapping his nose with a rueful look.

Guin ached to touch Corvin and comfort the gnawing hurt that she knew so well; his expression of bereavement, his guilt tugged at her heart. She strained to hear the rest of his words.

"I knew that she would leave, that she would never come back. I begged her to take me along even though I knew that my father would never allow it. Never had I seen her weep before, never! But she cried then. I still remember her words to me before the coach carried her and Emmaline away. 'Someday, Daniel, when you are old enough to do as you please, you will come to me. There will always be a place for you in my heart, my Daniel.' She was the only one who had ever called me 'Daniel.' That was the last time I saw her. She didn't return for holidays ever again. I never did seek her out,'' he said with regret as he watched the water flow by below. He looked up to see that Elaine was trembling, her face sad and pale and he knew that it was not the wind from the river that caused her to quake. Her empathy for his mother had been drawn from Elaine's own well of memory. He kept his hand upon the railing of the bridge, feeling the inadequacy of words once again when a touch could have said far more.

"You could not have understood," Guin said, trying to make him see what she knew. "You were but a boy. How could you have known that she was leaving to protect you?"

"Protect me?" Corvin snorted in disbelief.

"Yes. Don't you see? If your mother had remained you would have been forced to stand her defender against your father. He would have used you, hurt you or your sister, as a means to get at her. Such men will use any weapon fair or foul, milord. I remember, in Spain I had adopted a stray cat. It was a kitten, naught but a pitiful ball of fur and bones, but it was far more to me. When Toledo curled himself round my ankle, I felt that there was something in this world that loved me, that would miss me if I were gone. But I made the mistake of letting my husband see that I cared for the animal. One night, he came home drunk and dinner displeased him.

" 'That damned cat getsh better treatment than I do,' '' Guin mimicked Alfred's wine slurred words.

"Then he kicked Toledo with his boot. Sent the poor thing flying against the wall." Guin touched her cheek, surprised to find that her cheeks were wet. "How strange," she commented almost to herself. "I did not cry then. Why should I be crying so many years later?"

Corvin had offered his handkerchief with a half-smile. "Perhaps, you had already used up your budget of tears? I know that I depleted mine a long time ago," he said, realizing that although it must have cost her dearly, Elaine was attempting to use her own pain to try and comfort him.

"And I am using more than my budget of your handkerchiefs, milord," Guin said in an attempt to lighten the mood.

They had led their horses along the bridge making way for a produce cart that rumbled by. Guin could see that Corvin was lost in thought and made no effort to break the silence.

"You know, Elaine," Corvin said. "I believe that you have the right of it. If Mama had stayed my father would surely have destroyed the both of us and Emmaline besides. Why did I not see that?"

"It is like standing too close to a painting, milord. When you are looking at the small details it is sometimes hard to see the whole view clearly."

"And you, Elaine? How do you view yourself?"

"How others look at us is almost as important as how we see ourselves," she observed deliberately turning the subject from herself. "What does it matter that you and I know the whys and wherefores of your mother's actions, or for that matter our own. Unless those who appoint themselves our judges concur, we are punished."

"All the ton knows what manner of man my father is," Corvin agreed. "But as he is the wealthy and powerful Earl of Sinclair he is merely an eccentric old gent, useful as an object of fun and always to be relied upon to accept an invitation to dine so that he might spare his own provender. However, my mother's scandal will live on long after her death. It does not hamper me at all, but I fear my sister will suffer for it. It is unfair."

"Every individual bears some parental baggage. I am sure that your sister will carry her load with grace," Guin said comfortingly.

"I am beginning to believe that might be true," Corvin concurred. "Morton House is working wonders upon Emmaline. That Mrs. Courtney has turned the chit around. Remarkable woman! I have never seen my sister so happy and secure. For the first time in her life, I think, Emmaline feels cherished."

"Every child needs to feel themselves valued, special in some way," Guin said, forcing herself to speak circumspectly, masking the glow of pride at his words.

"But I wonder how many children never feel so?" Corvin asked, his face falling back into a brooding expression. "I know that the only unique quality that I was credited for was my ability to get into mischief. Nothing that I ever did was right. The times that I got caned or put upon a diet of bread and water for some minor infraction are beyond counting. However strange Emmaline's upbringing was, at least she was spared a childhood as a prisoner of St. Clair Abbey. I should bless Mama for that. Thank you, Elaine."

Guin felt a warm satisfaction spread through her, as she realized that his thanks were sincere, but she knew that she had only repaid a debt. It seemed to Guin that Corvin's sympathy and kindness upon the swan boat had lifted a burden that her heart had carried for a long time. She could only hope that his heart was lightened as well. Guin was amazed that she could share so intimate a part of her with a

stranger and tell this man things that she had dared
confide with no other living soul. The bond of secrets exchanged seemed to draw them closer and despite Guin's efforts, the wall between them began
to crumble.

For the first time in her life, she realized that it
was possible to be friends with a man. She discovered a wry wit, a cynical intelligence that masked
a vulnerable core within. Corvin cared deeply, not
just about the small personal world of people whose
lives were interwoven with his, but the larger
sphere that would shape the future. He had danced
at the Congress of Vienna, had manipulated against
Metternich, fought in the bloody field of Waterloo
and still counted the Duke of Wellington among his
closest friends. A listener was all he required and
the time passed quickly under the spell of his quiet
voice.

It was like listening to a piece of music that he
had heard long ago, Corvin thought, as she spoke.
He heard the echoes of his own experience in
Elaine's words, with the familiar themes of loneliness, the haunting melody of wasted lives. While
Elaine made every effort to conceal any clue to her
identity, the essence of her being had somehow
become open to him. Her insights were keen, and
the staid exterior belied a delightful sense of
whimsy and soaring imagination that appealed to
a like quality within himself that Corvin had never
before explored. The Viscount found himself
damning the oath that seemed to be the only wall
between them.

As they reached the end of the bridge, Guin
forced herself to confront the consequence of this
new found accord. Although Corvin remained true
to his word, never moving to touch her, Guin
found herself drawn to him more strongly than
ever before. Only sheer power of will kept her

from yielding to the invitation that was always present in his eyes—his very look was a caress. She knew that no matter how great her temptation, no connection between them could endure. Succumbing to the desire for the pleasure of his touch would only add to her growing burden of heartache.

to step across his fences, "How dare you demand that I leave Interloper's alone. I...

Nine

≪≪≪≪≪≪≪≪≪≪≪

THE BROODING expression of the two men at the
dinner table was accentuated by the evening
gloom. Ives drew the curtain and shook his head
imperceptibly. Trouble was brewing. Never had he
seen young Master Hopley's visage so marred by
scowls.

"I will do no more, Corvin," Hopley said, breaking the silence at last.

"You are my only link to her, Hop," Corvin said.

"Blast it, Corvin!" Hopley said, throwing down
his fork, nearly shattering the fine china. "I only do
what I should have done weeks ago, when you first
persuaded me to carry your billets for you. I refuse
to be party to a seduction!"

"I've given my word not to seek her out, but I
need more than a few meetings to accomplish my
aims."

"Just what are those aims?" the young man asked
in an uncharacteristically cynical tone. "Whatever
those questionable goals of yours are, milord, they
are of no matter to me. I do not care what kind of
damnable bargain you have made, or how you have
forced her to meet you. I will not assist you both to
perdition."

"I begin to see the makings of a parson in you,
my lad, for you have already begun to preach upon
matters that you know little of," Corvin said, trying

to keep a rein on his temper. "How have you determined that I have forced her to meet me?"

Hopley glared at his friend. "She was against furthering the acquaintance from the very start. It was only your constant badgering that caused me to aid you at all and now I regret it. I have come to know her, Corvin. She is a fine woman. She does not deserve to be hurt."

"I do not intend to hurt her, Hop," Corvin said, his voice soft but emphatic.

The obvious sincerity of the Viscount's assertion caused Hopley to lower his own tone. "I know. I realize that is not your intent," he said, rising from his seat. "But this is ultimately what will happen."

"Please, will you just give her the parcel."

"It is as I said. I helped you when I believed you nearly engaged to another woman. I thought you genuinely concerned about Mrs. . . . . I mean Elaine's welfare, but it has gone far beyond that, has it not?" Hopley asked earnestly.

Corvin avoided his friend's accusing eyes and rose to stare into the fire. "I look at her and see myself, years ago—alone, frightened, angry at the hurts that I endured."

"But those notes, they betoken much more. Do they not?" Hopley asked. "That is why I can carry them no longer."

Corvin tried to convince the young man, playing shamelessly upon his kind heart. "She needs my help and I owe her nothing less in return. Before Elaine, I had honestly believed that my past had lost the power to hurt me, but it was like a corruption, Hop, festering and fouling me. Thanks to her, I understand a great deal more about myself than I did before. Now, I want to help her. She needs me, Hop."

Hopley went to stand by his friend. "What noble arrogance! Doctor Corvin, healer of broken hearts extraordinaire. Even if you accomplish this laudable aim, do you truly wish to help her for her own sake or for what she may give you in gratitude? Once more, you evade the issue."

"A damnable question! You must think me the most selfish conniver."

"No, Corvin," Hopley said somberly. "I am just trying to make you see yourself in truth."

"I have never met a woman like her," Corvin said, with a shake of his head. "I found myself confiding in her, telling her things that I have never told another living soul. We talked of my boyhood."

"Deep waters, indeed. You have always kept that part of your life close to your vest," Hopley said, momentarily taken aback.

"I always carried that gnawing resentment with me. Yet, somehow it seems to hurt less now that I have told her."

"As if your burden has been lightened?" Hopley asked, searching his friend's face. What he saw there did not reassure him. When Corvin said her name there was a tone that Hopley had never heard previously, a possessive note that had never sounded when he had spoken of a woman before.

Corvin nodded, thinking of the depths of her blue eyes. "I find myself missing her company. Without Elaine, all is flat. Those mornings in the park are the only times I feel most truly alive."

"I think that you are in love, my friend," Hopley said, regarding the Viscount with profound pity, knowing that he was sure to be hurt.

Corvin regarded Hopley with a wisp of a smile. "Love? No, Hop! I have been assured that I am incapable of that." He spoke as if the emotion were some kind of fatal disease.

Hopley bent, threw a lump of coal into the grate and stared at his smudged fingers. "I doubt that she will consent to be your mistress," he remarked, looking up as Corvin's face tightened in anger.

"You go too far, Master Hopley."

"If I seem to do so, it is because I hold you both in high regard." Hopley looked his friend squarely in the eye. "This can only end in heartache, Corvin. Best to cut it quickly."

"Since you hold the lady in such high regard, I hardly see why I should cease to see her," Corvin said, regarding the young man coolly. "Unless you wish to tell me."

"If I only could," Hopley said miserably, thinking of what society would say if Corvin were to wed a mere schoolmistress. Given the Viscount's aversion to scandal, he would never stoop to such a mésalliance and a woman like Mrs. Courtney would not consent to a slip on the shoulder. "No wonder the Bible adjures us not to give oaths lightly. There was never a more damnable tangle! But I reveal no secrets if I tell you to puzzle it out for yourself. Think Corvin, why would the lady wish to keep her identity secret if she foresaw some honorable end to this folly? Obviously the revelation of the truth would cause her some injury."

"Scandal?" Corvin ventured.

"Most likely," Hopley agreed. "If you wish to continue meeting her, you would do well to ponder it. Would you be willing to bring more censure upon yourself? Your sister?"

"I will cross that bridge when I reach it. If I reach it," Corvin corrected. "As I have told you; after she has met me four times I will not seek her out against her will. There are but two meetings more and I will see her with or without your help. Now will you take the gift?"

"I warn you, if you think to send her baubles, she will throw it back in your face," Hopley warned.

"I know that," Corvin replied as he mounted a

ladder and handed down a slender volume from the shelves. "I would not insult her so. This should be perfectly within the bounds of decorum."

"Wordsworth?" Hopley asked, opening the book and reading the fly-leaf. "I say! I did not know that you were so close a friend of the versifier! Didn't know that you were fond of poetry at all," he said, looking up in surprise.

"How could you have seen what these shelves contain when you so rarely go beyond my table? There is a great deal about me you do not know. Indeed, there is a great deal about me of which *I* am not sure," Corvin murmured almost to himself as he came down the ladder. "Now will you give her this? Surely, a book is a most proper gift?"

"There is nothing proper about any of this," Hopley snorted. "And do not blame me if she casts it back in your face when next you meet."

"Then you shall do it!"

"I am a fool for getting my foot further in. Give me your parcel and I shall play errand boy." Hopley felt an aching hollow in the pit of his stomach at the open delight in the Viscount's face.

Corvin clapped him on the back. "You have my thanks, Hop. Now why don't you polish off your meal while I write a note to accompany the book?"

"I don't think so, Corvin," Hopley said. The truth would inevitably come out, he thought. It was doubtful that even the close friendship between them would absolve him for his role in this deception, no matter what oaths Hopley had given. Love did not tend to make men reasonable. "I suddenly find that I have lost my appetite," he said.

The wet weather continued till near the week's end, Friday dawning clear and bright. But after scant hours of rare sunshine the clouds returned once more, dumping their torrents with renewed vigor.

The curtain of rain parted momentarily as two bedraggled figures straggled up the marble steps of the mansion upon Hyde Park Corner. Due to the early morning hour and the downpour, not a soul was in sight, yet the woman peered about anxiously as if fearing discovery, while the man tried the key in the door.

"Cursed lock," Corvin mumbled as he rattled the key about. "Knew I should have had it fixed long ago."

"I think that I should return home, milord," Guin said anxiously as a gust of wind drove a sheet of water into their backs. "This is hardly a public place as we agreed upon. I will fetch Bombay from your neighbor's mews and return home."

"And have you catch your death? I shall have it open in but a moment," Corvin declared, giving the door a futile shove. "I do hope that Ives and the others have managed to remove the pianoforte from the park. I swear, that poor musician all but cried when the first drops began to fall."

"And you arranged it all because I mentioned that I was fond of Beethoven's pieces for the keyboard?" Guin asked. "I feel most guilty."

"No need. Although there was not a cloud in the sky before the sun rose, Ives insisted that we procure a waterproof canvas and even if the instrument is ruined, I can well afford the price of another. Still 'tis a pity, I would have enjoyed hearing the music in the arboreal setting."

"I found myself wondering whether Ives was going to cover you or the instrument, milord," she giggled as the water streamed down her face.

"It was quite comical, wasn't it?" Corvin said with a grin and jiggled the key once more to be rewarded with the rasp of the lock mechanism turning. He pushed the door open but his triumphant grin faded abruptly when he caught sight of his quivering companion. "You are shaking like a leaf! I should have insisted that you return with me to my apartments, will you or nil you!"

"Ah, but would you have been able to face the formidable Ives?" Guin asked, her teeth chattering too quickly to allow a laugh to escape.

Corvin looked down at himself with a rueful grin. "I allow the thought of my valet's wrath makes me quake."

The once-stylish waves of Corvin's hair were plastered flat upon his forehead. The snowy cravat was a soaking stump of linen hanging limply between his sagging shirt points and a trail of blue dye was beginning to run from his formerly elegant morning coat across the front of his shirt. Wet trousers clung impossibly to every curve of his well-formed leg. A pool of dirty water was rapidly forming on the marble floor at the base of his muddy Hessians.

Although Guin did not realize it, her attire, too, had been tailored by the rain. The velvet habit had been transformed to a sheath of second skin, outlining each limb with liquid accuracy. Curls had escaped from the knot that she wore and hung damply against forehead and nape. Her cheeks were flushed with the cold and the fringes of her lashes were limned with droplets that hung like jewels above her eyes. Corvin took an unconscious step toward her when a bolt of lighting flashed illuminating the fact that the door was still wide open to the weather and intrusive eyes.

Guin shuddered convulsively but it was not entirely the chill that caused her to tremble. She had caught that look of longing in his eyes. A moment more and she had no doubt that he would have swept her into his arms. The very thought of a man touching her in that way would once have been enough to send her into tremors of terror. Yet, now, she felt oddly disappointed at the missed embrace.

As another jagged flash lit his concerned face, Guin realized that she no longer feared him. A wave of emotion filled her and she was glad that he had turned away to shut the door, lest he read her dangerous thoughts. More than ever, it was hazardous to be alone with him, for the loss of fear made her vulnerable. As his broad shoulders forced the huge portal shut against the wind and threw the bolt home, Guin knew that whatever the weather, it would have been far saner to remain on the other side of that door, out of his reach, out of temptation's way.

"Come on, your teeth are chattering," Corvin said, the unlover-like remark chased the trepidation from her eyes as he had intended. He continued in a brusque, no-nonsense tone. "There are some clothes upstairs that you can use until your own things dry."

"I will be just fine. I think that I had better go," Guin declared, making one more weak attempt to escape. A clap of thunder made the panes rattle with its force.

"Into the storm?" Corvin asked, with a shake of his head as a fit of sneezes belied her claim of comfort. "Do you still fear me so much, Elaine? I did not bring you to my home to break my oath. I would not violate my word or this place."

Guin knew from the way that he spoke that this house was special to him, sacred somehow, and she nodded to indicate she would stay.

He beckoned and as she followed him up the stair, Guin exclaimed at the beauty of the tapestries that lined the hall, their jewel-box colors glowing even in the dim rainy daylight.

"The hunt of the unicorn," Corvin told her as he pointed out the creature hiding in the foilage. "It is said that there was once a full set depicting the hunt from start to finish, but only the chase and the seduction tapestries remain.'' Corvin opened a door and gestured for her to follow.

The furniture was shrouded in holland covers, but everything about the room still proclaimed it a female sanctuary. The rose and cool green shades of the decor combined to give an oddly lush air of relaxation and airy grace.

"This was my mother's chamber," Corvin responded to the unasked question. "In fact, this house was left to me by her." He opened the door of the wardrobe, the colors spilled into the gloom like a rainbow of fabric. "You will find the clothing sadly out of date, I fear. After my sister's birth, Mama never returned to England. Still, I assume you will find something that will suit. You are much the same size as she was."

"I could not . . ." Guin protested, feebly.

"You must and you will," Corvin declared, alarmed by the way she was shaking. "I vow, your lips are turning the most unattractive shade of blue. Will you cease these maidenly flutterings so that I may change from these wet things? I freely confess myself frozen to the marrow. The library, where we shall meet is the first door to the right at the foot of the stairs." He paused at the door. "You have nothing to fear from me, Elaine. I may be Sinclair's son, but I am not so lost as to forget my honor."

"It is not your honor I fear for, milord. It is mine," Guin whispered as he closed the door behind him.

Despite his chilled state, Corvin did not go to change immediately, but went downstairs to the library. Fortunately, it appeared that the caretaker had not been behindhand in his duties. Since the Viscount often came here when in need of a quiet place to contemplate, the hearth was in readiness and soon a merry blaze crackled, chasing the chill from the room. A trip to the larder yielded cheese, dried fruit and biscuits.

He poured himself a brandy, lifting the amber liquid in salute to the portrait of his mother above the mantel. The eyes of painted blue seemed to dance with fond mockery as he downed the distilled fire in a single gulp. As the spirits chased the chill from his body, Corvin could almost swear that she was asking him for the answer to some important question. A trick of the liquor and light, nothing more, he decided, shaking his head to clear the haze. Yet, he was left with a decidedly odd feeling as he went to seek some dry clothing.

The library was empty when Guin came down the stairs. Still shivering with cold, she knelt near the fire spreading the habit before the hearth to dry. While the borrowed sprigged muslin she wore became her far better than anything she had worn for years, the thin fabric was more suited to a summer afternoon than a rainy autumn dawn. Unhappily, the late Countess' wardrobe contained nothing warmer since the thinnest of muslins had been all the rage before she departed the country.

Guin pulled the Kashmir shawl that she had found more tightly about her, welcoming the warmth and concealment the wrap provided. She had chosen the gown she wore because of its deceptively demure décolletage, unaware until she attempted to button nonexistent fastenings, that the back plunged almost the full length of the shoulder blade. There had not been time to seek another garment but luckily, with the chill weather, there was ample excuse to keep the covering securely about her.

With the shawl draped about her shoulders, Guin let her hair loose from its pins, swinging its damp mass forward to dry as she surveyed her surroundings. In this room there were no holland covers to conceal the graceful lines of the Greek style that predominated the decor. The appointments had the mark of Robert Adam's influence, but it was clear that a woman's hand had brought about a harmony that made the library far more than the stuffy tomb for tomes that was common in so many of the homes of the ton. Several well-placed mirrors reflecting each other upon opposite walls made the room seem far larger than its actual size. This was a place of Apollo, all light and thought.

Above the marble mantle hung the Vesta of this room. The late Countess of Sinclair had chosen to be portrayed in Greek robes and the painting was the completion of the library's symmetry. Guin could see clearly that Emmaline was cast in her mother's image. The beautiful child was destined to become a striking woman.

"The goddess regards the goddess."

Guin whirled, keeping a tight grip upon the shawl. Corvin leaned against the lintel, a gleam of admiration lighting his eyes.

"It is a lovely room," Guin said.

"And we have been having most terrible weather of late," Corvin said, mocking her drawing-room tones, but his smile took the bite from his gentle ridicule. "Yes, it is exquisite. My mother entirely re-did the place when she married Sinclair which makes me think that she might actually have been fond of my father once. When I was a boy, the family would always meet here for the holidays. It is one of the few places in my life that was truly happy."

Guin watched as he crossed the room to a small table by the fireside and picked up the brandy decanter. A dark curl hung damply on his forehead and the light gleamed upon his wet hair. Something about him was different, but it was not the change in clothing; it was apparent in the way he walked, the softening of the lines in his forehead. He is truly at ease here, she realized. The tension that she had always sensed in him was relieved.

"I would live here," he said, pouring two glasses,

"but this place is far too large for one man to rattle about in. My father says I should rent it or sell it. There are many willing to pay a fine price to be the Duke of Wellington's neighbor, for Apsley House is just across the way. Maybe I am a fool to keep it vacant, but I would not sell it."

Guin shook her head, swallowing to clear the lump that had somehow appeared in her throat. "I could see that one would not wish to have strangers walking freely through the place you regard as your real home, milord."

Corvin looked at her, delighted at her perception; there was so much about him that she seemed to understand without being told. It seemed that each meeting strengthened that peculiar affinity, increasing their awareness of each other. He lifted the glasses of amber liquid, his eyes upon her. With the fire flickering behind her, the flowing muslin was almost as revealing as her wet habit and he tried to damp the growing flame of desire that swept through him, knowing it would only frighten her.

"Will you have a brandy?" Corvin asked, stepping towards her, pleased that this time, she did not move away as she had before. She looked far lovelier than he had dreamed possible, the wet strands of her hair falling like some lustrous waterfall against the red Kashmir shawl. So intent was he upon her face that he did not see the protrusion of the table leg before him.

His eyes held infinite tenderness and although Guin knew that she was in jeopardy, she was powerless before the magic in his gaze. Men had looked upon her in the past, with lust, with cruelty, with anger, with loathing but never before had she experienced this gentle look that she dared put no name to. But the contact broke, the spell was shattered, as he began to fall. Guin moved forward to steady Corvin before he plunged to the floor, but she was not quick enough to halt his downward progress.

The glasses flew from his hands, spewing their contents as Corvin grasped instinctively for something to break his fall. He caught the fabric of the shawl in his fingers and it was torn from her shoulders in a swift motion.

Corvin looked regretfully at the mess of shattered glass, knowing that his clumsiness had ruined the moment beyond salvation. He looked up at Elaine with a rueful smile, but the horrified expression upon her face caused him to hasten to reassure her that he had taken no injury.

"I am quite fine, if a trible bumbling," he said, scrambling to his knees and raising his hands to show her that they were uncut. It was a moment before the Viscount realized that he was not the focus of the woman's stare. He rose slowly, looking into the mirror at her now-bare back, now reflected into infinity by the looking glasses. Although the faint white tracery below her shoulder blade was faded, the story of cruelty it told was unmistakably clear. It was no wonder that she had flinched at his every approach, he thought. Indeed, Corvin marveled that Elaine had brought herself to trust him at all under the circumstances. The abuse charted upon her skin should have utterly destroyed her spirit. Yet, she had endured and miraculously, she trusted him enough to be alone with him. Or did she?

Guin saw her scars through the filter of memory, the pain spanning the gap of years. Once more, she was a young girl, dragging herself before the mirror, gasping in horror and agony at the raw wounds.

"Elaine?"

The sound of Corvin's voice recalled her to the present and she tore her eyes from the multiplicity of images to search Corvin's face. His stunned expression confirmed that he had seen it all. Her shame was no longer secret from him.

"So, milord, now that I have clearly given you a disgust of me, will you allow this farce to come to an end?" Guin asked as she snatched up the shawl and shook away the fragments of glass. She began to put it on, hoping that concealment would extinguish the revulsion in his expression, but she thought the better of it. *Let him see all. Let him know what manner of woman you are. Then you shall be free,* said a voice within. Guin deliberately turned her back to him and eyed him over her shoulder. "Now you know, milord, what I am; what I have deserved. My husband told me once that he would make sure that no other man would be deceived in me, that he would set my mark of shame upon me for any who would be so foolish as to think to touch me. Now you see the truth."

Corvin saw himself mirrored in her eyes. The tone of self-loathing, the look of utter despair, touched a chord within him that he thought had long been buried. From the depths of memory he dredged a young boy's humiliation and pain.

"No," he said, his voice unintentionally harsh. "I understand, Elaine."

"Do you, milord? Do you really?" she asked, rancor filling her as she dared him to look. "My husband would laugh when I screamed, so I did not scream."

Corvin felt a wave of shame at his facile words. Her mocking derision told him that he truly did not understand. Every joke about wife-beating that he had ever laughed at, every on-dit about a husband who used his fists that he had casually shrugged off, called him a liar. True, he had endured violence, but no one had deliberately sought joy in his suffering as Elaine's husband clearly had.

"Do you understand, milord?" Guin asked, her

voice trembling as she spoke. "Can any man know what it is to live in such constant fear? Never knowing if the man who is as much your lord and master as any black slave in the Indies will chastise you for some minor infraction with the rod or his fist? Can you understand what it is to hide for days in your rooms so that no one will see the bruises?" She swung her hair behind her to cover her back like a curtain.

"What of the law?" Corvin asked, his emotions in turmoil as he beheld her teetering on the brink of hysteria. "Or your family?"

"My father," Guin said with a bitter laugh, unable to stem the bile that rose to choke her at the memory. "I came pleading to him, begging for him to take me back, but he said that my wild ways had brought the shame upon me. I needed a firm hand upon the reins, as if I were a willful cart-horse to be broken. There was no one else. As for the law, a man owns his wife, person and soul, property and sinew. He can chastise his chattels as he chooses."

It seemed to Corvin that she was searching his very soul; all the hopelessness and despair of those times were in her eyes and then, as though some barricade within her burst abruptly, the words came spilling out.

"I tried to be a good wife, heaven and earth as my witnesses, I tried to do my duty, but he never believed in me. The promotions that he sought never came because of my infamous history. In his eyes, every glance was a flirtation in the making, so I kept to myself, mingled only with the other officers' wives, but then he claimed that I hampered him socially," she said trembling as the vivid image came to mind of that dark night when she had teetered on the edge of despair.

"May God forgive me for the lengths I drove him to, for it was my foolish youth that maddened him so." Like a spent runner, she took a breath and began once more. "After we returned to London, my husband changed for the worse. When he sold out, there was no longer any discipline at all to his life. Some friends of his dragged him home to me one evening. He was foxed and had lost every penny of our month's income. I could tell . . . I knew that he would strike me. I told him then that I was with child . . . but that infuriated him all the more. 'Twas then he took his riding crop to me; said that he would beat the bastard from me." Guin's tone dropped to a mere whisper. "He was true to his word. I spent weeks near death but by some cruel miracle I recovered."

Guin turned away from Corvin and closed her eyes unable to withstand the look of undisguised horror upon his face. "He came home drunk again and I knew what was to come when he awoke with an aching head. I took his gun and put it to his temple and held it there, for the longest time and listened to him breathe. I knew I could keep him from waking; I wanted to and for that I shall never forgive myself," she stated flatly, her voice breaking.

Corvin was at a total loss, unable to touch her, unable to comfort her as he longed to do. In the face of all she had suffered, anything that he could say seemed totally devoid of meaning, yet words were all he could offer.

"It is not you that needs forgiveness, Elaine. It is the man who called himself your husband," Corvin said, coming as close to her as he dared. "I admire you, Elaine, for your courage. If any one had done to me what your husband had done to you, I think that I would have pulled the trigger without regret." He lifted his hand to touch those quivering shoulders, then stopped as he realized that he could not.

"It was his right, milord, a husband's right," Guin said simply, turning to face him once more as she tried to explain. She tried to gather her courage so that she might tell him the whole.

"It is no man's right, dammit!" Corvin exclaimed, angered at her acceptance of the burden of guilt. "No one has the right to do this to another human being! We have societies to protect animals, but any man can play tyrant with his wife and children and no one will say him 'nay.' " Corvin quieted abruptly when he saw her backing away from him. "Forgive me, Elaine. I just cannot help but wonder how different our lives would have been if there had been someone to protect us. You are not responsible for your husband's actions, any more than I must answer for what my father did."

Guin bowed her head.

"Elaine, look at me," Corvin pleaded, feeling the sting of tears in his eyes. Frustration beset him as he feared that nothing could pierce her utter dejection. "You cannot reproach yourself. I spent far too many years trying to place the blame for all that went awry in my life. I condemned myself, my father, my mother, even poor Emmaline until I was awash in bitterness. It made me afraid."

Guin looked up at him in surprise and marveled at the glisten in his eyes. "I cannot picture you frightened of anything, milord," she whispered.

Corvin nodded. "I was loathe to trust anyone with any part of me that was subject to hurt. I am thought a very cold fellow."

"Why do you tell me this?" Guin asked, unwilling to believe what he was saying. She knew in her heart that the fault was hers, not Alfred's and she would have to carry that burden of blame for the rest of her days.

"Because you need to know that not all men are like your husband. You cannot spend the rest of your life in fear because of the past. Look." He pointed to the mirror. "The scars have faded."

Guin realized that he spoke the truth. She reached back to touch the faint white seam in amazement. Although she would bear those marks always, time had healed the physical traces of her wounds.

"Trust me, Elaine," Corvin begged, aching to take her into his arms. "Trust me, as I trust you."

"Yes, I believe in you," she whispered, watching in wonder as a tear began to course down his cheek. "But those who think you cold misjudge you, milord, for no other man has ever cared enough to shed a single tear for me."

Corvin watched in awe as her hand moved upward. He stood stock still, not daring to move as her fingers, feather-light and soft, brushed the tear away. He laid his palm on top of her hand and turned it to touch her hand with a gentle kiss.

"Thank you, milord," Guin said softly, ashamed of all she had not told him. "I would that you never regret your trust."

When Guin had returned to Morton House that morning, she had immersed herself in a flurry of activity, hoping to postpone the moment when she must reckon with herself. Now that the day was done, she knew that she could procrastinate no longer. Guin sighed staring at the posy that he had given her as a token of the day. He had purchased it from a street vendor on their way back to the park. The storm had cleared as abruptly as it had started and the new-washed streets had been bustling with the waking world when they had come upon the old woman with the baskets of violets.

"Blue, to match your eyes," Corvin had said, as she had sniffed at the delicate fragrance.

How many times had Guin heard similar phrases in her life as Elaine Borne? Yet the simplest of words gained profound meaning when they fell from Corvin's lips. Even silence, that fearsome social bane, seemed comfortable and right between them. There was almost no need to converse when a glance could speak so eloquently. Love had its own powerful language. Love . . . at last she had acknowledged it, if only to herself. She loved Corvin, yet the thought brought her no joy, for it was an affection poisoned by deception, destined to die in a future of bitter regret.

Guin put the blossoms down when she realized that her clenched hands were crushing the delicate stems. She knew that Crovin had given her a gift of trust and she owed him nothing less in return. Surely, the tenderness that he felt for her was a combination of infatuation and the pity of a kind heart. Once the mystery was resolved and his pity quenched by a final truth-telling, Guin was sure that he would probably never wish to see her again.

There was a rap at the door and Perkins all but burst into the room.

"It is him, Mrs. Courtney," Perkins' demeanor was calm, but his voice was atremble. "The fellow from Vauxhall Gardens and he wishes to speak with you, madame."

"Tell him that I am unavailable, Perkins. Ask him to leave a message," Guin muttered an oath under her breath. "If he causes difficulties, threaten to call the watch."

"Don't be foolish, Mrs. Courtney, or should I say, Marshall?" Sir Mortimer Septimus said, elbowing the butler aside. "You wouldn't treat an old friend so shabbily, would you now?"

Guin drew a breath. "You may leave us, Perkins, but please stay close by in case you need to show our visitor the door."

Perkins threw a baleful glance at the guest. "I'll be waiting, madame."

Sir Mortimer examined the elegantly appointed room appreciatively. "You've done well for yourself, Elaine. Landed on your feet it seems," he commented, seating himself uninvited.

"What do you want, Septimus?" she asked, thinking that he had declined over time. The former disciple of Brummel wore stained crumpled clothing; his eyes peered at her blearily, bloodshot from years of debauchery.

Sir Mortimer laughed. "Still blunt as ever! You always did come straight to the point. Ah, it is so good to see old friends, brings back wonderful memories. You recall when you dressed yourself up as a page and went with Caro Lamb to Lord Byron's rooms, do you not?" he asked.

"So, it was you? I had always wondered who was responsible for the spreading of that tale? I could never credit that Byron would be cruel enough to tell of it," Guin said, proud that her tone did not betray her fear.

"I am so glad that I have cleared that misconception," Sir Mortimer sneered. "We would not wish to malign Lord Byron's sterling character, would we? But since it seems that you are not in the mood to reminisce with me, Elaine, shall we discuss the present?" His eyes lit on the bouquet that she had left on the table and he picked it up. "How charming. Have you a suitor? Some cit, by the looks of it, violets—the poor man's posy, though a flowery sentiment will win a woman's heart every time, won't it? How will he feel, I wonder, when he finds out about your past, Elaine?"

Guin forced herself not to snatch the flowers from his hands. "Say what you have come to say, Septimus and let us not prolong this game of catspaw. If you are looking for me to shrivel up into a quivering jelly as I once did in fear of Alfred, you are bound to be disappointed," she declared.

Septimus sighed. "Ah, where is the old mousey Elaine? But I have forgotten, buried beneath that spinster's disguise is a goddess, is there not? A veritable goddess," he said, his look sending a chill of fear up the schoolmistress' spine. Before she could step away he had risen and pulled her into his arms, to kiss her with oily passion.

"Touch me again and I swear, I will have you thrown out and take the pleasure of a kick on your hindquarters for added speed. I do not care what it costs me," Guin said, pushing him from her, wiping her mouth with the back of her hand to clear the reek of drink.

"A woman of fire. Poor Alfred thought you a cold piece of fish, but he was always a fool," Sir Mortimer said, seating himself once more. "No, Elaine, it is not your lovely self that I desire. I only ask a simple favor as an old friend. I wish to court one of your pupils, Emmaline Stanton." He placed his hand over his heart. "I am madly, passionately, in love."

"And if I refuse to assist you?" Guin asked with a calm assurance that she did not feel.

"It would be so sad if society were to find out that a schoolmistress of Morton House is really the notorious Elaine Borne, would it not?" Sir Mortimer asked, as he pulled one of the violets from the bunch and tossed it to the ground.

Guin was silent for a moment. There was no doubt that Septimus would ruin her if he revealed her identity. The Borne scandal was an old one, but bad enough to taint the reputation of Morton House irreparably. Still there could be no question of handing Emmaline over to this monster in dandy's clothing. As the delicate flowers fell one by one in a heap at his feet, Guin wished that the girl could see him now, his breath stinking of liquor, his clothing ready for the rag-man. Surely that would cure Emmaline of her romantic delusions.

Guin smiled inwardly. Some good might be salvaged yet.

"Would you like some refreshment, Sir Mortimer?" Guin offered with an icy courtesy.

"So, the years have brought you some sense, have they?" Sir Mortimer said with an unpleasantly knowing smile.

Guin went to the door. "Perkins," she said aloud to the waiting butler, "bring up a decanter of port and some of Mrs. Bacon's scones." In an undertone she added, "Tell Lady Emmaline to go to Eddy's room immediately and listen by the hearth. She's in the music room. Then, find Doro Quigley and send her up as well, quickly."

"Yes, Mrs. Courtney," Perkins said, then hurried to do her bidding.

"Let us move over to the chairs by the fire, Sir Mortimer," Guin said in tones of strained courtesy as she closed the door behind her. "It is getting a bit chill and the window near my desk is somewhat draughty, I fear."

"Getting old enough to fear a draught, Elaine? Yet you didn't seem to be afraid of a chill in Vauxhall, did you?" Sir Mortimer mocked as he seated himself before the fireplace. "Hard to believe that a luscious body is hidden beneath that hideous bombazine. No wonder that none of your past acquaintances have recognized you. I know I wouldn't have, but there was something about your voice, that enchanting lilt perhaps. In the end, t'was your eyes that give you away. Never seen eyes quite that shade on any other woman. Mask or spectacles, that blue is unforgettable and the sight of you on a walk with your pupils this morning was enough to jog my memory."

Guin judged that Perkins would have gotten Emmaline in place. To be sure, she decided to draw Sir Mortimer out further.

"How flattering," Guin said drily, "that my Alfred's *dearest* friend should remember me still."

Sir Mortimer looked up in surprise. "Sarcasm? The years have changed you, Elaine. For all your fits and starts as a maiden, you were the meekest of little mice once you were married, were you not? I would have thought that Alfred had knocked all the fight out of you."

"Goodness knows you encouraged it, Sir Mortimer. When I refused to succumb to your blandishments, you made my husband think that I had attempted to seduce you. How I suffered."

"I always pay back those who thwart me, Elaine. In the end, I always get what I want."

His gaze raked her assessingly, but Guin returned his stare with icy disdain. He could not have realized how much she welcomed the knock on the door.

Perkins directed the footman to set the laden try on a table near Guin's chair. A look told Guin all she needed to know. "May I draw the draperies, madame?" Perkins enquired.

"Very good, Perkins," Guin said. "I shall pour. You may leave us now." Perkins drew the curtains and bowed himself out. It gave her some confidence to know that the faithful retainer would be waiting just outside the door should she need him. Guin filled Sir Mortimer's glass, suppressing a shiver as his hand touched hers briefly. "Perhaps it is best if we do not discuss the past, Sir Mortimer. We both know that you have me in the corner. If I refuse to cooperate with you, you will destroy me and Morton House. Knowing you, I realize that you have no compunction about compromising the reputations of the girls who study here."

"The situation in a nutshell, Elaine," he said, lifting his glass in a mocking salute. "You obey me, or I shall ruin you."

In the bedroom above, Doro looked at Emmaline questioningly. "Good Heavens, it is your Sir Mortimer," she whispered. "Why does he call her, 'Elaine?' "

"I don't know," Emmaline said, as she strained to hear more, "Something about Mrs C.'s past, I think."

No fires were laid in the girl's rooms until late evening and the friends sat close to the hearth. Doro took a shawl from the drawer and draped it around Emmaline's shoulders even though she doubted it was the cold that made her shiver so.

"What do you want me to do?" Mrs. Courtney's voice wafted up the chimney.

"Simply turn a blind eye to my little courtship of Emmaline, nothing more," Sir Mortimer's replied.

"I cannot believe that you love the girl, Mortimer," Mrs. Courtney said.

"Her fortune makes her eminently desirable." Sir Mortimer's derisive laughter echoed up the flue.

A tear rolled down Emmaline's cheek and Doro stroked her friend's hair as the conversation below continued.

"My pockets are sadly to let these days, Elaine. I would have had that blunt long since were it not for your interference at Vauxhall."

Emmaline began to shake, muffling her sobs in Doro's shoulder.

"Sad, Sir Mortimer, when your looks are not what they used to be. I suppose that you are totally beyond the pale now and cannot gull any of the heiresses with mamas to watch after them."

Doro clutched at Emmaline's hand as they heard the sound of a chair scraping back.

"You go too far, Elaine. Remember that I can ruin you with a word. You will do as you are told."

"You will unhand me, Mortimer!"

The girls recognized that Mrs. Courtney's imperious tones were much the same as those she used for recalcitrant schoolgirls.

"You would do well, Sir Mortimer, to remember that you need me and that I, too, with a word, can ruin your plans. I may destroy myself, but I will have the satisfaction of taking you down with me. Release me at once or I shall have you thrown out. I will give you my decision tomorrow evening."

"Little fool!"

"Wiser than I once was, Sir Mortimer. I have no faith in your continued silence once you gain your objectives. What is to prevent you from injuring me once you have married Emmaline? I need time to think, to devise some way to insure my position. Perhaps then, we can come to some agreement."

Sir Mortimer taunted. "So the mouse has teeth. Very well, I shall give you until tomorrow, but no more. The duns will not wait." There was the sound of the door closing and a brief silence.

"Emmaline, did you hear?" Mrs. Courtney's voice came echoing from below, "I am so very sorry, my dear."

"She heard, Mrs. Courtney," Doro called, as she hugged her weeping friend to her. "Every blasted word, the bloody swine."

"Ladies do not curse," the chiding voice called up the chimney, "no matter how great the provocation."

Doro thought that she could detect the traces of a sob in the schoolmistress' voice.

"Help Emmaline, Doro," she said, "I shall be up there in a few moments."

"Sounds like you need some help yourself, Mrs. C.," Doro whispered.

As Ives lit the last branch of the candelabra, Lord Corvin nodded dismissal and turned his attention once more to the man before him. Even though he had employed John Fless several times, it still amazed the Viscount that this nondescript little man was one of the most successful investigators outside of Bow Street.

"I would have been here sooner, milord, but after Septimus left the school, I followed him to his apartments where he met with his mistress, as luscious an armful as I've ever seen—"

"His mistress is of no interest to me," Corvin said, cutting him off. "What concerns me is that he apparently has enlisted Mrs. Courtney's cooperation. Tell me once more. What did you see?"

"'Tis as I said, for the past few days he's been hanging about the place. Then this evening he walked right up to the door, bold as brass. The draperies at the front was open, so I caught a glimpse of who he were talking with, the dark-haired stick of a woman."

"Mrs. Courtney," Corvin supplied.

"Aye, she's the one," Fless allowed. "Then he kisses her, passionate-like, but the butler draws the curtains and I could see nothing more till Septimus is back on the street. Says to the footman, 'When I come back tomorrow evening, t'will be as much as your job if you ain't civil.' "

"So, Mortimer has finally made his move."

"Aye, so it seems. The gentleman has been leading us a clever dance though, never going near the young lady, meeting with that mistress of his. I should suspect that he's been stringing your sister along by writing to her. Must have been a lot of scribbling going back an' forth atwixt 'em."

"I had never thought to have the school watched as well," Corvin sighed. "We shall have to handle this very carefully, since I have no wish to drive my sister into that villain's arm and as yet, we can accuse him of nothing except kissing the schoolmistress. Septimus must be desperate, indeed, to cozy up to Mrs. Courtney. I think Fless, that I shall have a little talk with the schoolmistress after Sir Mortimer's visit tomorrow. She cannot deny it if I come in upon his heels.''

Ten

<<<<<<<<<<<<<<

GUIN TURNED her damp pillow over to the other side and lay back staring into the darkness. The endless review of her circumstances had brought her only frustration. It would take little more than a whisper from Sir Mortimer and the carriages would be lined up before the door with angry parents demanding their daughters before they were further tainted by association with the notorious Elaine Borne Marshall.

In the hours before dawn, Guin set upon her course of action. Mrs. Courtney would be obliged to disappear, dismissed by Mrs. Haven before the first breath of rumor. The ensuing scandal might buffet Morton House and a few pupils would be lost, but the school had gotten to the point where it could endure without her. However, as she tossed about, Guin realized that Septimus, in his desperation, might not allow himself to be deterred by Emmaline's new repugnance.

It was little use to seek sleep. Guin fumbled for the tinder box and a lit a candle. Pulling a wrapper about her shoulders, she seated herself at the escritoire that stood by the window. She touched the polished oak lovingly and remembered the day that she had purchased it years ago, the first piece of furniture that she had ever truly owned. Now, she was to become a wanderer once more, with nothing that belonged to her that could not be carried in a carpet-bag.

Guin wiped away a tear and resolutely dipped her pen into the inkwell. Corvin was bound to connect the Elaine he had met in Hyde Park with Morton House once the rumors about Elaine Borne began to circulate. Although they were due to meet in the park at dawn, Guin knew that she could never bring herself to tell him face to face. It would be unbearable if this last memory of him were one of anger and recrimination. She was determined to make this last meeting a recollection that she could treasure. Far easier to put the words to paper than to tell him that she had betrayed his trust.

Once she had explained all, Guin recorded everything she knew about Sir Mortimer's intentions, so that the Viscount would be better able to protect his sister. Finally, she sanded, sealed and addressed the missive, setting it up against the inkwell so that she would remember to send it with a footman before she left Morton House.

In the wan light of early morning, Corvin looked about him in satisfaction. Although the canvas walls of the tent did not totally shut out the morning chill, the worst of the drafts were kept at bay and the glowing brazier sent out a spreading warmth. Everything was in place. A carpet covered the damp ground. Tapestry hid the canvas wall giving the illusion of elegance. The table was set and the light of a branched candelabra suffused the china and silver with a soft glow. Through some amazing servant's magic, Ives had managed to keep the food warm and delightful smells wafted from beneath the covered dishes. All was in readiness. The only thing lacking now was the lady.

"She's coming, milord," Ives announced.

"Can our little surprise be seen?"

The servant shook his head. "Almost invisible till you're right upon it."

"I shall go out to meet her. It is time for you to vanish, Ives," Corvin said, giving a nervous tug at his shirt points, ignoring his valet's frown.

"Yes, milord," Ives agreed, pausing to move a piece of silverware ever so slightly into perfect alignment before he followed his master outside.

As he waited, Corvin felt a twinge of apprehension. After this final meeting, he was honor bound to let Elaine go and never seek her out again. It was a vow that he had never expected to keep and the thought that she might choose to take him at his word filled him with desolation. As long as she did not trust him with that most vital of secrets, her name, the future was uncertain.

Corvin's imagination had supplied any number of unpalatable explanations for her secrecy, but he somehow could not credit them. Such fine sensibility and essential goodness could not spring from a soiled source. She had revealed so much of the horror of her past, yet she obviously felt that this final secret was beyond his ability to understand and forgive. He vowed to use every means within his power to breach this last barrier. She must be compelled to believe in him sufficiently to allow him to love her, to release him from his vow forever.

She dismounted with swift grace. It was obvious that she had been crying. The dark shadows beneath her reddened eyes made the lines of her high cheekbones more prominent.

"I have a surprise." Corvin said, realizing he sounded like an excited schoolboy. In his eagerness, Corvin forgot himself and put out a hand to lead her. He was about to apologize and withdraw when she placed her fingers in his grasp.

His look was a silent question and she nodded slightly. In answer, he raised her fingers to his lips, tucked her arm beneath his and led her to the bower that had been prepared.

He grinned as her eyes opened wide in wonder. She hesitated as he parted the entrance for her and Corvin understood her apprehension.

"My promise still holds until you absolve me permanently, even though you have been so good as to grace me with your hand. Trust me, please?" Although Corvin was reluctant to let go of her, even briefly, he released his hold. She stepped inside.

"Amazing. However did you manage?" she asked as she looked about her.

"I cannot take all the credit," Corvin admitted. "Ives is a conjurer. The weather is growing colder and I do not wish you to take a chill." He set the chair for her and she seated herself. Corvin picked up the coffee pot but poured clumsily, splashing rivulets on the snowy linen.

"If you will allow me, milord," she said, smiling shyly. "You are obviously not used to serving."

"Daniel," Corvin said, staring down into her eyes. "Call me, 'Daniel.' "

"Daniel," she murmured with a catch in her voice.

He had read once of a heathen belief that a true appellation holds power and that the force within the name could be used to shackle its owner. Corvin knew now that it was true. To hear his own name whispered so moved him beyond any word of love he had ever heard. Will he, nil he, Daniel was bound to her and somehow, he had to find a way to persuade her to reveal herself to him.

"Coffee, milo . . . Daniel?"

He nodded assent, not trusting himself to speak.

Guin forced herself to eat but did not really taste a morsel. An ache of sweet tension seemed to grow with every glance. Guin tore her gaze from his face and rose to explore the richly appointed tent. She recognized the brilliant tapestry hung beside the table as the one from the hall near his mother's chamber. A young woman sat on a fallen tree and the unicorn was on its knees before her, resting its horned head in her lap. The hunters hid in the background waiting for the kill.

"Elaine?"

She started; his tender look causing her heart to beat faster.

"You seem lost in thought," Corvin said, drinking in the sight of her, the thought of losing her almost like a physical pain.

"I had not seen it clearly in the hallway the other day," Guin said as she dropped the edge of braided wool. "I was just pitying the poor unicorn and the girl."

"The girl?"

"Knowing that that wonderful creature is to die because of her. Doubtless, she had never seen the magnificent beast before, didn't understand what it meant to slay such a wonder and now, it is to die," she said sadly.

"But it never does," he said, coming to stand beside her. "It is always suspended in that moment of discovery, finding its happiness, unaware of betrayal. Perhaps that is better than never having had any joy at all."

"And she is always caught in the agony of regret," she whispered, wondering if the memory of his touch could be worth a future of misery. He held out his hand and seemingly her body supplied an answer, acquiring a will of its own as she moved into his arms.

Safe within the circle of his love, her doubts began to ebb. She closed her eyes and savored the sensations that threatened to overwhelm her as he kissed her. His hand brushed softly against her cheek and she raised her own tentatively to trace the outline of his mouth. As she rested her head against his shoulder, she caught a glimpse of the girl in the tapestry and felt the terrible sadness in her eyes.

It was wrong, dreadfully wrong to deceive him for the sake of a memory. No matter what happened, the end would be the same when he found out the truth, but the hurt and betrayal would be far worse if she followed where he led. She pushed herself away. Her heart hammered as she tried to find the words to make him understand. If she told him all . . .

"What is wrong, Elaine?"

His voice was harsh with passion, but a distinct note of irritation penetrated her confusion. The veil of conflicting emotions tore just enough to allow suspicion to enter. In her worry about Daniel, she had thought little of herself. As her gaze swept beyond him, Guin began to realize that she might not be the only one guilty of subterfuge. From the strawberries upon the table to the silk cushions upon the floor, Corvin had created a perfect setting for seduction.

She deliberately nursed her doubts. Clearly, it had been his intent to tantalize her from the beginning and he had succeeded only too well in entangling her feelings until she had somehow lost sight of that truth. Surely, she had never truly believed that mere friendship would satisfy such a man. Or had she really wanted him from the start and refused to acknowledge the ultimate price?

"Elaine?" Corvin looked at her with puzzlement. "You have no need to fear me. I will take care of you, I swear. You will never be in want again."

She took his words to confirm the worst of her fears. Although the implied offer of carte blanche was not unexpected, her mind reeled at the enormity of her own self-deception.

"No," she said softly. "I could not bear it, Daniel. May heaven forgive me, but I should have realized where this would lead. Far better that I had stopped coming regardless of your threat. Each time, I told myself that I was a fool to risk it, but you have become like an addiction. I could as soon stay away as do without food and water.''

"What are you trying to tell me?" Corvin asked, holding out his hand, but she stepped back.

"I cannot do this, Daniel. It would hurt us both." She kept her hands rigid at her side, resisting the urge to take the hand he offered. "I told myself that we could part as we were, comfortable and fond of each other's companionship, but I do not think that it can ever be entirely that way between a man and a woman. I had thought that after you had seen my shame that you might be satisfied with simple friendship."

"Do not call it your shame, Elaine," he said, puzzled by the sudden change. "I hope that you will give me credit for seeing beyond such superficialities. It makes you no less beautiful in my eyes."

"What you seem to propose goes against everything I believe in. I will not debate the morality of love without marriage, for I have seen marriage without love and I cannot think it a worse sin," she said, trying to ignore the hurt in his voice. "But what will happen when you tire of me, milord? The mystery tantalizes you, but once you have found all that is secret, what then?"

"It is far more than that," Corvin protested. "You do not understand."

She raised her hand as if it could stop the flow of lies. "Ah, but I do, Daniel—all too well. My mind is reeling, searching for some means of doing what you ask, yet I can see no happy outcome. If our relationship endures and you do not discard me, what will happen when you marry, as you eventually will? It is expected. Tell me, then, am I to ignore your spouse's existence? What of the terrible injustice I do her and your children? Children—consider that possibility. What if there is a child, Daniel? Our child, the result of my loving you?''

Her cadence was almost that of a teacher asking a question of a dull pupil. ''Are there not ways of preventing children?'' he asked bluntly, his much vaunted diplomatic skills seemingly deserting him as the conversation took another unexpected twist. Even as the question came from his lips he knew that he had made an error.

His words doused her as would a pail of cold water, washing away any shred of pretense that was left her. There could be no doubt now of what he wanted, what he had always wanted. She could not keep the sarcastic inflection from her tone. ''If they were effective, do you think that there would be any harlot with a baby clinging to her breast?''

''Elaine, you are mistaken. Listen to me.''

His pleading tone caused her to soften. ''Daniel, did I truly mistake you or are you indeed, offering me a carte blanche?''

His silence was an answer.

Tears welled in her eyes. ''I was almost willing to be your mistress, Daniel, because I love you beyond any hope of salvation that I might have. But I refuse to let any innocent pay for my sins. It has happened once in my life. I cannot allow it to happen again.'' She turned and fled.

Corvin heard the echo of hoofbeats fade into the distance. She was gone and he cursed himself for his stupidity. It had been clear to him from the start that Elaine was not a common woman, certainly not the sort that would easily give herself to the life of a Cyprian. Yet, he had deliberately set out to win her, never stopping to examine his motives or goals. He wanted her more than he had ever wanted any other woman, but it had long gone beyond a simple matter of desire.

Trembling on his tongue had been an offer of marriage. Marriage, to a lady who would not even vouchsafe her name; the thought was numbing. Never in his life had Corvin felt so confused. He had always kept clear sight of his aims, never allowed his appetites to interfere with the pursuit of his ambitions. Even his passions had been courted with deliberate calculation. For the first time in his memory, Corvin was unsure as to just what he wanted. The thought of scandal was anathema to him. The Stanton name was buried under years of shame. Did he believe in Elaine enough to risk heaping more dishonor on his tarnished family? And what about Emmaline? Another disgrace might spoil the child's chances of social success.

The tent had grown cold. The last embers in the brazier had died.

"Milord?"

Corvin heard the tentative whisper from outside. A glance at his pocket watch showed him that hours had passed.

"Rip it down, Ives," Corvin said as he strode outside. "And do not bother to rehang the tapestry. I have grown tired of it."

By mid-afternoon, Guin had nearly finished packing and her room, the bane of the chambermaid's existence, had lost its usually cluttered look. After a maid carried the last bundle from the room, leaving the two women alone, Aunt Hermione decided to plead with her niece once more.

"But Guin!" Mrs. Haven protested. "I could never run the school myself."

"You will have to. The other teachers will help you," Guin declared, taking up a plum merino round gown and examining it carefully. "This is plain enough, don't you think?"

Mrs. Haven snatched the garment from her hand

and threw it on the bed. "Will you listen to me, gel? I tell you this is folly! We shall weather this storm, child. If we lose a few pupils so be it, but I cannot allow you to do this."

"Aunt Hermione," Guin said with a sigh. "Septimus intends to tell all unless I cooperate with his scheme."

"What could he possibly gain from spreading such tales, Guin?"

"Revenge. Revenge for thwarting him. I do not doubt that he will tell the story with all the relish of a participant. My past will be present once more. All will hold me to blame for driving my husband to die for my honor," she said, looking at her aunt, willing her to be convinced of the necessity of the course that she proposed. "If you let it be known that you dismissed me as soon as you got wind of my history, the ton might even sympathize, but if I stay, well, there is nothing society likes less than being played for fools. Morton House will not last beyond a week after Septimus begins his campaign of innuendo."

"There is more to it, isn't there? Those meetings with Lord Corvin that you have told me of—"

"I had no choice," Guin said angrily. "I thought you understood."

"I do," Mrs. Haven spoke with quiet certainty. "You are running away from Lord Corvin ain't you?"

Guin picked up the gown and folded it carefully. "I am doing what I think is best for all of us, Aunt."

"You ain't got the courage to face him and tell him the truth? I am surprised at you, Elaine Guinivere Morgaine Borne!" Her aunt's voice quavered.

"Are you? Why is it that people always feel that they have the license to tell me that I must fulfill their expectations? First Papa? Then Alfred and Corvin and now you, Aunt Hermione?" she said, placing the gown in the faded carpet-bag. "I love him. I suppose that I always will, but there can be no hope for me. He would never marry me and I will not take carte blanche."

"If he knew the truth . . ." Mrs. Haven persisted.

Guin wrapped her brush in a nightgown. "He will know. I have written a note telling the whole. He will hate me, believe that I deliberately made a fool of him. Heavens, listen to me whine when it is all my own stupid fault. Pride, silly pride, my besetting sin," she said with a bark of bitter laughter. "If I had listened to you from the first, we would not be at this pass."

"And where would young Emmaline be?" Mrs. Haven asked. "Doubtless miserable by now in the realization that her husband was not what she believed—as you did. Would you want that on your conscience, gel? For knowing you, you would have taken the blame for that upon yourself as you have for everything else. Why do you forever make yourself the martyr? Stay child, we will fight them together."

"You will not persuade me, Aunt," Guin said, giving the woman a fierce hug. "Although I love you dearly for trying. I must do what is right, for the school."

"But not for you, Guin, never for you." Mrs. Haven took the dress that Guin was attempting to fold and shook it out. Then, she began to prepare it properly. "I would make an excellent abigail, I vow, but you had best stick to teaching. Perhaps, after all this blows by, you could return."

"Perhaps," she murmured, knowing full well she could never return. "Who shall I be, I wonder?" Guin said aloud, attempting to keep her tone light. "I have written myself a glorious reference. I am sure that I shall have a new place before the scandal becomes common knowledge." Guin brushed at her eyes. "Have you ever seen such a watering pot as I? I vow, I have cried more these last weeks than I have in all my life."

"Love can do that," Aunt Hermione said sadly as she took the miniature of Guin's mother and wrapped it carefully, then nested it within the pile of clothing. "Anything more?"

"I will send for whatever else I need. Best to travel light until I know my ultimate destination," Guin declared with forced cheerfulness. "Come, now, Aunt Hermione. I smelled buns baking. I might as well enjoy Mrs. Bacon's cooking while I still may. Besides, a full stomach gives courage and I shall need all I can muster to send Septimus on his way this evening."

Mrs. Haven took her niece's hand, matching Guin's tone. "La, I am famished myself," she agreed. "There is nothing to match buns fresh from the oven."

They closed the door behind them.

Lord Corvin turned his collar up against the wind, as he peered out into the darkness of Green Street toward Morton House across the way. "It is after seven. Where is Sir Mortimer?" he asked.

"Milord," Fless said, his tone betraying his annoyance. "If you continue to crane your neck like that, then our quarry will be warned off."

Lord Corvin turned his back on the square. "Better, Fless? I will watch this rather interesting bit of brick wall until you inform me that I may take a peek."

"Very good, milord," Fless agreed.

It was unfortunate that Fless was a taciturn man, Corvin thought as he stiffened against a gust of wind. A bit of conversation would have been a welcome distraction from his inner visions of Elaine's tear-stained face. He had come to a decision. As soon as this business with Septimus was brought to a conclusion, he would set the estimable Fless upon her trail. Oath or no oath, he would find Elaine and make it right with her.

"Milord, keep your eyes upon the wall. It's him." Fless said. "He came afoot; is walking up the stairs. Turn now."

Corvin turned just in time to catch a glimpse of Sir Mortimer's back as he entered the door of Morton House.

"The drapes are drawn, milord," Fless whispered. "We shall just have to wait until he leaves."

"You will follow him and see where he goes once he departs," Corvin said grimly. "I think that I shall stay and have a chat with Mrs. Courtney. She has some explaining to do."

Guin had seated herself behind her desk and watched the clock tick away five full minutes before she allowed Perkins to usher Sir Mortimer in.

"Why did you keep me waiting?" Sir Mortimer blustered as Perkins showed him in.

"Did I? How rude of me," Guin said, deliberately keeping her voice bland. "No need to trouble taking a seat, Sir Mortimer, for you will not be staying long since I refuse to help you."

Sir Mortimer's face blanched. "You do not realize what you are saying, you little fool. I have the power to bring this cozy little existence of yours down around your ears. A few words from me is all it will take."

"I know," Guin said. "Nonetheless, I refuse to be part of your scheme, Septimus."

Sir Mortimer looked at her, nonplussed. Then his bewilderment changed to calculation. "You are far shrewder than I thought, Elaine. Looking for your share, are you? Very well, then, help me and you shall be a wealthy woman once more."

Guin laughed at his coaxing tone. "I think not.

You will have to find another dupe for your scheme;
if you have the time before they haul you off to
Fleet.''

His dumbfounded expression moved her to
laughter and he charged at the desk. ''You will regret this, Elaine Borne. By tomorrow evening your
name will be on everyone's lips. Every detail of your
youthful exploits and your husband's miserable
death will be bandied about over dinner. See how
your precious school fares then!''

''Perkins!''

Upon hearing her call the butler entered with a
speed Guin would not have previously credited.
With a footman's aid, he pulled the irate Sir Mortimer from the room. The old roué's imprecations rang
through the halls as the servants escorted him un-
ceremoniously to the door.

''He is gone, madame,'' Perkins allowed himself
a grin. ''We will hear no more from that rogue.''

Guin's answering smile faded as the servant
closed the door. She could not be so sanguine. The
sound of footsteps overhead informed her that the
girls had been allowed to return to their room. It had
not been necessary that anyone hear her second interview with Sir Mortimer.

''Can't see much of his face,'' Fless said. ''Weren't
much of a lover's tryst, I'd say. He were in there
barely a quarter hour.''

''Follow him, Fless. In the meanwhile, I shall have
a talk with Mrs. Courtney,'' Lord Corvin said.

The man nodded agreement and slipped out after
Sir Mortimer.

When they were out of sight, Corvin walked
across the street and knocked upon the door.

The snarl on the footman's face was replaced by
a look of stupefaction.

''I realize that I am unexpected, but still that is

not a proper way to greet visitors," Corvin said, putting his hat in the stunned servant's hand. "Is Mrs. Courtney in the parlor?"

The footman nodded dumbly.

"I shall show myself in."

Guin sat before the fire, staring into the flames. She did not look up as the door opened.

"Mrs. Courtney. I have serious matters to discuss with you."

The woman rose, her eyes wide with shock.

Elaine. Without the spectacles, Corvin saw it at once. The firelight flickered on the mass of hair drawn tightly from her wan face.

"Daniel," she murmured, rising from the chair.

It was a plea for forgiveness. Her whisper was so soft that he almost did not catch his name. It angered him that she should dare to beg for his sympathy, even use the name he had vouchsafed her.

"I must congratulate you, Mrs. Courtney." His controlled tones surprised even himself considering the turmoil within. "You should consider a career upon the stage for I vow, the disguise was excellent. Why you were the very picture of injured innocence, too virtuous to be soiled by an illicit love."

She turned away unable to endure the hatred in his eyes.

"What did you hope for, Elaine, if that is your real name? Did you think to lure me into marriage ultimately? What a triumph that would have been! Promote a marriage between my sister and your lover and then marry the future Earl of Sinclair yourself. After all, we do have a history of marrying whores."

He whirled her round to face him. The look in her eyes was stunned, as if she had been physically struck.

Guin felt a flash of anger. The words came slowly, as if each one was wrenched from her. "Yes, my name is Elaine, Elaine Borne Marshall."

The name struck a chord. Elaine Borne. He remembered her at the core of Caro Lamb's circle, a group that his stodgy younger self had shunned like the plague. They were the very type of people that were prone to the embarrassing excesses of his parents.

Elaine Borne. Mothers used her as an example and a warning. The news of her husband's death in a duel had even traveled to the Spanish Peninsula. It had not surprised many that a woman with so soiled a reputation had led her cuckolded husband to the field of honor.

As he gazed at her, Corvin was frightened to realize how poor his judgment had been. The woman before him represented everything that he loathed: impulsiveness, wantonness, disdain of sensibility. Yet, she had so bemused him that he had been at the point of scouring London for her with the object of asking her to be his wife. All the time, she had, no doubt, been laughing with her lover at the naiveté of the love-crazed Viscount.

Everything made horrifying sense from the farcical meeting at Vauxhall where he had "rescued" her from her lover's arms—Saint Corvin, the knight erroneous—to the trysts in the park. As a former diplomat, he could appreciate the exquisite calculation with which she had manipulated him. The finely-tuned dance of tantalize and retreat had nearly driven him to a declaration of marriage. Now, she dared to face him with a look that he could only characterize as one of defiance.

"You amaze me, milord, in your remarkable assessment of the situation. You spy upon me, follow me, force me to meet you unwillingly and plan my seduction, then name me a whore," she declared, her eyes searing him with fury.

"Deny then, if you will, your meeting with Sir Mortimer Septimus."

"I cannot. But then, unless you were listening at the keyhole, milord, you could not know the circumstances of that meeting. If you truly understood my purpose, you would not make these ridiculous accusations."

"Purpose," he sneered. "Can there be any other purpose to this?" He pulled her into his arms. All the passion of his contempt went into that kiss. He held her struggling body tightly, bruising her mouth with merciless force, ignoring the hands that pummeled helplessly against his chest until he tasted the salt tang of blood and realized that it was hers.

"Elaine!" It was a groan of despair. Although it was against all reason, he still wanted her. Corvin brushed his finger against her bleeding lip. He had not meant to hurt her and he would have said as much but she pushed away from him. His neck snapped back with the unexpected force of her slap.

"Get out of here," she growled like a cornered animal. "Get out or I shall call the servants. You will not ill use me again, not you or any other man. I have had far too much of that in my lifetime."

Corvin rubbed his hand against his stinging cheek, glaring at her.

"Daniel!" Emmaline burst into the room followed by an anxious looking Doro and Eddy.

"Pack a bag, Emmaline," Corvin commanded. "You are coming home with me."

"But Daniel, you do not understand," Emmaline begged, grabbing hold of his hand.

"Pack your things, I said," Corvin roared. "We will send for the rest of your possessions tomorrow." He felt a twinge of irritation as Emmaline looked at Mrs. Courtney, as if for direction.

"Do as your brother tells you, Emmaline. It is best," Guin said, reassuringly as she escorted the girls to the door. "Do not worry about me, dears, I have weathered far worse storms."

"You are making a mistake, Daniel, and when you find out you will feel like the veriest fool," Emmaline said before she pulled the door shut behind her.

"Is this what you teach them?" Corvin asked. As he looked at her, he wondered how he could have been so blind. "To contradict and defy their elders. I would expect such lessons from Elaine Borne."

"Milord," she said taking a scarlet stained finger from her lip. "I will endure any insults that you may tender but do not touch me again. As you yourself informed me, no man has that right."

He grasped her wrist. "I did not . . ."

"I remind you of your oath, Lord Corvin. Or does it no longer bind you now that you know that I am so sunk beyond reproach?" she asked, surprised at the depths of her disappointment in him. He had shown himself to be a man, just like all other men. She had been a fool to expect more.

Corvin released her wrist, feeling suddenly ashamed.

"Ah, chivalry has not disappeared, it seems," Guin said with a laugh that was dangerously close to a sob.

Her bitter, mocking laugh jarred him. How was it that she made him feel like an inattentive scholar who had missed the answer to an obvious question? Corvin lashed out at her in his confusion. "Once the ton finds out who you are, you will not have a student left," he declared.

Blue eyes cut him with daggers of anger. "It seems that I misjudged you again, Lord Corvin. I thought you a fair man, but I was mistaken. I did not think you malicious enough to harm the reputations of innocent pupils out of spite, but I was wrong there, too. You need not trouble yourself with the matter of informing polite society of my identity, milord. Sir Mortimer will take care of that."

"What do you mean?" he asked.

Guin was unable to hold herself back any longer. The disillusionment and hurt had become too great to bear. "I suddenly find that I cannot stand the sight of you. I will see what is keeping your sister," she said and she fled the room.

The room clearly belonged to a bachelor without a valet. Clothing was strewn carelessly about and the remains of yesterday's luncheon sat upon the table. From the noisy street came the cry of a rag-man selling his wares.

"He brought her home to St. Clair Abbey last night. He was livid, I tell you, Mort, absolutely livid. The chit was crying buckets and Sinclair was raging. It was a madhouse!" Norah said, gesticulating with her hands as she described the scene.

"And Corvin did not tax you at all?" Sir Mortimer asked.

"If anything, he was almost apologetic about disrupting the household."

"Exactly what did he say?" Sir Mortimer rubbed at his stubbled chin.

"Very little. Assured his father that it was not Emmaline's fault and that he had found out some information about Morton House that made it undesirable for the girl to remain under the school's influence. You were not mentioned at all."

"Must have found out about Elaine Borne somehow . . ." Sir Mortimer murmured. "Dash it all, I can never get to Emmaline at St. Clair Abbey and even if I did succeed in snatching the chit, I would be caught before I got to Gretna. You must contrive to deliver her."

"And where does that leave me?" Norah whined. "You cannot involve me directly, Mort. I cannot simply hand the child over to you." Norah fumbled with her reticule searching for a sweet. "If Sinclair connects me with this, he'll bloody well kill me."

"And what about me, eh? The schoolmistress knows all about me," Mortimer said, as he tied his cravat into an untidy Mathematical. "Now that Corvin has found her out, it would be just like that woman to queer my pitch out of spite. We have to do something, and quickly, Nore. My creditors have me under siege."

"But what can we do?" Norah pulled at the wrapping. "The schoolmistress obviously realizes that you can do her little damage. There is nothing the Quality likes less than cold scandal broth."

"There is the duel," Mortimer pointed out. "Is there not?"

"You would not dare," Norah said, her hand stopping midway to her mouth. "If you were to revive the whispers, the truth might come out, Mort. That could be very dangerous for us both."

"It cannot fail to come out now, Nore," Sir Mortimer said with a frown. "Now that Corvin knows that Mrs. Courtney is Elaine Borne they will dig it all up once more, the duel will come to light again."

"How can we prevent it?" Norah asked as she chomped nervously. "You know how it is. Once the cats have hold of that ball of yarn, they will worry it till every thread is unraveled."

"We might salvage the situation yet," Sir Mortimer said, a grin spreading slowly across his face. "If we embroil Mrs. Courtney in a far greater scandal, one that will make the tabbies unsheathe their claws and tear her to shreds, the duel will pale by comparison, will it not? As you said, why sip cold scandal broth when there is hot, spicy disgrace to savor?"

"I dunno, Mort," Norah said doubtfully, wiping her sticky fingers on her sleeve. "What if she peaches to Corvin, first? You will never be able to get near Emmaline then."

"True enough, but if Corvin is as angry as you

say he will not be in a mood to hear her until his temper cools. We must make certain that she does not have a chance to speak to him and that means we must snatch Emmaline tomorrow,'' Mortimer declared as he smoothed the wrinkled folds of his cravat. ''If we make the schoolmistress part of the conspiracy, she can accuse all she wants and nobody will believe her. Moreover, no one will even think to question the circumstances of her husband's death once they learn she has aided in her pupil's elopement. A far better revenge than I could have hoped for, is it not? Emmaline's trust in her teacher can be used to our advantage.''

MY LADY SCANDALOUS'S TROUSSEAU 238

Wildmore to marry? She knows now that you are able
be bill her in dispose carr 24

Eleven

‹‹‹‹‹‹‹‹‹‹‹‹‹

GUIN PAUSED at the end of the street to look back
upon the place that her dreams had built. As
she had instructed, there had been no farewells or
fond leave-takings, for the manner of her departure
had to be consistent with the story that they had
concocted. The ton adored retribution as long as it
did not apply personally and Guin could just imagine Aunt Hermione saying in her most injured tones,
"I turned her out into the street, I tell you, milady,
as soon as I got wind of what was about."

As Guin turned the corner, a jarvey slowed to a
stop before her. The door opened and she found
herself pulled into the cab, baggage and all.

"How very convenient." Sir Mortimer laughed as
the carriage began moving once more. "You are
ready for our little journey."

"You might as well stop the carriage, Sir Mortimer." Guin dusted off her sadly battered hat and
pinned it firmly atop her head. "Emmaline is no
longer in my care."

"I know that her brother removed the chit last
night. However, you underestimate your value to
me, Elaine. Propriety dictates that my little Emmaline have some suitable escort to the altar. What better chaperone than the proper Mrs. Courtney?"

Guin shook her head. "Emmaline will never go

with you easily. She knows now that you are after her only for her fortune," she said.

"Willingly, unwillingly, it is all one. I had hoped to snatch you while you were out for your daily ride, and hold you until the time." He pulled the watch from his pocket. "Faster!" Sir Mortimer called to the driver. "There's extra in it for you, Crum, if you don't spare the horses."

The alleyway where they finally came to a stop was not far from Hookham's. "Not a word," Sir Mortimer warned and Guin saw the dull gleam of a pistol in his hand. "Remember, Elaine, I am a desperate man and if they fish the body of a disgraced schoolmistress from the Thames, there will be none surprised. Is that correct?"

Guin swallowed and nodded her understanding.

"Mrs. Courtney?" Emmaline called. Guin could see the girl's face through the grimy glass and tried to warn her with her eyes. The gun did not waver as the handle of the door turned and opened. Sir Mortimer pulled Emmaline inside and slammed the door shut behind her, banging to signal the driver to go on.

Guin helped the confused girl to a seat.

"What is happening?" Emmaline asked. "I received your note saying that you wanted to speak to me. Why is Sir Mortimer here? Let me down this instant!"

"I think not, my love," Sir Mortimer sneered.

Emmaline's eyes widened with fear when she saw the gun in his hands.

"I want you ladies to act naturally. Smile as if you are pleased, especially you, Mrs. Courtney. There will be many people abroad at this hour, people who will later recall that they saw you with Emmaline Stanton on her wedding day."

Emmaline grasped Guin's hand tightly, shrinking

against the woman as Sir Mortimer's mocking laugh rang through the carriage.

"I am sorry, Emmaline," Guin whispered. "I did not know that he meant to use me as bait to snare you. By the time I realized, it was too late."

"How noble, Elaine." Sir Mortimer laughed unpleasantly. "Would you have preferred to be shot then? That too can be arranged if you do not make your visage a little less grim. Smile, for we are going for a little outing."

"We searched everywhere, Corvin," Lady Sinclair daintily applied a lace handkerchief to her streaming eyes. "Hookham's, up and down the streets outside. Then my maid found that note in the book that poor Emmaline had chosen."

Corvin looked at his stepmother skeptically. It was lucky that Lady Sinclair had left Drury Lane for her courtesan's career, he mused. Her act of concerned anxiety was overdone beyond belief. He read the note once more.

" 'I must talk to you, Emmaline, so that we may clear up this terrible misunderstanding. I shall be waiting in the alleyway. Mrs. Courtney.' "

"I tell you Corvin, you are dead wrong about her. She would not have helped Septimus in this scheme." Hopley declared. "It was Mrs. Courtney who warned me herself about his intentions and begged me to drop a warning to you."

Corvin cast Hopley a look of pure ice. His friend's duplicity had cut deeply.

"Why would she put you on to her own game?" the younger man persisted. "It does not make sense I tell you."

"Trying to divert suspicion, no doubt," Lady Sinclair broke in. "If she is Elaine Borne, as you have told me, then she is the worst kind of shifty jade. Why Lady Crombie herself told me she saw Emmaline with the schoolmistress and they were grinning like a pair of fools. 'Tis clear that the two of them had it all planned between them. How could you have deceived your friend for such a woman, Mr. Hopley?''

''I could tell you nothing, Corvin, because of an oath,'' Hopley protested.

''It seems the lady is prodigious fond of oaths,'' Corvin said. ''If you two would cease your brangling! I have called in help.''

Lady Sinclair abruptly ceased her sniveling and looked at her stepson. ''The Bow Street Runners? Think of the scandal, Corvin.''

Corvin looked at her with growing curiosity. Norah had never troubled herself about scandal before. Indeed, he would have wagered that she would welcome intervention by Bow Street. It would be just the ticket to sully the child irreparably in her husband's eyes.

''Not a Runner,'' Corvin explained. ''This fellow has performed some investigative services for me in the past. His discretion can be absolutely relied upon.''

''You must do as you think is best, of course,'' the Countess said, pulling a twist of peppermints from her pocket and popping one into her mouth. ''I have always found peppermints to be so soothing. Would you care for one, Corvin?''

Lady Sinclair wilted beneath her stepson's withering glare.

''Milord,'' Ives entered with a letter on a salver. ''This was just delivered by a footman from Morton House.''

''A ransom note, perhaps?'' Lady Sinclair suggested, slurping noisily on the candy. She edged closer as Corvin unsealed the missive.

Corvin cast an annoyed glance at his stepmother. "I shall read this in my study. Ives, when Mr. Fless arrives, show him in immediately."

Corvin closed the door behind him. He settled into a chair and began to read Elaine's letter. The woman's effrontery was amazing! She apologized for her deception, but perversely pointed out that he had forced her into it. Her description of the events leading to their meeting in Vauxhall stunned him. She made herself out as a victim. Did she really think him stupid enough to believe such faradiddle? But his anger changed to bewilderment when she begged him to protect Emmaline.

John Fless was shown in. "I see you have the situation well in hand, milord," he said. "T'was a good idea to bring Sir Mortimer Septimus' other mistress in for questioning."

"Whatever do you mean, Fless?" Corvin asked, rising from the chair.

"The woman with the henna curls out there," Fless said. "She might be able to give us a clue to Septimus' whereabouts."

"How would she know?"

Fless sighed and spoke slowly as if to a child. "That woman I saw in your parlor, milord. She's the bit o' muslin Septimus spends his time with."

Abruptly, all the pieces of the puzzle fell into place. Elaine's words made bitter sense. Corvin threw the door open and advanced upon his startled stepmother. "She will tell us what she knows, Fless, if she knows what's good for her."

The door flew open and Sir Mortimer herded his two captives into the room. Emmaline cowered against Mrs. Courtney as he locked the door behind them and pocketed the key.

"Welcome to the bridal chamber," Sir Mortimer proclaimed, pulling the flask from his pocket and taking a celebratory swig. "I regret that our wedding journey will have to be postponed a day or two, my dear. Your brother will be expecting us to head straight for Gretna and will surely not be looking for us in the slums of St. Giles. When his attention is turned in other directions, we can do it up right and tight, my sweeting. Until then, this is our little love nest," he said cupping the horrified girl's chin in his hands. "I realize that this is not what the Lady Emmaline is accustomed to, but we will be cozy, let me assure you, cozy indeed." He brought his lips down on hers.

"Leave her!" Guin grabbed at his hand, but found herself pushed to the ground.

"Do not interfere between a man and his wife, Elaine!" Sir Mortimer sneered down at her. She whimpered as he raised his hand to strike and he laughed mockingly. "Hard to believe that such a lovely woman could be so pitiful, unable to hold as poor an excuse for a man as Alfred Marshall. He was a fool you know, invested in every crazy scheme that anyone of us could think of," he said, then paused for another long pull at the flask.

"Then when he found out that he was sharing his mistress with me, the idiot challenged me to a duel. His timing could not have been more perfect, for the little scheme that I had caused him to invest in was coming to light and his evidence could have meant prison for me. The only person who could have connected me to it, you know? One shot and it was over. Of course, I fled the country for a bit, but it was soon safe to return."

"Over a mistress . . ." Guin whispered.

"A mistress!" Sir Mortimer taunted. "You were not even good enough to hold Alfred Marshall, Elaine."

A mistress. All those years of guilt and Alfred had died for a common tart. Guin had believed that the stories of her youthful escapades had stoked his jealousy beyond the bounds of reason and goaded him to his death. Every version of the tale had styled him a cuckolded fool defending the honor of his promiscuous wife and she had accepted her burden of shame and scorn as due penance.

Now, without realizing it, Sir Mortimer had given her a powerful weapon. At last, Guin realized that what Corvin said was true. She did not deserve the cruel turns that her life had taken.

Emmaline twisted from Septimus' hold and pounded upon the door. "Help us!" she screamed. "Please somebody, help us!"

"This is St. Giles, Emmaline," Guin said, getting to her feet. "You saw what it is outside that door. No one here would lift so much as a finger."

"Sensible at last, Elaine." Sir Mortimer lifted the flask to his lips, tipping it back further and further, then shaking it in irritation. "Empty," he cursed. "A man cannot be without refreshment on his wedding night." He pulled the key from his pocket and went to the door. "I would suggest you do not attempt to leave, ladies. A fate far worse than marriage to me would await you out there, Emmaline."

"Get us something to eat while you are gone, Mortimer," Guin said. "If we are to be here for some time we must have nourishment."

"So woman does not live by love alone either," Sir Mortimer chortled. "Very well, I shall bring us some provisions. In the meanwhile, Elaine, I would suggest that you teach your pupil the obedience owed by wife to husband. I recall that you learned that lesson well." The key grated rustily as he locked the door behind him.

Guin took the weeping Emmaline into her arms, brushing back her hair attempting to soothe her. After a few moments, she seated the girl upon the bed and went to explore the adjoining chamber, but it contained only a second bed and a single narrow window that led out to the steeply pitched roof. She tried to pry it open but to no avail.

"Let me help," Emmaline said, her red-rimmed eyes still streaming as she began to pull at the other side of the jamb. "I have behaved like a useless fool long enough."

Guin squeezed her hand, then applied all her strength to the window. Abruptly, it swung open. Emmaline peered outside.

"Where does it lead?" Guin asked.

"It overlooks the roof of the house next door, but it is a long drop." Emmaline sniffed in despair. "I cannot see too much."

"There does not seem to be any way to get to the street," Guin said, sitting down heavily on the bed. "And even if there was, Septimus is right, we would not last a moment alone in St. Giles."

"You could not get through the window anyway, Mrs. Courtney. It is far too small." The girl began to tremble. "There is no way out, Mrs. Courtney. He means to make sure of me and we are trapped. I would rather die. I swear, I would rather die than let him touch me."

"No!" Guin exploded. "I will not let it happen! I will not!" She bunched the threadbare coverlet in her hands. A gleam lit her eye. "Emmaline, did he bring the carpet-bag up with him?"

"I shall check," she said and returned directly with the dusty bag. "What do you plan to do?"

Guin pulled the musty sheets from beneath the blanket. "Sometimes, Emmaline, the appearance of something can be almost as powerful as reality. We are about to create an illusion." She pulled her scissors from their worn case and began cutting the tattered linen.

* * *

It was almost dusk when Sir Mortimer returned. To judge from his lusty singing as he mounted the stairs, he had refilled and emptied his flask many times over. All for the better if his judgment was befuddled, Guin tried to reassure herself as she sat waiting for the door to open.

"Where is my blushing bride?" Sir Mortimer asked, surveying the room as he dumped his load of parcels on the table. "I have brought us wine, wine to toast my lovely fiancée!" he said, waving the bottle over his head. Guin sat silently upon the chair.

"Where is she?" Sir Mortimer asked once more. His eyes went to the closed door of the small room. "Ah! The blushing maiden hides herself. No need, my darling, to fear me. The lock don't work anyways, made sure of that." He pushed at the door and was puzzled when it did not yield immediately. "Barricaded in, Emmaline. Come out now; you only make me angry." He pushed harder putting his full weight upon the door. "Tell her, Elaine. Do her no good."

Sir Mortimer cast a venomous look at the steadfastly silent woman. "Pay dearly for this little trick, Elaine, you will. You put her up to it, no doubt." He slammed himself against the door once more and at last, it yielded enough to allow him through the gap. His gaze immediately went to the open window and the rope of twined sheets that was tied to a chair leg wedged beneath the frame. Sir Mortimer craned his neck out the window.

"She's flown, Septimus."

He turned round in fury at the laughing voice behind him.

"Gone and may God speed her!"

He grasped Guin by the shoulders and shook her. "How long?" he roared. "How long?"

Guin pursed her lips as she pretended to consider. "Now let me see, about a half hour to twine the sheets. I would guess you've been gone about three hours?" She tried to stifle a gasp of pain as he twisted her arm cruelly.

"Elaine!"

Septimus' look was murderous. She dared not push him much further in this drunken state.

"I would say at least three hours now," Guin said. "You missed a small cache of coins that I had in my baggage. My advice to her was to find the soberest soul she could, preferably a shopkeeper and give him the money, promising more if he would get her safe home. I suspect that she should be with her brother by now and no doubt on her way here with the authorities."

"Bitch!"

Although he had not released his hold upon her, Guin was unprepared for the wrenching pain as he forced her arm further behind her and despite herself, she screamed as he threw her to the ground.

"That girl was my last hope, Elaine!"

Septimus advanced on her. Guin steeled herself for the force of the blow that was sure to come. At least, this time there was a reason to take the abuse. Every minute that she could deflect his interest, keep him from thinking, investigating, was crucial. She had hoped that he would go haring off immediately in fear of Corvin's retribution. Then she and Emmaline could escape together. However, she had miscalculated the depth of Septimus' desperation. Rage seemed to be overcoming his sense of self-preservation.

There was a clattering sound as the pistol fell from his pocket but he did not bother to retrieve it. Guin inched backward along the floor until she was against the wall, then raised her hand to cover her face.

"Mortimer!"

"Emmaline, no!" Guin groaned. It had been for nothing! For nothing.

The dusty and disheveled girl had emerged from beneath the bed and snatched the pistol.

"My darling!" Septimus wheeled about at the sound of the girl's voice.

Emmaline leveled the weapon at him.

"You wounnent hurt me, my love, you wounnent," he said as he advanced.

"Stay back! I warn you, Mortimer. My mama taught me to use this." Her voice trembled but the barrel remained steady.

"My love." He stumbled towards her.

There was a roar and the acrid smell of spent powder. Septimus doubled over and fell. Emmaline's horrified eyes met Guin's and she ran to her teacher. "I have killed him, Mrs. Courtney. I think I have killed him," she cried.

Guin tried to lift her hand to stroke Emmaline's trembling shoulder and gasped at the swell of pain. "Tell them I did it," she murmured. "I would be glad to claim the credit. Now go, as we planned . . . get help."

"Not alone. I cannot leave you here," the girl protested.

The door burst open. Corvin entered with Fless and Hopley following.

"Daniel!" Emmaline ran into her brother's arms. "Please Daniel, Mrs. Courtney. He near to twisted her arm off, I fear," she said, dragging her brother to Guin's side.

Corvin muttered an oath.

"Looks like the ladies took care of matters themselves," Fless commented loudly as he knelt and put a hand to Mortimer's throat. "Trouble with amateurs is they don't do it right. The blighter's still breathing." He turned Septimus over and looked at the wound in his shoulder. "And this don't look none too bad neither. Phew! Like as not t'was the drink what put him out.''

"Then I did not kill him?'' Emmaline whispered.

"You, puss?'' Corvin asked as he probed Guin's arm gently. "I shall have to push this back in place. It will hurt quite a bit. Fless, a bit of that brandy if you will.''

"Very brave . . . your sister, quick thinking,'' Guin whispered. She was floating away on a sea of pain. Familiar waters. She had sailed here many times before. Why did she persist holding on to consciousness?

"She saved me from him.''

Guin heard Emmaline's voice as if from a distance and felt gentle hands brushing the hair away from her cheek.

"I have the brandy flask here, Corvin.''

The voice was familiar. "Hopley?'' Guin whispered.

"Hush, my darling. Try to swallow.''

It was Corvin's voice. His arm lifted her gently and the liquid stung her lip, trickled down her chin. *My darling?* But as consciousness gave way to the spreading warmth and blessed oblivion, Guin was unable to consider those words.

Twelve

◀◀◀◀◀◀◀◀◀◀◀◀

"SHE TURNED him away again!" Emmaline declared, flouncing onto the bed in irritation. "I vow, she is almost as stubborn as my idiot brother."

"Perhaps, she is still in pain?" Eddy questioned.

"Nonsense," Doro said with a shake of her head. "Her shoulder is entirely back to normal."

"Why doesn't your brother sweep past Perkins and storm her door?" Cat asked. "That is what they always do in novels."

"Daniel seems to feel that it is up to him to make up for all the errors of all scandalous Sinclairs before him and now that Norah has run off to the Continent with Sir Mortimer, he has to contend with every wagging tongue in the ton, as well," Emmaline frowned. "The only one who seems to be happy is my father. He declares himself glad to have Norah's expenses off his hands."

"I still say that your brother should have brought them before the law," Eddy declared.

"And create more scandal?" Cat shook her head. " 'T'would have been foolish beyond permission, Eddy."

"I believe that Mrs. Courtney might actually have convinced my brother that she has taken him in disgust. After all, he did treat her very badly," Emmaline said.

"What about Mrs. Courtney?" Doro asked.

"Surely the scandalmongers have been chipping away at her."

"To the contrary," Cat said, "Mrs. C. has become quite the heroine. You know how perverse the ton can be about these matters. Sir Mortimer was quite hated and the brave schoolmistress' salvation of her pupil's virtue has become the story of the season."

"Hush," Doro said, putting a finger to her lips.

Mrs. Courtney's voice drifted up the chimney from the room below.

"You are sure, Aunt, that the girls are not above."

"Positive, gel. I was only just up there myself," came Mrs. Haven's reply.

"But she knows we are here," Emmaline whispered. "She saw me enter the room."

". . . set on this course, Aunt Hermione. Do not try to talk me out of it again. I have already spoken to Mrs. Aubrey's agency about a new position."

"Nonsense, child! You are being lauded all over town."

"For now." Mrs. Courtney's voice was glum. "But what happens when someone remembers Elaine Borne once more? It is inevitable, you know."

"You have lived that down, Guin. Admit it! It is not your past that you are running from, it is the Viscount Corvin."

"That is ridiculous," Mrs. Courtney said. "I have nothing to fear from him."

"Why do you continue to deny him an audience?"

"What would be the purpose of such an interview, Aunt Hermione? He is grateful for Emmaline's sake, although 't'was Emmaline's quickness that saved us both."

"Does gratitude prompt flowers sent every day? And haunting your sickroom?" Mrs. Haven's tone was sarcastic. "And despite all the hum about his stepmama, he has shown up on our doorstep regular as clockwork to speak with you, only to be turned away with some poor excuse.''

''I admit it! Is that what you wish, Aunt Hermione? I love him!''

Her despair echoed up the chimney.

''I love him so much that I cannot bear the thought of having to receive his sincere thanks and watch him walk out the door to live the rest of his life without me. Surely, I have had enough pain.''

There was the sound of a slamming door and a sigh rose up the hearth. ''La, she is a stubborn one. If only there were some way that she would give him a hearing. For unless I miss my mark, that young man is as befuddled as she.''

Emmaline grinned. ''I think, Maidens of Morton, that we have just been given permission to meddle.''

Although the weather was dismal, Guin's second leave-taking was far happier than the first, a month before. Her new employer had sent a well-sprung carriage to convey her to his home in Yorkshire and the entire staff and student body was assembled before Morton House for the send-off.

As the vehicle turned round the bend, Guin's deliberately cheerful expression was erased. Desperation had driven her to accept the first position that she was offered. Luckily, the Baron of Westwold had not known that she would have taken the position for half the munificent salary he offered, so anxious was she to leave London. Corvin had not even tried to see her these past few days. His only communication had been a formal note wishing her well in her new position, confirming that he felt little more than a sense of obligation.

The journey proceeded at a spanking pace, with changes of horses arranged at the various inns along the way. Her new employer was a generous man, Guin thought. Private parlors had been secured for each stop and at the inn where they sheltered overnight, her room was spacious and luxurious. The schoolmistress found herself growing more and more curious about an employer who would take such care of someone little more than an upper servant. The girl she was to care for must be a handful indeed, for a mere governess to merit such gentle treatment.

The sun was setting as they reached the gates of the estate in Yorkshire. The long beech-lined drive ended in the mellow brick of the Elizabethan manor, its simple splendor lit with the afterglow of day. Mrs. Pern, the housekeeper, greeted Guin at the door and immediately escorted her upstairs to a room that could only be described as magnificent. The carpet of deep blue seemed newly laid, and the draperies and furnishings were all done in the same unusual shade.

Guin's curiosity about her mysterious employer had become overwhelming. Although she was not normally given to gossip with the servants, she tried to direct the conversation to the subject, but Mrs. Pern would give her no clue.

"Ye'll be meeting him yerself soon enough, madame," she said. "He wishes to see ye as soon as yev refreshed yerself. Lily will assist ye."

The maid shyly bobbed a curtsy.

After a quick wash, Lily assisted Guin into her gown. The severe cut and high neckline did little to enhance her figure, but the color made her eyes seem a deeper hue of blue. Although Lily wished to arrange Guin's hair in a softer style, Guin insisted that it be brushed back into its usual knot. The last thing that she wished to do was attract her employer's attentions.

As Guin walked down the staircase, she found

herself wondering about the man she was to meet. Even though Mrs. Aubrey's employment agency was most respectable and had recommended the Baron highly, she began to question if it had been ill-advised to come so far without first finding more about her employer. Something seemed amiss.

Guin paused at the entrance of the library. Well, it was too late for foolish misgivings. The footman opened the door and Guin raised her chin. She knew that she was just being childish, seeking an excuse to run back to Morton House, an excuse to see . . .

"Welcome, Elaine."

"Milord," she said, her throat constricting in a combination of anger and shock. Corvin stood before the fire, smiling at her like a boy who has duped his nanny. His dress was formal, a study in black and white as decreed by the long-banished Brummel. A diamond pin gleamed in his cravat, the sole relief to his severity.

"You will send me back at once, milord," Guin demanded.

"Daniel, also Baron of Westwold, one of my minor titles. As you have no doubt found, the roads are bad enough in daylight, Elaine. There are also highwaymen to consider," he remarked, as he poured a glass of wine and offered it to her. "I have no intention of letting you risk your pretty neck."

She dashed the glass from his hand. "Why, milord? Why have you deceived me so?" she asked. "Is abduction the manner in which the house of Sinclair pays those who do their family a service?"

"Yes, it is terrible of me, I grant, to serve you so ill. But then, I am due to be the Earl of Sinclair in time and as you know, we are notorious," Corvin said, pulling a handkerchief from his pocket and dabbing at the wet spot on his waistcoat. "Poor

Ives; I vow, I never used half as many handkerchiefs before I met you, Elaine.'' Suddenly his jocular tone disappeared. ''Before I met you, I did not think myself capable of feeling. Yet, you touched that long-dead part of me and now, to my utter dismay, I find that I do have a heart. Do you forgive me, Elaine? For hurting you? For doubting you?''

His vulnerable expression melted Guin's anger. ''Yes, milord,'' she said softly. ''I forgave you long ago, for you enabled me to forgive myself. Any pain that occurred was as much my fault as your own, for I deceived you and for that I must ask your pardon. Now, I beg you, let me leave here before we have cause for further regret.''

''I cannot allow you to leave me,'' Corvin responded, in mock seriousness. ''Abduction is a family tradition. That is how my great-grandpapa obtained a good portion of the family fortune, but I shall not bore you with long stories. I shall have ample opportunity to regale you with the Sinclair history.''

''I think not!'' Guin said acerbically, her ire rising once more as she beheld the peculiar light in his eyes. Did he intend to offer her a slip on the shoulder once more? ''Since you refuse to see reason, I shall be returning to my room now. Tomorrow, I intend to be on my way to London if I have to walk every step. Unless, of course, Sinclair family tradition dictates that you keep me against my will.''

''You anticipate me,'' Corvin said. ''Great-grandmama did, in fact, require a bit of persuasion to see the wisdom of marriage. I do mean to have you, but not in that awful dress. I draw the line there. If the measurements that your aunt gave me are correct, one of the other gowns in your dressing room should be quite satisfactory. Most of them are blue. I fear that I shall make a tyrant of a husband, my love. If I have my way you shall always wear blue. You have spent far too much time in black.''

''Aunt Hermione cooperated in this scheme? I cannot credit it!'' She began to rail, then broke off as realization dawned. ''Did you say 'husband'?''

''It must be listening to that lot of jabbering chits that has affected your hearing, my love.'' Corvin moved closer and cupped his hands around his mouth. ''Husband!'' he shouted. ''Marriage! I love you!''

''No need to yell at me,'' Guin said, trying to control the riot of her emotions. ''Your wits must be addled. You cannot wish to marry me, milord. It is inevitable that someone will remember Elaine Borne again and my past will be a current scandal once more.''

''Elaine Guinivere Borne Marshall Courtney, you are a most exasperating woman. How can you think that your childish antics will at all compare to the glorious record of debauchery and notoriety accumulated by generations of dissipated Stantons? Why, my ancestors were pirates, murderers, thieves and traitors, albeit most of them were wily enough to use their nefarious skills in the service of the Crown.''

Corvin poured another goblet of wine as he continued. ''Do not doubt, Elaine, that their ladies were more than their equals. If you would but accompany me to the portrait gallery, I can show you one acknowledged traitress and no less than two ancestresses who were known poisoners. They dispatched the second and fifth Earls of Sinclair respectively, but who could blame them? The second and fifth were rotten to the core. As for the present courtesan Countess, my papa, alas, did not wish to put out the blunt to paint her.''

''An impressive family tree,'' Guin conceded.

Corvin bowed in acknowledgment. ''Difficult to live up to, even for one born to such a heritage. Certainly it would be ludicrous to lay your paltry achievements in infamy beside theirs. In fact, Elaine, you will probably be the most respectable Countess of Sinclair in centuries.''

''Will I?'' Guin said bemusedly.

''That is what I want to know,'' Corvin said, the plea apparent despite his tone of gentle raillery. ''Will you? For I love you, Elaine Guinivere Borne Marshall Courtney. Are there any other names? I have obtained a special license and the minister who awaits in the chapel will need to know.''

''Morgaine. My mother was fond of the Arthurian legends, you see.''

''The sorceress?''

Guin nodded.

''Appropriate, for you are a witch. Aha! You do fit right into the family scheme. A witch was all we have been lacking.''

''You are mad,'' Guin declared with a laugh of pure joy. ''Yes, I will marry you.''

''A madman and a witch,'' Corvin said, moving closer to her. ''We will do the Sinclairs proud, my love. And now if you do not mind, I should like your permission.''

''My permission?''

''To touch you. I made a vow you know, and although we Sinclairs are a treacherous lot, we always keep our sworn word. I swear that I will love you always, Elaine Guinivere Morgaine Borne Marshall Courtney; and to think I once wanted to know your name,'' he mused. ''I cannot tell why, for it is far too much of a mouthful.''

"Then why, Daniel, do you persist standing here chattering when you could be kissing me?" Guin asked, delighted by the promise in his eyes.

"Forward wench! We shall make a Stanton of you yet!" He took her into his arms and proceeded to show her just how.

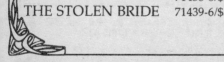